THE MASCARA MURDERS

THE MASCARA MURDERS

A COSMETIC CRIMES MYSTERY

ARLENE KAY

LEVEL
BEST BOOKS

First published by Level Best Books 2023

Copyright © 2023 by Arlene Kay

This novel is entirely a work of fiction. The names, characters and incidents portrayed in it are the work of the author's imagination. Any resemblance to actual persons, living or dead, events or localities is entirely coincidental.

Arlene Kay asserts the moral right to be identified as the author of this work.

Author Photo Credit: Kim Rodriguez photography

First edition

ISBN: 978-1-68512-436-6

Cover art by Level Best Designs

This book was professionally typeset on Reedsy.
Find out more at reedsy.com

To those who enhance the world by molding young minds and creating beauty.

Praise for The Mascara Murders

"...Another funny, witty, twisty mystery full of love, loss, friendship and heart."—Devon Ellington, *Tracking Medusa*

"... Fast-paced with a clever cast of characters. *The Mascara Murders* will keep you guessing until the last act."—C. Michelle Dorsey, *Gone But Not Forgotten*

Chapter One

Gemma Reed Watts eyed me like a cat at a mouse hole. "What do you mean he's gone? Disappeared? Daniel Flynn can't just vaporize. He's got a big job. He's famous, sort of."

As usual, my friend and business partner had ignored the preamble and skipped right to the main event. My attempt to gently break the news to her hadn't worked. Frankly, I felt a tad shaken myself, but steely self-control kept my emotions in check.

"You heard me. He left for Oxford yesterday."

"Oxford. Like in England?" Gemma still refused to get it.

"Yep. Oxford University. A chance of a lifetime came up, and he grabbed it. Who could blame him?"

I swallowed the bile accompanying that lie and summoned a smile. Admittedly the chance to study at Oxford University was an incredible opportunity, especially for a fledgling district attorney with big ambitions. Just because we'd been practically inseparable the past year didn't mean anything permanent. At least not in Daniel's eyes.

Gemma's mouth gaped open as if she were the village idiot. Frankly, it was an unappealing look for someone who peddled cosmetics and focused on appearance. "What about you," she asked. "Got your bags packed too?"

She'd forced my hand as she often did and unmasked the awful truth. My hopes for a future with Daniel had been dashed. He sugarcoated the bad news by suggesting that we "pause" our relationship during his absence. After all, England was a continent away, and in fairness to me, he couldn't hope to tie me down. That was so much bilge water, and it didn't fool me one bit. With her typical bluntness, Gemma immediately cut to the chase.

"He dumped you! I can't believe it. He dumped you." Tears welled up in her big green eyes as she squeezed my hand. "Man, oh man. For someone who has everything you have the worst luck with men I ever did see. Last guy tried to kill you and the one before that…" She gave me a hard look. "Did you do something, Marky? You know men don't like being bossed around, especially a hottie like Daniel Flynn. That man has plenty of women just panting after him."

I shook my head. "We weren't ready for the next step, so it makes sense. After all, there's plenty of time for the serious stuff later." That analysis was strictly from the head, not the heart. Truth be told, I had few illusions. The man wanted his freedom, from Michigan and especially from me. Why else would he vanish to the Old World like a fleeing felon? Despite my brave words, l was devastated. We'd spent quality time together during the murder trial of my former friend. That time had been special, at least to me. Taking stock of my situation helped. At 26 years of age, I was a strong independent woman, graduate of the prestigious Art Institute of Chicago, and a successful business owner. Folks called me pretty, or at least attractive. Long blonde curls and blue eyes still meant something to most people. My mother thought I was the most beautiful girl in the world, but unfortunately, her vote didn't count for much in the romance sweepstakes. I'd faced setbacks before and had emerged stronger. Friends told me I had trust issues, and they were probably right. This seemed like a betrayal by a man I had grown to care for, and it hurt more than I could ever have imagined.

"What'd Violet say?" Since my Aunt Violet had spent years in Paris, Gemma considered her the ultimate authority on all things, especially romance. For those of us in small town Harbor Bay, Michigan, that said it all. Come to think of it, Gemma was right. The first person I'd called was my aunt, a gifted artist, and entrepreneur who knew more than a bit about life and love. With my parents now living in New Zealand, she was closer by proximity and personality than anyone else I knew.

"You know how philosophical Violet is. She sees love affairs as fungible assets. Sort of what doesn't kill you makes you stronger."

Gemma frowned. "I'm not sure what fungible means, but it can't be good. Not if it means breaking your heart. Well, look on the bright side. You can concentrate all your energy on making Poppet the biggest thing in the state. Maybe the entire country. That'll show Daniel Flynn a thing or two. Score one for Marketta Davis!"

Gemma and I owned and operated a business—Poppet— a temple of restorative beauty. Right now, it was strictly small potatoes, but we aspired to much more. My original goal had been quite lofty. At the Art Institute of Chicago, I'd plunged into the world of Mary Cassatt, Georgia O'Keefe, and Berthe Morisot, convinced that I too, had the seeds of painting genius. That dream crashed and burned when my instructor gave me a reality check. Forget about reaching artistic heights. My prospects were limited to local shows and mediocre results. Thanks to Aunt Violet, I poured my energy into a different aspect of creating beauty, and Poppet was born. I still painted and secretly nourished hopes of someday breaking through the barriers, but the beauty business was my first concern. Harbor Bay, a bustling town of 1200 full-time residents, had always been my touchstone. Reliving the glory days of Marketta Davis, golden girl, and prom queen, was not my style, but I loved the close-knit community that had spawned me and my family. When Daniel Flynn galloped into my life, I acquired another dream. Perhaps the time was finally ripe for a permanent relationship. Even Gemma had a steady beau, although deputy sheriff Benny Soto was certainly no prize package. Life in a small town presented very few suitable candidates for romance and even fewer for marriage. I promised myself that I would never settle out of desperation, even though my parents cast anxious looks at their only offspring each year when their peers flaunted photos of grandchildren. Aunt Violet had never married, and she was perfectly content with her decision. Perhaps I should follow suit and live my life as an independent woman. Alone but not lonely. Those words didn't thrill me, but they didn't terrorize me either. I told myself that I needed time to heal. Why obsess about things I couldn't hope to control? Onward and upward was the ticket. Gemma wasn't finished yet. She folded her arms and rocked back and forth. She'd be spinning like a top soon if she wasn't careful.

"Those British women have great complexions," she snorted. "Peaches and cream. Plus, they get all dolled up in twin sets and pearls. Makes a man think they're real classy. Look what happened to Benny's mom."

Josephine Soto, local bookstore owner and mother of Deputy Benny, was scarcely a case in point. Several years before, her husband had abandoned her for a British librarian on a tourist visa. Although the culprit apparently met Gemma's idea of a man-stealing vixen, the truth was something different. Josephine was a formidable female who had hectored her poor spouse almost to distraction and paved the way for his escape. I'd seen photos of the vixen in question, and she appeared quite refined and understated despite the creamy complexion, pearls, and twin set. Besides, all that was irrelevant. Daniel Flynn had made his choice. I was neither his jailer nor spouse, so his behavior was strictly his affair. Now both of us had to live with it.

Gemma was unconvinced, but she withheld further comment. Meanwhile, I found solace in my rough collie Fantasia. She accepted my embrace stoically, although I may have gone a bit overboard. After fastening her harness, we jogged through the adjoining park land and stood for a long time overlooking Little Traverse Bay, a tributary of Lake Michigan. If a few errant tears fell during the process, I would deny it. Besides, no one could prove a thing.

Spring days flew by, and after a while, my thoughts of Daniel were less frequent. More of a dull ache than a sharp pain. I ignored his emails and heaved those postcards of Big Ben and Buckingham Palace straight into the trash. Poppet was flourishing, but like most small businesses, it required constant attention, adjustment, and tinkering. We hadn't yet found the formula for success, but at least the store was in the black and trending upward. Life was busy and slightly boring, but I could live with that. Little did I know that, once again, fate would intervene and give me the opportunity to change course.

One afternoon, the screech of brakes announced the arrival of our landlord and principal advisor, Violet Davis. Although her driving skills were more suited to Paris than Harbor Bay, everything else about Aunt Violet was exceptional. She parked her Mercedes in a reserved slot and sauntered into Poppet wearing an enigmatic smile and a sizzling red ensemble. Naturally, her makeup was flawless, and her raven locks looked salon perfect. Discreet touches of jewelry completed the effect. Violet waited until we were comfortably situated, sipping lattes, before springing her big surprise.

"Things have been quiet for a while, Marky, and I know how you love to solve puzzles."

"I do?" Sometimes my aunt was so enigmatic that I missed the point. Her depiction vastly understated the impact and danger associated with my one "adventure" unless risking my life, confronting a murderer, and bringing him to justice was akin to solving a crossword puzzle. I said nothing knowing full well that Aunt Violet would soon fill the conversational void.

"You probably read about Tori Aaron, the teacher who was murdered last month. It got plenty of press even in this part of the state."

"The art instructor at Sherborne School? I met her once or twice at gallery openings. Such a waste! She was quite talented." I recalled a petite woman with a tangle of dark curls and eyes that sparked with life. "Have they solved it yet? I didn't see anything on the news."

Violet coughed. "The authorities are stumped. Random mugging was the official verdict, although plenty of people have doubts." She thrust a newspaper account from the *Detroit Free Press* into my hands. It was a sparse rendering of a grisly crime that made no sense. Tori Aaron's skull had been crushed with some heavy object, and her belongings stolen. No sexual assault, thank goodness, but no evidence of a motive either. One bizarre detail seemed especially cruel. The killer had decorated—some said desecrated—Tori's face with a garish array of cosmetics. No specifics except for a slash of black across her eyelashes and a discarded tube of mascara. Naturally, the press had latched on to that and dubbed it "the Mascara Murder." The headmaster of Sherborne mouthed the usual meaningless platitudes—wonderful woman, inspired teacher, admired by all—but those words seemed hollow. No call for justice was issued by either the school or the surrounding community. Within a week, her murder had fallen from the headlines and superseded by new, equally appalling crimes. Sherborne School was a pricy prep school nestled in an affluent suburb, twenty miles west of Detroit, where violence was practically unknown. Most residents

5

preferred to keep crime at a distance, satisfied that their little communities were insulated from the atrocities so common in the big cities. Tori Aaron's death was considered an anomaly and relegated to the back burner of history.

"I was surprised that they let it go so easily," I said. "After all, slaughtering a teacher at one of the area's most prestigious prep schools would cause a stir in most places. And the makeup angle was particularly disturbing." I wondered where the discussion was leading. Violet Davis seldom indulged in idle chatter or flights of fancy. One look at her face told me that there was a personal angle to this story. I saw pain and something else in her eyes.

"You knew her, didn't you? I can tell this means a lot to you."

Violet cleared her throat and dabbed at her eyes. "Tori studied with me in Paris. She was so gifted...so full of life. Kind of a force of nature. A lot like you, Marky, except she eschewed any cosmetic touches. Lord, that girl was quite militant about that and plenty of other things. Still, she deserved better than this. I'm afraid the administrators care more about bad press than justice. It's almost as if she was expendable."

It was a sad tale but not unusual. Anxious parents, outraged alumni, and schools with dollar signs in their eyes. That scene was played out in many settings with predictable outcomes. Bad press slowly faded away, replaced by a steady onslaught of happy talk.

I studied my aunt for a moment before speaking. "I agree that her death was a tragedy, but where do I fit in?"

Violet avoided my question by reminiscing about her lost student. "I admired Tori, even though she was often indiscreet. Such a little bit of a thing but quite a spitfire. She called herself a social justice warrior. You can imagine how that went over in a staid place like Sherborne. Not well."

From that, I assumed that the deceased had embraced controversy and rocked the boat until it capsized. Challenging the status quo anywhere was risky but in a venerable institution like Sherborne, it was downright perilous. Still, it was far more likely that Tori Aaron would be fired than killed. Violet was angling for me to do something, but her plan wasn't clear. She knew that I was a sucker for the defenseless, human, or animal. In my own way, I too, was a social justice warrior, but I lacked the courage or inclination to disrupt my life.

We sipped our lattes in companionable silence. Then, Violet sprang the trap. "I want you to help me find her killer. I owe her that much." Her eyes narrowed as she spit out the rest. "Rumor has it that the police are sniffing around one of her students. Some scholarship kid, of course. He needed money, and they got an anonymous tip."

Something didn't add up. "I thought you said the police were stumped. This sounds like they're actively pursuing leads. What could I possibly do? You know how they hate having amateurs interfere in their business." I shuddered, recalling the reaction of town Sheriff Gideon Hall during our last adventure. He made his position abundantly clear. So clear that he had threatened to charge me with interfering in an official investigation. He was far more tolerant about Aunt Violet's activities, but then I think he secretly revered and feared her.

"Besides, I'm an outsider. You know what a closed society those prep schools are. A very privileged one at that. They'd close ranks immediately if some stranger came poking around."

None of my protests fazed Violet at all. She merely nodded and smiled as if she were placating a fractious child. "Exactly. That's why you're perfect. Your degree from the Art Institute carries a lot of weight, you know. Of course, my endorsement won't hurt either. They're desperate to find an instructor for the summer term they call it summer camp to take Tori's place. I got a call from the headmaster only today. Naturally, he offered me the slot, but I couldn't possibly accommodate him. When I mentioned you, he leapt at the idea. Once you become a faculty member, you'll fit right in."

I sputtered some sort of response that made little sense. After all, I had a business to run and a life in Harbor Bay. Summer was our busiest season. It was impossible. Besides, I didn't want to fit in at Sherborne. Peel away the lofty goals and mission statements of such institutions, and class distinctions were laid bare. I wondered if Tori Aaron had sensed that same thing.

Violet favored me with her special smile, a combination of wit and whimsy that never failed to charm everyone in her orbit. "Don't worry about Poppet. I promise to fill in while you're away. Oh, and I forgot to mention that

Sherborne is dog friendly. You can take Fantasia with you."

I felt myself weakening. Fantasia was both my constant companion and muse. Including her in the package wasn't a dealmaker but it surely helped. I envisioned spending the summer term surrounded by privileged brats with plenty of attitude and little talent. I folded my arms and maintained a steely silence. Violet seemed to read my mind. Before I uttered one word, she brushed aside my protests with a practiced hand.

"Sherborne emphasizes community service, you know. No student can graduate without participating in a meaningful project. The parents get involved too." She beamed a smile my way. Something in her gaze made me suspicious. "I pitched this little idea to them, and they gobbled it up."

"What?" Violet's little ideas tended to have big strings attached. On the other hand, I owed my aunt so much. She had financed our business, advised us on strategy, and purchased the building that housed it. Could I refuse devoting three months to a cause that meant so much to her? Only an ingrate would turn her down. I felt myself weakening but continued a half-hearted effort to resist. When she played her hole card, I finally caved.

"I proposed a community art project to raise money for scholarship students. Dedicated to Tori Aaron. You would coordinate the work of local and Sherborne students and at the end of term, we'd have a competition. I volunteered to judge the results."

That idea intrigued me, but I still resisted. Aunt Violet would never beg. That simply wasn't her style. She relied upon my gratitude, guilt, and sense of adventure to carry the day.

"A little change would do you good, Marky. Besides, you need to show Daniel Flynn that you've moved on. He probably expects you to hole up in Harbor Bay, pining for him while he trots around England making conquests. Men adore that. It reinforces their egos at no cost to them. Don't let him pigeonhole you like that. Trust me, I know."

As usual, she was right. A change in scenery was also a change in perspective. Painting was my first, most ardent love, and I'd abandoned it for too long. Perhaps I could leverage artistic talent with my penchant for seeking the truth. I surrendered without firing a shot.

"Okay. I'm in. No promises, though."

Violet embraced me with more fervor than she typically showed. "I knew I could count on you. We'll keep Tori's memory alive and find her killer. Count on it."

Chapter Two

My first week at Sherborne was unremarkable—for me if not for them. Getting settled was surprisingly easy, especially with Aunt Violet leading the way. Frankly, the way the staff bowed and scraped to my aunt was embarrassing, although I was glad to fade into the background and play the humble handmaiden. In short order Fantasia and I were ensconced in a comfortable set of rooms that epitomized the term shabby chic. A sitting area lined with bookshelves and anchored by a stone fireplace was furnished with a plump sofa and well-loved wing chair. Tori must have made this space her own. Her presence inhabited every corner, from the carefully curated accessories to the abstract paintings that graced the walls. She was indeed a talented artist if these works were indicative of her output. Fantasia immediately dove under the couch and unearthed a relic of owners' past, a squeaky cloth toy in the shape of an elephant. She trotted around the room, grinning that toothy collie grin and brandishing her prize. Who could resist that display of simple joy? I certainly couldn't.

According to their website, service to others was a core value at Sherborne School. Headmaster Coleman Ross emphasized that to me at our first meeting. He was a tall, imposing figure with lush silver hair and austere patrician features that resembled a tortured saint. A famous portrait of St. Sebastian, complete with arrows, came to mind. Although he radiated gravitas and executive presence, Violet revealed that the headmaster was rather a dim bulb intellectually. No matter. Coleman had enough wit or good fortune to marry an heiress to a major manufacturing fortune, thus securing his place in the firmament. He was adept at fundraising, soothing the spirits of anxious parents, and coddling their precocious offspring. Those critical skills far exceeded the need for intellectual heft.

"You come highly recommended, Ms. Davis," he intoned. His voice was deep and mellow, rather like a fine bourbon. "We were frantic when we lost your predecessor. Our summer art program is key to the school and the community. They depend on us."

Not one word about the tragedy that had befallen Tori Aaron. Coleman sounded aggrieved, as if Tori had deliberately ruined his schedule by her death. I decided to prod a bit.

"Tori's murder was such a tragedy," I said. "My condolences. It must have devastated the school."

Coleman hastily closed the gap by averting his eyes and nodding solemnly. "We were shaken. Still recovering from the shock. Ms. Aaron was a beloved member of our Sherborne family." It was a practiced response that lacked passion but covered the essentials. His body language revealed that this uncomfortable subject made the headmaster squirm. He shuffled papers on his desk and checked his watch. "You'll be guiding fifteen students from the middle and upper form. Some of them have real potential but all have a great deal of enthusiasm for the project." He handed me a printout with their names, ages, and addresses. As I scanned the list, I noticed an asterisk next to two of the names. "Anything special about these two?"

He brushed aside my concern as if it were lint. "Nothing at all. Most of our young people come from fine families. The area's best. Those two students, Tomas Devereaux and Abigail Jenkins, might need a delicate touch at times, but I'm sure you're up to it. Artistic temperaments and all that."

He rose and nudged me toward the door. "You'll have to excuse me, Ms. Davis. I have another engagement. Claire Howe Smith can fill you in on any other details. She's our resident published author. Quite respected by the literary establishment, you see. Perhaps you've read her novel, "My Sister's Secret"?

I shook my head. "I don't read much fiction, but it sounds like something worth reading." Coleman seized on this admission, reached into his desk drawer, and thrust a copy of a hardcover volume into my hands. "Here. With my compliments. You'll find Claire very helpful. Knows everything that goes on at Sherborne." With that, Coleman Ross firmly but politely ushered me out of his inner sanctum.

* * *

Fantasia attracted a throng of both students and faculty wherever she went. Even timid souls recalled the old Lassie show and couldn't wait to approach her. One of her admirers was Claire Howe Smith, a roly-poly woman of middle years with a fresh face, smooth cocoa complexion, and friendly demeanor.

"I'm glad I caught you," she said. "May I pet her?" She crouched down and scratched that special spot between Fantasia's ears. "I love dogs, cats, and just about anything with four legs. In my younger days, before my joints gave out, I rode horses. Couldn't get me and my sister out of the barn. My family always had plenty of animals around."

I immediately warmed to her. "Do you have any pets, Claire?"

Her smile faded, and for a moment, I feared that she would break down. "It's okay. I have an irascible tabby Mr. Rogers, and I just adopted a golden retriever." A tear slid down her face as she said that. "Forgive me, Marky. You must think I'm a fool. It's just that Raleigh was my friend's dog. They were inseparable, and I can't seem to see him without visualizing Tori." She wiped her eyes with a white, starched handkerchief. "You probably heard the story. Raleigh was with her when it happened."

I knew enough to stay silent. Losing a friend or a pet took an enormous emotional toll on most people.

Claire gulped and continued her story. "The cops called it a routine mugging, but I don't buy that. Tori was cautious, almost paranoid, about crime. Carried Mace with her everywhere she went, especially at night." She took a deep breath. "Poor Raleigh was no help at all. You know how genial Goldens are. He ran down the block and just sat there shivering. Everyone's a friend to him, even a killer." Claire sat down on a bench and patted the seat next to her.

"Are you sure?" I asked. "If you need to be alone, I understand."

"Brooding doesn't help, does it. Besides, I'm supposed to be your spirit guide to the wonderful world of Sherborne School."

I mentioned how the headmaster had praised her. "He didn't want to linger with me after I mentioned Tori's murder. That's for sure. He got very antsy, but I did score a copy of your novel. Congratulations. I can't wait to read it."

Claire's grin was genuine this time. "That's my boss. He parades that book out like a trophy every time someone new shows up."

"Have you published anything else?" I asked. "The cover blurb says this was a New York Times best seller. Pretty impressive!"

She bowed her head. "Nothing yet, although I'm still working at it. Now concerning Coleman...We call him the summer soldier and sunshine patriot. At least those of us who admire Thomas Paine do. Life among a weird bunch of academics, Marky. You'll get used to it."

"Was Tori like that?"

Claire explained that Tori was the Samuel Adams of the bunch, a firebrand who didn't shrink from controversy and relished it. "An avenging angel—that described Tori perfectly." Claire looked around and lowered her voice. "You heard about the incident in the gym, I suppose."

Time to downplay things. "Only the newspaper account, and it was sketchy."

"It was truly awful, Marky. They were using Kahoot."

She noticed the puzzled look on my face and patted my shoulder. "I forget that not everyone's into those gaming things. Kahoot is an interactive game. Lots of fun in most cases, and the kids adore it. They devise quizzes or submit answers, kind of like on Jeopardy, except they use their cell phones. Answers are projected on a big screen so everyone can participate."

I kept my expression blank wondering how in the world this gaming thing related to Tori Aaron. Patience, I told myself. The answer will come sooner or later.

As Claire recounted the experience, I realized just how painful the memory was for her. "Anyhow, this time, some troublemakers used swastikas and

13

racial epithets as their usernames. We shut it down right away, but the damage was done." She spread her arms out wide. "Big blow up with parents exploding and the media snooping. Coleman Ross went berserk trying to track down the culprits but no luck."

I chuckled, visualizing the elegant headmaster in a tizzy. "Not quite the image of Sherborne he tried to project."

Claire paused as she stroked Fantasia's lush coat. "Thing is, Marky, we're pretty sure it was one of those community project kids. Your new group. Not that we could prove anything."

It didn't shock me. Adolescent humor was often obnoxious and hurtful, even in the most rarified spaces. Most teens outgrew it, but occasionally, it festered and grew into something worse. I'd seen it with my Harbor Bay classmates. Every high school had its share of bullies, male and female. Claire mentioned that racist graffiti had desecrated the whiteboards in an Indian teacher's classroom, and a noose had been discovered in the boys' gym. Again, plenty of suspects but no proof. How ironic. Beneath the glitter and glamor of Sherborne, the same cauldron of evil existed as in the poorest school systems. I sensed there was more to the story and that it involved Tori Aaron.

"Surely someone raised Caine about it."

Claire closed her eyes while she composed herself. "I'm ashamed to say that none of us had the courage to really pursue the matter. No guts, no glory. Too afraid of losing our precious jobs. As a Black woman, I wasn't unfamiliar with those stupid racial taunts. Go along to get along and all that. Don't make a fuss. Tori didn't feel that way. Her grandparents were Holocaust survivors, and she never forgot it. She was fearless and look where it got her."

After that bombshell, we changed course. I asked Claire about her writing, particularly her most recent novel. Every writer, even an acclaimed one like Claire, loved to discuss her work. Artists react the same way. Never enough praise.

"My sister was a writer too. Far better than I ever could be." Claire hesitated. "She passed at a very young age. Carla suffered so much, but she never gave up. She kept writing until the very end." Fantasia pushed her head onto Claire's lap and gazed up at her with soulful eyes as if she sensed her sorrow.

I changed the subject by asking about my new colleagues at Sherborne. Claire relaxed immediately and provided thumbnail sketches of her coworkers, complete with amusing anecdotes. "Of course, we're not at full strength now. Summers mean sabbaticals and vacations for those who can afford it. I think you'll enjoy most of the staff." I sensed a big caveat coming my way. Hardly surprising in a group of hard-charging professionals vying for promotion in a field where there were few monetary incentives. The atmosphere at the Art Institute often grew savage as students and instructors vied for prominence.

Claire took her time, choosing her words carefully. "Have you met Harry Putnam yet? Correction: Harrison Putnam, junior. It really ticks him off if you call him Harry, so naturally, I always do." The spark of mischief in her eyes encouraged me. Perhaps Claire was a kindred spirit, after all.

"Harry chairs the science and math department. Loves to sprinkle words and phrases from six different tongues into his conversation just to show how literate he is. I've always thought that the word "supercilious" was coined to describe him. He's a Dartmouth grad who never quite left the campus."

After that, I couldn't wait to meet Harry. Claire continued her narrative, grimacing as she did so. "He and Tori sparred constantly at faculty meetings, although they always managed to keep things civil. Any time she made a proposal, he tried to shut her down, but it didn't work. Not with Tori."

Claire also mentioned two other colleagues, Roddy Park, and Gin Hastings. "You'll recognize Roddy instantly when you see him. Astoundingly handsome but not conceited. The pride of Amherst College. Almost every sentient female around this place hankers for Roddy, but he rises above it all. Totally consumed by Political Science and finishing his doctorate at the University of Michigan." Roddy's approach sounded sensible to me in an era where real or perceived misdeeds could instantly end anyone's career.

"That's Gin Hastings, now," Claire said, pointing at a young woman who was sprinting toward us at an alarming rate of speed. "She's the youngster of our group. A tad naïve but quite a darling girl. Thinks the best of everyone. Gin's a Julliard grad who teaches drama and performing arts to our little darlings."

At first blush, Gin reminded me of an Irish Setter pup, all gangly and full of good cheer. I found it impossible not to smile at her freckled face, shiny auburn locks, and mile-wide grin. She plopped on the ground beside Fantasia and embraced her.

"What a beauty," she enthused. "Such a good girl." Gin raised her head and stared into my eyes. "I've read all about you, Marky. Great website for your store, by the way, and I love your paintings." She paused for dramatic effect. "That murder trial you testified in got plenty of press down here. Do you plan to find Tori's killer too?"

Chapter Three

I gulped and sputtered, dumbstruck by the blitzkrieg confronting me. Gin was impertinent and unapologetic but instead of snapping at her I was tempted to pat her head.

"Wow!" Claire said, barely repressing a grin. "Quite an introduction. Our Gin means no harm even when her manners suffer."

"Nice meeting you," I said, shrugging it off. "We'll be working together a lot this term."

"Don't mind me, Marky. I'm trying to do better." Gin bowed her head in faux penitence. "Like the show says, "Curb your Enthusiasm." Hasn't taken yet, more's the pity." She shook her curls and laughed. "Now tell me. What's this detective stuff all about. I've always wanted to play a private eye. You know, like Miss Marple or Jessica Fletcher."

While she wove her fantasies, I leapt into my cover story.

"Don't believe everything you read. You know how the newspapers are. Besides, my only goal is to survive this summer and share my love of painting with the kids. No hidden agenda. My Aunt Violet loves this place, but she wasn't available, so I agreed to substitute." I seldom lie but when the occasion demands it, I can prevaricate with the worst of them. Gin was knee-deep in dreamland, but Claire gave me a speculative look that said she wasn't buying my act.

"Too bad," she said. "We could use some help avenging Tori. She'd be the first one to jump in if one of us had been hurt, and I'd like to return the favor."

Gin scrambled up and perched on the arm of the bench. "The cops took the lazy way out. Mugging and robbery. Just routine. That's so much bunk!"

Claire nodded. "Like most of us, Tori never had a spare cent. Not that I knew of. We used to joke about pinching pennies amidst all this splendor. Tori always said that the teachers at this school were the only ones who could qualify for food stamps. We even talked about striking, not that we would."

Despite the levity, there was the ring of truth in her words. Staff salaries were comparatively low, especially when yearly student fees rose north of forty thousand dollars. Had Tori led the push for more money and paid the price?

"Was she nearing her home when it happened? I'm not certain where Tori lived?"

Gin jumped right in with the answer. "She lived on campus like most of us. In the faculty lodgings. You're living in her place, matter of fact. One of the few bennies about working here. She was the most disciplined person I ever met. You could count on Tori being at the dog park at six p.m. sharp. Kind of anal about her habits. We all joked about it."

Claire shivered as the story unfolded. I doubted if she had used that dog park since adopting Raleigh. Too many painful memories at play. I was no big fan of dog parks, but they were very popular. Surely someone had seen Tori that fateful evening.

"No CCTV in the area, I suppose?"

Claire hesitated. "Nope. The suburbs aren't exactly high crime havens. That's why Tori's death was so shocking."

Gin turned to Claire and grimaced. "You mean her murder, don't you? Death sounds so peaceful. I want everyone to remember that our friend was savagely murdered."

Claire put her arms around the younger woman. "Of course." She dabbed at her eyes again. "The police questioned all of us after it happened, but they never followed up. Just sort of swept everything under the rug. They do that in minority neighborhoods quite regularly but it's shocking when it happens in a place like this. I guess a nobody doesn't rate much attention around here."

I shared the pain and frustration these two women expressed. If Tori had been wealthy or world renown, the outcome might have been different. Suburban police forces were often more equipped to handle traffic patrol than homicide cases. That was the reality we were confronted with. I plucked the folder Coleman Ross had given me from my satchel.

"Any insights about my students?" I asked. "Two of the names have an asterisk next to them but I haven't a clue what it means. He was pressed for time and didn't explain."

Claire scanned the list, then turned the sheet over. "Bet he told you to ask me, didn't he? That is so Coleman. Delegate the dirt to the peons."

Gin gave her a hearty slap on the back. "Congratulations, girlfriend. You've got a new title. Well, better you than me. Gotta go." She literally skipped away from us and disappeared down the path. It took a while, but Claire ultimately did her duty. She explained that Tomas Devereaux was an exceptionally promising painter and writer but a bit hard to handle.

"In what way? Temperament or talent?"

"Both, I'm afraid. Tomas is passionate. Totally consumed by his art and unconcerned about his other studies. He's a scholarship student but that's not the issue. With his talent, he can win a place at almost any university if he agrees to study. Calls himself TD and has a bit of a chip on his shoulder. Most teachers steer clear of Tomas, but not Tori. She was a real bulldog when it came to nurturing and wasn't afraid of cracking the whip if needed." Claire sighed. "You know, at the end, I think she was beginning to finally get through to Tomas. Tori's family background wasn't that different from his, but her raw talent and drive helped her overcome obstacles."

I wondered what Aunt Violet would make of Tomas Devereaux and his painting. Had he allowed his passion for art to extend to his instructor? I made a mental checkmark next to his name. He warranted closer scrutiny. I pointed to the other listing; the only female who had been singled out. Claire had a different perspective on Abigail Jenkins.

"She's a very nice kid. Sensitive but hardworking and pleasant. Her family has big bucks and cosseted her all her life. Abby is trying to assert herself, but she lacks confidence."

I cut to the chase. "Any thoughts on her artistic aptitude?"

Claire shrugged. "I'm not the one to assess that but Tori felt that art was a good creative outlet for Abigail. You know, to free her from her inhibitions."

I interpreted that to mean that Abigail was no superstar. Just a motivated student who loved painting. No surprise there. Plenty of aspiring artists channeled their skills elsewhere. I knew that from personal experience. Art History was a field that demanded a pinch of talent and a discerning eye. Having family wealth was also a plus when it came to future placements in the field. Perhaps that was the right path for Abigail. I'd dealt with tender adolescents before and felt confident in doing it. In fact, not long ago I had been one of them. Claire's frown told me that there was more to come. "What haven't you told me?" I asked.

"Doesn't her name ring a bell?" she asked. "She's the much-beloved daughter of Senator Robert Jenkins, Senate majority leader. He absolutely dotes on the girl and when that nonsense about Kahoot came up he was livid. Flew in from DC to give Coleman a verbal thrashing." She grinned. "I've never seen my boss look so shaken. The Senator threatened to open a civil rights investigation and to pull Abby out of Sherborne."

That reaction stunned me. From everything I'd read, Robert Jenkins was an even-tempered moderate known for his use of reason over hysteria.

Claire saw my confusion and enlightened me.

"Abby's mother was Jewish, you see. She passed several years ago, and the Senator still grieves for her. No surprise that the swastika business enraged him."

No wonder Coleman Ross had singled out Abigail! I pointed to another name with a checkmark on the margin.

"What about this one? Anything to worry about here?"

Claire closed her eyes and sighed as if she had grown weary of the discussion. "Oh yes. You can thank me for that little reminder. Coleman is oblivious to that kind of thing as men so often are. How to describe Priscilla Sayers, or Miss Pris, as we call her, behind her back?" I tried not to react, but Claire's disdain was a surprise. It seemed out of character for the calm, collected woman in front of me.

20

"Forgive me, Marky. I know it's unkind and highly inappropriate for a teacher to dislike a student—at least openly. But the one thing I loathe is a sneak. Priscilla heaps all kinds of praise on her comrades until she sees an opportunity. Then it's lights out."

That reminded me of a quote from the late, great Oscar Wilde. Something about true friends stabbing you in the front. I shared Claire's dislike for backstabbers and avoided them whenever possible.

"So, does this kid have any artistic talent?"

"That's the sad thing," Claire said. "Priscilla is quite gifted and can be very charming. Just keep your guard up around her. Tori found that out."

"Oh?"

"After Tori's murder, Priscilla told several people that Tori got what she deserved. That she was up to no good. I think she resented the fact that Tori saw right through her little game."

Claire didn't share any more details, and frankly, I was more than ready to take a break. This teaching assignment promised to be more challenging than I had bargained for. I longed for a chance to thrash things out with Aunt Violet. She always put things in perspective for me. We parted at the residence hall to freshen up before the evening's festivities. The official opening of the summer term was apparently a big deal at Sherborne School, with a formal dinner and party. All my prospective students would be there, as well as most of their parents. I could hardly wait.

* * *

I chose a cobalt blue dress for my debut. It had the advantage of being sophisticated but subdued, something that might prove advantageous in this strange environment. Gemma told me that this outfit highlighted the color of my eyes, but I can't attest to that. I only know it made me feel good. Bearing in mind that my business was Poppet the spot for beauty, I applied a dab of shadow and a coating of my favorite mascara. Truth in advertising, I always say.

The social was held in the main auditorium which had been reconfigured for the big event. The summer session typically attracted fewer than two hundred students, but those who attended were motivated either by the chance to redeem themselves academically or by the fervent wish of their parents for a respite from teenage angst. The buffet table was laden with wholesome choices, including a succulent platter of jumbo shrimp and a mound of crab cakes. I eyed the possibilities and sidled toward those with the most promise. Naturally, as a newcomer, I was subject to more scrutiny than the rest of the crew, and bearing that in mind, I tried to refrain from stuffing my face. While mulling over these considerations, I felt a familiar tap on my shoulder. It could only be one person, the same person who had inveigled me into this charade in the first place. My beloved aunt, Violet Davis, beamed at me with an angelic expression that was totally misleading. Naturally, she was an immediate standout in a wispy silk confection from the Paris runway and mile-high stilettos that would cripple any normal being.

"I wanted to surprise you," she whispered. "Coleman asked me to make a few opening remarks. Looks like a good opportunity to scope out the suspects while we're at it."

Before I uttered a word, Violet was surrounded by a throng of admirers. Her fame as both an artist and an entrepreneur was widespread, and her status as a part-time Parisian added even more cachet. A feature of the opening event was an auction of one of Violet's paintings with all proceeds directed to a scholarship fund. I recognized Senator Robert Jenkins as he headed our way, trailed by a bustling Coleman Ross. The Senator radiated ease with power; the headmaster emitted an artificiality that puzzled me. Surely, he was accustomed to squiring the rich and famous around his school. Perhaps the residue of the Kaboom fiasco still lingered.

Robert Jenkins took Aunt Violet's hand and kissed it. He knew exactly how to accomplish that, cleanly and elegantly, without slobbering over her fingers as men often did. "I've long been an admirer of your work, Madame. In fact, my late wife collected your paintings whenever possible." Jenkins was a tall, slender man with a full head of silver hair and piercing brown eyes that missed nothing. His physical presence, combined with that aura of power, made him a very attractive specimen and a possible romantic interest for my aunt. I considered myself an accomplished matchmaker for others. Not so able when it came to furthering my own interests.

"Perhaps you'll be the successful bidder in our auction, Senator," Coleman Ross chimed in. It was a rather surprising misstep for a man who frequented the haunts of the rich and famous. Robert Jenkins nodded and brushed Coleman Ross off like lint.

Aunt Violet introduced me to the Senator, noting that I would be instructing Abigail for the summer. At the mention of his daughter's name, his face brightened, and he beckoned to a sweet-faced, gangly girl with long, curly hair and warm brown eyes. "My daughter, Abigail."

It's both misleading and dangerous to make snap judgments about people, but I plead guilty to the occasional lapse. I was drawn to Abigail Jenkins immediately, recognizing in her a kindred spirit whose confidence needed a boost. A cosmetic touch would have been useful, but I put that thought aside for the moment. Poppet, my beloved store, would provide a treasure trove for this child when the time was right.

"Have you designated the charity for tonight yet?" Violet asked Coleman. "Because I had a thought." I shivered, knowing that my aunt's little ideas frequently had far-reaching implications. Coleman smiled blandly and walked into her trap. "No. What were you thinking of?"

Violet's smile was beatific. "In view of everything, I propose we establish a fund in the name of Tori Aaron. She was an ardent supporter of finding and funding artistic talent, especially amongst the underprivileged."

Coleman Ross gulped, but before he could respond, Abigail clapped her hands in joy. "What a wonderful idea! I loved her. Ms. Aaron was so kind even if you weren't a superstar." While they discussed details, I excused myself and made a beeline for the group huddled around the punch table. I'd spotted Claire and Gin there laughing with a man who could only be Roddy Park, the political scientist and unwilling heartthrob of Sherborne. Claire welcomed me into their group and promptly introduced Roddy. If you favor tall, handsome men with beautifully sculpted features and a museum-quality physique, Professor Park fit the bill. Despite the obvious, he seemed unaware of the effect he had on women. His smile was warm and welcoming, and his handshake firm. I refused to speculate on the firmness of any other features he possessed, although it was a pleasant prospect. I focused instead on more neutral topics, such as the turnout and the chance to glimpse some of my pupils.

"Marky, check it out," Gin said, grasping my wrist. "That's Priscilla Sayers." She pointed to a petite blonde who had taken center stage near the front of the room. The girl had presence, that I recognized. Most seventeen-year-olds hang back when adults draw near, but Miss Pris had no such inhibitions. She had a well-proportioned figure, shoulder-length blond ringlets, and the assurance of a much older girl. Small wonder that Claire tried to avoid her. Priscilla Sayers was a force to be reckoned with but not in a good way. She turned suddenly, spotted Roddy Park, and made a dead set at him.

"Oh, Professor," she trilled, tugging his arm. "We've been looking for you to settle an argument." Roddy shrugged helplessly until Claire intervened.

"We're busy here, Priscilla. Come meet Ms. Davis, your coach for the summer term." I extended my hand, hoping to build at least a temporary bridge with the girl. Fat chance. She nodded briskly, ignored my outstretched hand, and quickly turned her attention back to Roddy. In the end, it was Gin who saved the day by reaching out to a short, muscular lad standing next to Priscilla.

"Marky, this is Tomas Devereaux, a most promising painter. No slouch as a writer either."

Aha. Another student with an asterisk next to his name. Was he the person the police had flagged as Tori's possible assailant? What struck me about Tomas was the intensity of his blue eyes and the blaze of energy that surrounded him like a force field. Unlike his fellow students, Tomas had an untidy mass of black hair that could have used a comb and perhaps a thorough scrubbing. His garb included tattered jeans more suited to a studio than a social. I disregarded his tattoos since they now tended to be the rule rather than the exception with the younger crowd and even people my own age. My business partner Gemma sported several and fiercely defended what she considered to be body art. Personally, I preferred to save the artwork for my canvases rather than deface my body. I'd read that the police maintained a database of tattoos which tended to identify those on wanted posters rather than the fashion pages. To each his own. As an artist, I'd trained with all kinds of creative types, so very little shocked me. I sized up Tomas Devereaux as a kid playing a part, determined to defy the establishment by portraying a James Dean type of rebel no matter what it cost him.

He glanced at me and made a few desultory remarks. Perhaps Tomas was shy and socially awkward, the type who spoke through his work. That was my initial assessment although until I saw his canvases, I couldn't validate it. Meanwhile the headmaster cleared his throat and called the meeting to order. He introduced Aunt Violet and asked her to discuss her experience and the art auction. I watched the reaction when the name Tori Aaron was mentioned. At first, the crowd grew silent as those assembled digested the news. Suddenly a cheer, initiated by Tomas Devereaux, grew in volume, and reverberated throughout the room. Chants of Tori, Tori, Tori rang out. One notable exception was Priscilla Sayers, who wrinkled her pert little nose and pouted.

"Something wrong, Priscilla?" Gin managed to keep a neutral tone.

With a head toss, Priscilla spat out a response. "Why glorify her? She got what she deserved."

I saw shock and disdain on the faces surrounding her. Gin uttered one unseemly response, but it was Tomas Devereaux who said it best.

"Cut it out, Pris. Just because Ms. Aaron kept you in line, don't get nasty. She helped plenty of us." He stepped away from Priscilla and melted into the crowd. Meanwhile, I joined Claire, Gin, and Roddy at a side table reserved for faculty. Aunt Violet concluded her remarks and displayed the painting up for bid. It was a charming oil of a young woman done in the impressionist style. I recognized the model and ducked my head to avoid detection. Who knew that my aunt would feature my portrait at this event? Roddy Park smiled as he viewed the painting. "That model looks familiar. Don't tell me you posed for the painting, Marky?"

I nodded as my cheeks burned with embarrassment. "Guilty. It happened a long time ago, and I'd forgotten all about it. Anyone is fair game with an artist in the family."

Did I detect a spark of interest interspersed with his teasing? Perhaps political science wasn't his only pursuit after all. On the other hand, it was probably wishful thinking on my part.

"It's lovely," Claire said. "Too bad you need deep pockets to compete."

A spirited bidding war followed Violet's remarks, with the final sticker price reaching ten thousand dollars. Senator Robert Jenkins acknowledged the applause of the crowd and stepped up to claim his prize. Based on the looks he exchanged with her, he seemed as enamored of Aunt Violet as her work. His daughter clapped her hands and hugged her father when he handed her the portrait.

"Daddy's little girl wins again," said a caustic voice. I turned to face the newcomer, a thirty-something man with intelligent grey eyes, a slight frame, and a bad combover. Claire pulled out a chair for him and introduced us. "You haven't met Harry yet, Marky. He chairs the math and science department."

He bristled as we shook hands and corrected her. "Harrison Putnam, Ms. Davis. At your service."

I was curious about Harry and what prompted his reaction to Senator Jenkins. "Not a fan of the Senator?" I kept my smile letter-perfect to deflect any suspicion. "I hope that wasn't a commentary on my aunt's artwork."

"Certainly not. I simply oppose the deification of someone like Tori Aaron." He gave what sounded like a snort. "Tradition and values are the cornerstone of this institution. Anything or anyone that threatens them erodes the foundation of Sherborne School itself. Tori Aaron lived for that. A real drama queen." Realizing his gaffe, he quickly added. "Her death was a tragedy, of course."

His emotion startled me but not his other colleagues. Gin rolled her eyes, and Claire grimaced, as if they had heard this song before. Roddy Park reacted.

"Come on, Harrison. That's unfair. Tori was as committed to the school as any of us. She just had different perspectives on issues." He paused. "I often wished I had her courage. It's not easy to stand out from the crowd."

"Social justice warrior. Nonsense. I knew her game. Suck up to the students no matter how absurd their demands. We're molding minds here, not running a popularity contest." Harrison folded his arms as if that ended the discussion. I wondered what Tori had done to excite such emotion. Most institutions, such as Sherborne, were dry as dust relics of the past. An infusion of new blood could only improve the landscape. On the other hand, every great social revolution had its casualties, and the tug-of-war between traditionalists and rebels was nothing new.

"Don't you want her killer to be found?" I asked. Before he responded we were joined by Aunt Violet. "Am I interrupting anything?" she asked. "This is such a charming event. Motivated students and parents. Who could ask for anything more?" I introduced her to my new friends and watched my aunt activate the charm machine for which she was rightfully famous. Before long, even the dour Harrison Putnam had a smile on his face as he conceded that Paris was indeed his favorite world city and French his language of choice. He then switched effortlessly into a torrent of French designed to prove his point. Any further discussion of Tori Aaron was temporarily shelved for a more propitious time.

While they chatted, I stole a glance at Roddy Park. No doubt about it, the guy was worth seeing. Brains, brawn, and beauty. Quite an alluring combination. I reminded myself that the unlamented Daniel Flynn, as well as several of his predecessors, were also comely lads with some very bad habits. While in the throes of infatuation, I'd missed the classic warning signs until it was far too late. The price was much steeper than I had bargained for. All things considered, I resolved to stick to painting and cosmetics. They were inanimate but predictable, satisfying pursuits that were unlikely to break my heart.

Violet checked her watch and excused herself. She had a dinner engage-ment with the headmaster and several guests. I wondered if Senator Jenkins was among the elect. Come to think of it, he would be an ideal mate for my aunt. Gemma called my matchmaking a gift. I considered it a curse. Either way, I resolved to monitor the situation. Our gathering broke up soon afterwards and I sought refuge in my new digs, the former home of

Tori Aaron. Several tasks awaited me, including a thorough review of the lesson plan and an outline for my first session. All eyes would be upon me tomorrow, and I was anxious to make a good showing. The students deserved my best effort, and so did Tori Aaron. Perhaps if I were lucky, I might gather a scrap of information that would lead to her killer. After walking Fantasia around the quad, I spent some time meditating. I'm uneasy with the paranormal but not a total naysayer. Perhaps with a little effort, I could channel Tori's spirit. If so, she might lead me to her killer and justify this excursion into academia.

Chapter Four

I slept soundly, aided by a fluffy down comforter and Fantasia's presence. With her at my side I felt almost invulnerable. She was my guardian angel and pillow pal, a force whose keen hearing never missed a sound and banished any fear of intruders.

Sunlight streaming through the window awakened me with a jolt. Fortunately, I had just enough time to exercise before my debut. I fastened Fantasia's harness, slipped into my jogging suit, and headed outdoors. Yesterday I'd scoped out a wooded trail abutting the perimeter of the school grounds. According to the welcome brochure, it was a "verdant two-mile track ideal for the novice jogger." That sounded tailor made for my abilities and desires. I gauged that I was somewhere between a novice and intermediate runner with nothing to prove to myself or others. The day promised to be mild with a high temperature around eighty degrees. I avoided extreme heat whenever possible and considering Fantasia's furry self, she flourished best in cooler climes as well. After warming up, we started out at a moderate pace that allowed us the luxury of enjoying nature while virtue signaling. Several speed demons whizzed past us, including one determined bike rider who wielded his machine like a weapon and ran us off the path. *Ignore him,* I told myself. *Don't let a thoughtless jerk spoil your day.*

After completing our run, I fed my girl, showered, and readied myself for class. We'd been allocated a large light-filled studio that was configured classroom style. Easels with blank canvases for each student ringed the desks, as if awaiting inspiration. I arrived early and scrutinized the eager

THE MASCARA MURDERS

faces as they took their seats. Fantasia curled up in a corner on her dog bed and promptly took a snooze.

Abigail and Priscilla arrived first followed by Tomas and a gaggle of students I had yet to meet. Each of them clutched a sketch or oil, from the previous term, some shyly, others quite audaciously. Promptness was emphasized at Sherborne, and they abided by that rule. Several of my paintings were displayed around the room, and I hastened to share my artistic journey both triumphs and bumps with the students. They seemed relieved to know that even after a disappointing experience like mine, the budding artist could persevere.

One rude comment stung, although considering the source, I was not surprised. Priscilla Sayers scrutinized my paintings and uttered a loud sigh. "Don't you run a cosmetic store now, Ms. Davis? Seems like a long way down from the Art Institute." Her saccharine smile fooled nobody, and in my younger days, I would have slapped it off her face. *Remember. She's a child. A child who needs guidance.*

Self-control was my superpower now and I used it to my advantage. "I'm proud of my business," I said. "But Priscilla brings up an important point. Painters seldom reach the heights immediately. Many of the greatest were discounted until after their deaths. Tenacity and resilience are almost as important as raw talent. Besides, there are plenty of fields other than painting where artists can flourish." I beamed a faux smile at Priscilla. "For me, Poppet, my cosmetics studio is one of them."

That dissipated the tension in the room. Tomas Devereaux shot a triumphant glance at Priscilla and gave Abigail a fist bump. "Ms. Aaron told us the same thing," he said. "Anyone can be a critic."

After spending some time discussing goals and expectations, I asked each student to describe an artist whose style he or she admired and how that compared to their own painting. Priscilla spoke first, extolling the work of Georgia O'Keefe.

"What excites you about her painting," I asked. Perhaps we were finally on the right track.

Priscilla eyed me boldly and smirked. "There's an erotic component to them, isn't there? It suits my personality." I ignored the subtext and focused on the artist's life and influences. O'Keefe was an American icon who was worthy of admiration and imitation. Several other students joined in and contributed their perspectives.

"Ms. Aaron said that O'Keefe was disregarded because she was a female." Abigail Jenkins ducked her head after making that statement as if she feared rejection. On the contrary, I thought it was an excellent opportunity to discuss the artist's bold use of form and color. If there was a feminist slant to the topic, all the better. The chatter was useful since it allowed me to gauge both the artistic scope of the students and their reaction to Tori as well. Most avoided any reference to their former teacher, but several spoke openly and candidly about her.

I was particularly curious about Ru Taylor, a Eurasian student from Hong Kong. According to Claire, his family was fabulously wealthy and dedicated to their son's education. Like Abigail, Ru's artistic talent was exceeded by his zeal for art history. He confessed that he hoped to serve as a curator in his family's gallery someday, or an appraiser at an auction house. He was an engaging lad with a warm smile that drew me to him. "My name Ru means scholar, Ms. Davis," he teased, "but don't expect too much from me. I love abstract painting, particularly Picasso and Pollack. Ms. Aaron used to tease me about splatter art."

I reached out to Tomas Devereaux next. The samples he provided were astounding—raw talent with the promise of much more. No wonder Tori had mentored him. His style was reminiscent of Degas, one of my personal idols. Surely the authorities had no basis for suspecting Tomas of murder. I refused to even consider it. If anything, he seemed to revere Tori Aaron.

As I examined each student's work, I felt the glare of Priscilla Sayre's eyes boring into me. The girl was a curious study in passion and personality, not something that would bode well for her in the future. Priscilla's oils were adequate, workman-like if anything. She favored bold splashes of color and vivid depictions of landscapes. With her looks and initiative, however, I had no doubt that Miss Pris would fare well in almost any field that had a substantial male component.

We concluded the morning session on a high note. Our time together would be divided into both discussion and a painting "lab" that would encourage each student to work on individual projects. Overall, I was encouraged by the enthusiasm of the group with a few notable exceptions. As I tidied up the room, Abigail Jenkins approached me. The girl was tentative but very sweet and I was drawn to her.

"Did you know Ms. Aaron," she asked. Her voice was almost a whisper and had a tremor in it when she said Tori's name.

I described my brief acquaintance with her but added that my Aunt Violet knew her quite well. "She was very impressed with Tori's talent," I said. "You must miss her."

Abigail nodded. "She was so brave. I'm not like that, but Ms. Aaron encouraged me. "

I patted the girl's shoulder. "I understand that she stood up for what was right no matter what."

Abigail looked around as if she feared being overheard. "You probably heard about that Kaboom stuff. Most teachers ignored it, but not Ms. Aaron."

"Were you hurt by it?" I asked.

She lowered her eyes. "Yes. I guess so. My dad says there are mean people everywhere, and you must fight back, but I just wanted to cry."

I was so absorbed in our conversation that I didn't hear anyone approaching. Tomas Devereaux was as stealthy as a panther and for a moment, his sudden presence made me feel uneasy. "Social justice warrior. That's what she called herself," he sputtered. "Fat lot of good it did her. They always win in the end. Look what happened to her, and nobody even cares. My dad says you just can't beat them."

Abigail lifted her head and showed some spunk. "That doesn't mean you quit trying. You can't just let them win, Tomas. Look what happened during the Holocaust."

He waved his arms as if this was an old argument they had had before. "Easy for you to say, Abby. You're somebody. Just look at your family versus mine." He turned away, but before he said anything more, Ru Taylor poked his head in the doorway. "Hey, you guys. Let's grab some lunch before the next session." He winked at me. "I hear the teacher is really tough."

I begged off on the excuse that I had Fantasia to feed and attend to. I was very eager to pursue that conversation about Tori and her brutal death, but restraint was called for. I needed to use what Aunt Violet called "finesse." After all, these teens didn't know me, and I needed to win their trust before venturing into such a sensitive subject. I also hoped to track down my aunt before she left the campus. Knowing Violet, she had wormed information out of her dinner companions last evening while charming their socks off. A tiny part of me was also intrigued by her friendship with Senator Robert Jenkins. Violet was circumspect in matters of the heart, but she might just drop a few clues.

I hurried back to my lodging, fed, and watered Fantasia, and headed for the faculty lounge. A bountiful buffet for the staff was supplied by a local caterer each day and constituted one of the perks touted by Claire.

Aunt Violet was already there enjoying a fruit salad, baked salmon, and iced tea. The rest of my colleagues were less abstemious. Claire tucked into a burger and fries with great gusto while Gin picked at vegetarian fare. The male contingent, including Roddy Park and Harrison Putnam, piled pasta, garlic bread, and gigantic meatballs on their plates.

Claire grinned at me. "So. How was the first session? Don't see any blood or obvious bruises."

"Early days yet," Gin said. "Most are probably evaluating you and gearing up for the kill."

I shrugged and took a big swallow of Perrier. "Mostly peaceful. One or two bumps in the road, but that's to be expected."

"Was one of those bumps named Priscilla?" Claire rolled her eyes. "She always reminds me how dull literary fiction like mine is compared to best sellers like *Fifty Shades of Gray.* Not that I'd turn down the royalties from a big success. My imagination just isn't up to the task, and unfortunately, neither is my experience."

Violet laughed. "Believe me. Marky can take care of herself. Beneath that angelic exterior beats a lion's heart."

Roddy Park gave me a speculative look. "I'll have to remember that.

Tangling with an apex predator can be hazardous to one's health."

I locked eyes with him and gave my best impression of a feline growl. Tangling with Roddy was a pleasant prospect any woman would enjoy.

"I suppose they mentioned Tori Aaron," Harrison sneered. The man seemed totally devoid of humor, always on the prowl for conflict and cynical to a fault.

I brushed off his comment with a nod. "Most of them really adored her. It's nice to see the kind of impact a good teacher can have."

Harrison wrinkled his nose. "Hmph. Too bad one of them probably killed her. The authorities seemed confident of that. Personally, I have my suspicions, and I told the police all about them."

Violet leapt into the fray to play her part. "What possible motive could one of these youngsters have to commit such a brutal crime? It seems unreal."

That led to a vigorous discussion of teenage angst, unrequited passion, and congenital evil. Harrison ended it with a comment that chilled my blood.

"One of your little charges has quite the criminal record, Marky. It's not much of a leap from assault and robbery to murder, now, is it?"

Lunch ended on that sour note. I joined my aunt for a leisurely stroll through the common, and a quick bout of girl talk. "How was your dinner?" I asked.

Violet pinched my cheek. "Don't be coy, Marketta. It hardly suits you. My meal was fine, and the company was even better. Plus, I managed to pry loose a few interesting tidbits about Tori and that dust-up with Kaboom."

"First things first. What do you think of Senator Jenkins, and more importantly, how did he act toward you?"

She didn't blush. Violet was way too sophisticated for that, but she did respond. "Robert is a charming man. Cultured, and filled with social graces. I hope to see him again sometime soon." She frowned. "Now that's out of the way, I found out that the police are still baffled by Tori's murder but are *actively pursuing leads*, whatever that may mean. According to Coleman, it might connect directly to one of the students, a townie, unfortunately. Perhaps Harrison wasn't too far afield."

My heart sank as I pictured the untapped genius of a student like Tomas

34

Devereaux being crushed in the penal system.

"I don't suppose they mentioned any names?"

Violet shook her head. "Lots of hints but no specifics and nothing helpful about a possible motive. Could be that the police were right all along. Maybe Tori was the victim of a random attack. It does happen even in affluent suburbs." I absorbed the truth of her statement and the uncomfortable feeling that Tori's assailant might go unpunished. It seemed so unfair.

We parted soon after, with Violet headed back to Harbor Bay and my beloved Poppet. She assured me that things there were well under control and that Gemma and her mom were up to the task of running the business. Violet was tactful, so she avoided any mention of Daniel Flynn or my nonexistent love life. I consoled myself with the thought that desperation breeds disaster. Desperation might drive some poor creature to get saddled with the likes of Harrison Putnam as a spouse. Far better to live a solitary life than to be harnessed to a perpetual doomsayer like him. Besides, I had an important task to fulfill. By living in Tori Aaron's old digs, I had absorbed through osmosis some of her spirit. That sounded fanciful, but somehow, it was accurate. She had an unquenchable thirst for justice, no matter what the price. Was her murder connected to the disruptions at Sherborne, or had something more sinister arisen?

I scurried back to my classroom just in time for the afternoon session. Several students, including the irascible Priscilla, were already at their easels. I stopped to observe each one and offer suggestions or comments where appropriate. Natalie Tolliver, a student from Detroit, was hunched over her canvas, perfecting a charcoal sketch of a female nude. We hadn't met before, and I was interested in Natalie's aspirations and artistic background. She was a tall, lithe girl with big brown eyes and the exquisitely molded cheekbones of an Etruscan princess.

"Nice work, Natalie. Did you use a live model or draw from memory?"

She stepped aside and flashed a smile that enlivened her entire face. "I spent last weekend at the Detroit Institute of Arts. Talk about inspiration! Couldn't wait to try some of the techniques myself."

The DIA was one of the Motor City's crown jewels, particularly the murals created by Diego Rivera. People often overlooked the museum, although it was ranked among the top ten nationally. I recalled my first expedition there as a youngster, accompanied by Aunt Violet during one of her infrequent jaunts from Paris. I was transfixed by the beauty and wonder of the place and still am to this day. That gave me a sudden idea.

"Perhaps we could arrange a class trip to the DIA. Do you think the group would like that?"

Natalie clapped her hands. "Oh yeah! My aunt is a docent there, and I know she'd arrange things."

I polled the class and found that everyone, even Priscilla was excited at the prospect. After explaining that I had to get permission from the headmaster, we tabled the idea and buckled down to work on our individual projects. Abigail asked permission to use Fantasia as her model, and I readily agreed. She still grieved for her spaniel, who had recently passed after fifteen years, and she had quickly bonded with Fantasia. Loving animals was a good sign in any human, and I admit that I suspected anyone who ignored or disliked them of being emotionally stunted, even potentially criminal. It was a prejudice that I happily admitted to and refused to change. As my class labored on, I mulled over other ideas to keep them engaged. To my surprise, Claire had suggested that I conduct an evening session on cosmetics and artistry. After all, from ancient Egypt on, the urge to enhance one's grooming had appealed to both men and women. Many of the classic paintings featured elaborate jewels, hair, and cosmetics on both genders. I knew Gemma would participate and Aunt Violet as well. Naturally, I had an ulterior motive. Anything that drew the interest of the students and got them talking might help us find Tori's killer. I had a short window of time and owed it to her and Aunt Violet to do my best. A chat with the local authorities might prove useful but I wasn't certain how to engineer that without committing a crime myself.

Evening meals were a communal event at Sherborne, with faculty seated among the students. I deliberately chose an aisle seat next to Tomas Devereaux in hopes that he would open up to me. The boy was hiding something, but I had no clue what it was. Priscilla patted an empty chair and beckoned to Roddy Park to join her. He laughed it off with good cheer and chose a space between Ru and Natalie instead. Thunderclouds appeared on Priscilla's lovely face, but he ignored her reaction. Meanwhile, Abigail and Tomas engaged in a spirited debate about the virtues of vegetarian eating.

"Sorry," Tomas said. "I like meat. Red meat and plenty of it." He forked a breaded pork chop on his plate. "Ms. Aaron tried to convert me too, but I resisted."

That gave me an opening. "What was she like," I asked. "Ms. Aaron."

Tomas grimaced. "It's hard to talk about her. Even now. I never met anyone like her before. She was one of a kind. She really cared about us, not like some of the phony baloney you hear."

Natalie agreed. She lowered her voice. "When Ms. Aaron discovered that Kaboom thing, she went after it like a detective. Sherlock Holmes or Miss Marple, even. Everyone knew she was hot on the trail. She questioned just about every student and teacher. More than the cops did."

"Wait a minute." Tomas raised his voice. "Are you trying to tell me she found out who did it? No way! Someone would have been expelled or worse if she blabbed."

"Maybe that's why she died." Harrison Putnam pasted an unpleasant smile on his face and claimed a seat. "Just so you know, Sergeant Stevens will be stopping by tomorrow to interview some of you again. Seems he found some additional information and has questions. Naturally, he can't speak with you unless one of your teachers or a parent is present. Rules, you know."

Tomas bit his lip but didn't respond. Roddy Park put down his fork and stared. "Probably nothing to worry about. Personally, I'll be glad when they solve this thing. Some of the parents are antsy about it, and I'm uneasy myself. It's hard to look at your friends and students as potential killers."

So, the local gendarmes were coming to Sherborne. Talk about kismet. I interjected myself headlong into the discussion. "I can help with that if you need someone. I have a bit of experience dealing with the police, so that might be useful." Modesty is not my style, but I lowered my eyes and tried to look humble.

"You're an outsider," Harrison snorted. "What possible good will you be?"

"Calm down, Harrison." Roddy looked ready and able to deck the smaller man. "It's a great idea. Being an outsider makes Marky impartial. That's an asset."

Gin pointed her index finger my way and plunged into the fray. "Hey, that's right. You were mixed up in a murder case not that long ago. You can be our resident expert on mayhem."

I politely declined that honor, but Gin wasn't finished. "Makes you wonder about the value of justice, doesn't it? Right before she died, Tori was hot on the trail of something or someone. She told me it would blow the doors off Sherborne when it came out. Then poof. She's gone, and so are any leads."

The students exchanged uneasy looks as if they feared the outcome. They were still young enough to trust their friends and believe in basic human decency. I'd shared that view once until I learned firsthand that even one's closest pals could harbor dark secrets.

To lighten the mood, I mentioned my proposed seminar on cosmetology and art. Roddy Park loved the idea. "There's a real tie-in with historical figures, plus it sounds like a lot of fun. Count me in if you need any help. We could choose some interesting subjects."

Several others voiced the same thought, including Ru Taylor. He spoke about the highly stylized Chinese opera and the paint used by the performers.

"Sounds kinda sissyfied," Tomas teased. "Guys in pajamas using makeup."

"Boy, have you got it wrong. Lots of the best martial artists, like Jackie Chan and Jet Li started out that way. Helps give them agility. I'll bet no one has the stones to call them sissies either."

That got a laugh from everyone and shifted the conversation back from the abyss to brighter topics. Several of us debated which actor was the best martial artist. Votes for Bruce Lee, Jackie Chan, and Jet Li ranked high until Roddy mentioned Chuck Norris and Steven Segal. That caused a sensation with nobody willing to yield his or her favorite to others. It was a vigorous discussion that was fun as well. The only naysayer was Harrison Putnam, who folded his arms and refused to participate. He questioned the academic value of action films and hinted that they helped to pollute young minds.

"Mark my words," he warned, "such things encourage violence and stunt the intellect." While saying that, Harrison glared at Tomas Devereaux as though he proved the point. When we finished our meal, the students dispersed, and Gin, Roddy, Claire, and I were left alone. Thankfully Harrison had excused himself, pleading another engagement. Gin suggested that we reconvene in the faculty lounge to enjoy adult beverages. That sounded fine to me. I needed more insights into the Kaboom incident and Tori's reaction. Frankly, although the entire thing was abhorrent, it struck me as more of a childish prank than a harbinger of murder. If the culprit hoped to cause a reaction, that goal had been attained and exceeded, but I saw no linkage to murder.

We found comfortable wing chairs in the instructors' lounge and sipped scotch while Claire delighted us with a poetry reading. Everything was so peaceful that I almost forgot my mission, especially when the lines from Sylvia Plath's *Bell Jar* rang out.

Roddy closed his eyes and leaned back in his chair. "Tori loved all of Plath's work. I think she memorized most of it. At least, it seemed like it. Always praised that confessional poetry."

"Plath was obsessed with death," I said. "She described it almost sensually. Tori wasn't that way, was she?"

Claire pounced on my question. "Absolutely not. Tori loved life and was determined to wring every ounce of pleasure from it. She certainly didn't fantasize about death. That girl never quit."

I could see that Gin had another view. "True, but let's face it, Tori took risks and made some stupid moves. Poking around other people's business probably got her killed."

"You mean about that Kaboom stuff?" I tried to sound innocent and slightly disinterested. Roddy gave me a sharp look that suggested I had failed miserably, but Gin couldn't wait to speak.

"There was more to it. I'm sure of that. Trouble is, Tori kept it to herself. Waiting for what she called the final shoe to drop. Whatever she found out, it would have caused someone around here some real pain."

Claire looked troubled. Her normally placid features were contorted in either pain or grief. "That was just like her. Tori was fair to a fault. Whatever rabbit she was chasing, she wouldn't say anything until she was positive. Wanted to be fair, and where did that get her."

I wished that Aunt Violet or even Gemma was there to back me up. After all, what did I really know about these people? One of them might very well be Tori's killer. Silence was golden in this instance, and I buttoned my lip. Roddy poured more Scotch and glanced at Claire. "You're suggesting that someone at Sherborne killed Tori? We don't know that, and it's a serious accusation to make. Academics aren't exactly known for their homicidal tendencies. We tend to think more than act."

Claire shrugged but didn't back down.

"All I know is that I lost my best friend, and nobody seems to have any answers. There's plenty of intrigue around here, Roddy, just like everywhere else. You just don't recognize it. Sex, jealousy, power—common motives no matter where you work. We writers feed upon it. Conflict fuels our novels, after all. The human dynamic at work."

No one spoke for what seemed like an eternity until Gin piped up and filled the void.

"I overheard something weird the other day. I was getting the mail from my cubbyhole and Coleman had his door ajar." She straightened her shoulders and ignored Claire's outraged look. "I wasn't eavesdropping, but you know how his voice gets high when he's agitated. It's impossible not to overhear the conversation. Anyway, I couldn't catch everything, but he was almost hysterical, ranting about a scandal that could ruin the school's reputation and land people in jail."

"Really? Who else was in the room?" I forgot my pose as disinterested stranger and plunged into the fray.

Gin shook her head. "Couldn't tell. Unfortunately, his secretary wandered in and gave me one of those mean looks she's famous for, so I grabbed my mail and skedaddled."

"Were any names mentioned?" Claire's hand trembled, shaking the liquid in her glass.

"Just one. Tori Aaron." Gin had the final word, one that curtailed further discussion.

* * *

I had plenty to think about when I returned to my suite. Fortunately, my dear Fantasia dispelled much of the gloom by covering me with doggy kisses and prancing about the room, squeaking her toy elephant. I owed her a comfort break before bedtime and that was her way of reminding me. Before leaving, I slipped my trusty flashlight into a side pocket along with several disposable waste bags. I'd already replaced my necklace with the police whistle I'd received courtesy of Gemma's beau Benny Soto. No sense in taking chances, particularly when word of my previous exploits had spread around the campus. I mulled over Gin's comments about scandal in the school. What action by a Sherborne inmate could lead to jail time? Embezzlement was always a possibility, of course, and an institution like Sherborne had a tidy endowment fund as well as several donation centers. Sexual misdeeds provided another temptation in a closed society where vulnerable teens abounded. Had one of the teachers breached their sacred trust? Nubile coeds like Priscilla could lure even a saint into perdition. From what I knew of Tori Aaron, she wouldn't hesitate to report that type of malfeasance no matter whom it hurt. *Not Roddy, I prayed. Surely, he had more sense than that.*

Fantasia took her sweet time inspecting every bush and blade of grass in the common area. I'm normally calm in a crisis, but when I heard rustling among the trees and the steady tread of an unknown person, I leapt to the side and screamed. In my defense, it was a refined, ladylike sound, nothing raucous. After all that had happened, who could blame me? Instead of danger, I heard laughter, the sweet sound of Claire's musical voice.

"Whoa there, girl. Don't panic. Raleigh and I were trying to catch up with you." The big Golden wagged his tail and touched noses with Fantasia while I took a very deep breath.

"You didn't hear anything?" I asked. "I'm positive someone was following me."

She patted my shoulder. "Just a case of nerves, not that I blame you. Gin never did learn to shut her mouth. Now everyone will think you're snooping." She shot me a quizzical look. "You're not, I hope. Playing detective, that is.

Can't stand to lose another friend."

I can deflect a topic when the occasion demands. "Don't worry about me. I was mulling over what Gin heard in Coleman's office. Have you got any ideas about it?"

She shook her head. "Could be anything or nothing. Our leader is more feckless than fearless if something threatens his school. He touts those college admissions stats like Sacred Writ."

"Oh?"

"You know. What percentage of our kids get into prestige schools, particularly the Ivys. I must hand it to him. Sherborne does exceptionally well even with kids who didn't impress me much."

I gave that some thought. Parents probably expected superior results after shelling out over fifty grand a year for their little darlings. Most prep schools were feeders to the big leagues, so it wasn't unusual unless someone gerrymandered the results. Even then, suspecting something and proving it were very different things.

"What if there was cheating and Tori found out? People do jail time for that. Just check out the news articles."

Claire frowned. "Gee, I don't know. It's not so easy to get away with something like that, especially when kids are involved. You know how they share everything on social media."

Speaking of social media gave me pause. "Suppose some teacher exposed his tender parts on the internet like one of those creepy politicians did? Tell me that wouldn't be worth killing for."

She plopped down on a bench and hid her face in her hands. "Forgive me, Marky. I know you're just trying to help, but I had a sudden vision of Harrison Putnam in the altogether, and it was too much to endure." We exchanged smiles that quickly turned into laughter. I'd never considered Harrison anything but an obnoxious scold. Certainly, never saw him as a centerfold. The very idea gave me chills, and not the good kind.

"Isn't he married? Prowling the singles bars just seems beneath Harrison Putnam. Besides, none of these students are even old enough to drink legally."

"He's divorced," Claire said. "At least some poor woman had the good sense to dump him. As far as money, supposedly, the Putnam family is loaded." She winked. "Just think, Marky. Someday our Harry will be quite a catch when he inherits a packet."

"Ugh. Give me penury over plenty with a guy like that. I meant to ask you; did Tori leave any notes that might give us a clue? I think the kids know very well who did that Kaboom caper and the other graffiti stuff as well. I quizzed them, and they looked very uncomfortable."

I had plenty to learn about the adolescent psyche. Claire shrugged it off with an aside. "You know kids. Nobody squeals even when they despise the culprit or disapprove of the act. It's a point of honor with them."

We ambled back to our quarters in silence, both of us deep in thought. I tried to marshal the clues I'd managed to collect, but from her expression, I suspected that Claire was mourning the friend whose life had been extinguished so brutally.

Chapter Five

Sergeant Jake Stevens arrived promptly at eight a.m. the next morning and asked to see me. Frankly, his physical presence was unimpressive—nothing like the lawman of screen or page. For one thing, he was vertically challenged, short by even the kindest description. I stand five feet seven inches tall and it's unusual for me to tower over most men. In addition, he carried enough extra weight to strain the buttons on his uniform to capacity. Artists notice these things, but they can be misleading. The moment he spoke I discarded such superficial observations. Stevens was nobody's dreamboat, but he was nobody's fool either. He glared at me with intelligent blue eyes and barked a question.

"Who are you, Miss, and why are you here?"

After I explained my role in loco parentis, he relaxed somewhat but still regarded me with suspicion.

"Okay, but don't interfere. I've got a job to do, and I intend to do it."

People often describe me as charming, especially when dealing with susceptible males. Unfortunately, any claim I might have had to womanly wiles was quickly dispensed with and ignored by the good Sergeant. The soft approach would never work with him, so I regrouped and tried another tact. If only I had come bearing donuts.

"Do you have any suspects yet? Most of these kids loved Ms. Aaron and they want to help."

He stared at a file on his phone. "You've been here what—three days? So, you're already an expert, Ms. Davis? Don't make me laugh. Most of them are spoiled brats more interested in pleasing Daddy than catching a killer.

Any one of them could lie to your face and stab you in the back."

I needed his help, so I swallowed the tart comment on the tip of my tongue and nodded approvingly. "That's true. I can see that you've assessed things quite neatly. I am an outsider but that's an advantage here. I can gain their trust and maybe find out things they won't share with you."

He heaved a big sigh. "I get it. You're a mystery buff. Loved Nancy Drew and all those girly books and think you know all about crime solving."

That aroused my anger. My cheeks grew warm and against my better judgment, I swallowed the bait.

"See here. No need to be patronizing. As a matter of fact, I recently helped solve a crime—a double murder. Just check with the Harbor Bay sheriff if you don't believe me."

That drew a smile or what passed for one from Stevens. His alarmingly large teeth reminded me of the evil gator grin I'd seen in wildlife shows.

"Trust me, I did. Checked you out with the deputy there. A guy named Soto. He used words like "meddling" and "conceited." Not quite the warmest endorsement I've ever heard, Ms. Davis."

I sputtered something vile but before I continued, Stevens held up his hand.

"Then I spoke with the chief. His assessment was much more positive although he did describe you as impetuous and bull-headed." He fixed those beady eyes on me once more and said, "Let's start again and clear the air. I'm in charge and your role is to sit on the sidelines in case any of these delicate young souls needs protection from big bad me. Period. Got it?"

I managed a civilized response, and the games began. Stevens divided the students into two groups of six and summoned them into the room. They scrambled into the classroom and sat silently, eyeing the sergeant, and casting the occasional glance my way. No one seemed overly concerned. If anything, with one exception the students in group one looked bright-eyed and eager for action. Tomas Devereaux was that outlier, and his attitude disturbed me. As a local scholarship student, he lacked the status and parental backing of his peers. Aunt Violet had referenced a townie who was on the police radar, and I feared it might be Tomas. His slicked-back hair, cutoffs, and battered tee shirt only added to the profile of a juvenile delinquent able and willing to offend.

"We found something odd under Ms. Aaron's body," Stevens said. As an opening salvo, it was effective. Several of the students cringed and Abigail Jenkins gasped.

There was silence in the room. Dead silence as if the ghost of Tori Aaron hovered above us watching the proceedings. Finally, Abigail asked the question.

"What did you find, Sergeant?"

Stevens nodded as if he had won round one in this battle.

"Well Miss, we found makeup. Cosmetics I guess you'd call them." He gazed into his phone again although I knew it was only a ruse designed to ratchet up the tension. "Let's see. One lipstick, gypsy red; loose face powder; eye shadow in some shade called Vamp; and one big tube of mascara minus the top." Stevens raised his eyes and watched the reaction of the students.

"But that can't be." Natalie Tolliver's voice was almost a whisper. "Ms. Aaron didn't use makeup. She said it was demeaning, bowing to society's view of women."

"Huh! Maybe she had a secret life you didn't know about." Priscilla Sayers had a malicious grin on her face. "Those mousey types can surprise you. She was probably meeting some man."

That gave Stevens the opening he sought. "So, you didn't like her much, Miss. I thought everyone loved Miss Aaron."

Priscilla didn't flinch. In fact, she doubled down.

"Don't look so shocked, all of you. I saw her one day kissing some guy under the bleachers. Not such a goody two shoes after all."

"You're a liar! You were always jealous of her." Tomas leapt to his feet and confronted Priscilla. "Maybe she found out some things you wanted to hide, Priscilla. Maybe you stopped her."

Sergeant Stevens showed no emotion. He plowed right through his questions without acknowledging the animosity in the room.

"You should know that Ms. Aaron discovered which one of you instigated that Kaboom incident in the auditorium. It's right here in her notes."

He was lying and I knew it. Claire already told me that Tori's notebook and iPad had disappeared and presumably had been stolen by her assailant.

Ru Taylor's face was ashen as he looked at his classmates one by one. It was an awakening of sorts for the lad who had obviously never suspected them of such a hideous crime.

"None of you saw anything out of the ordinary that night?" Stevens' tone suggested that they were lying. "There was a full moon, as I recall. Rather a mild night for that time of year."

"We already told you," Tomas said.

"Well, tell me again. Ms. Aaron's calendar showed a meeting at 6 p.m. I'm betting it was with one of you."

"What name did she have on the calendar?" Abigail leaned forward, clutching her purse as if her life depended on it.

Stevens knew how to manipulate suspects. He let silence fill the room like an uninvited guest. Finally, he glanced down at his file saying, "No name. Just 'student conference.' Leaves the field wide open, doesn't it?"

Priscilla Sayers brushed his comment off with a snarl. "We have over six hundred students here. Why zero in on us? It was probably some sleazy rendezvous. For all we know, she might have been *close* to a student. Too close. It happens you know, and Ms. Aaron was just the type."

"How *dare* you." Natalie jumped to her feet and pointed at Priscilla. "She was the most honorable person I ever met. If she knew who started that Kaboom stuff, Ms. Aaron would have faced him directly. You're the sneak, Priscilla, always trying to start trouble. Look how you pester Mr. Park. Everybody notices but he ignores you." Both girls faced off in what could have become a sticky situation. That's when Tomas intervened.

"Cut it out, you two. That night was the Jeopardy tournament of champions. We ate dinner early so that we could all watch it. Ms. Aaron was going to join us, but she never did. She was our team coach for the high school academic challenge." His voice broke. "She never missed an episode until that night."

"So, you're saying you all ate together and watched the show? No one left the room. Not even for a few minutes?" Stevens gave them that hard cop stare he'd perfected over the years to intimidate criminals into confessing. Unfortunately, it had absolutely no effect on these students who had probably grown-up watching television cops do a much better job of it.

I was torn between letting the scene play out and avoiding mayhem but was forced to choose the latter.

"Let's calm down and allow the Sergeant to ask his questions," I said breaking the spell. Between Abigail Jenkins's sniffles and Priscilla's smirks, Stevens was unable to regain the momentum.

Perhaps that was just as well.

Afterwards, I joined Gin and Roddy for a late lunch. They had chaperoned the second group and reported that very little had been achieved despite Stevens' tough tactics. Only one interesting point had emerged: Stevens confirmed that Tori had indeed uncovered the culprit in the Kaboom caper.

"He told Roddy but of course he ignored me," Gin huffed. "Sexist pig. All this man-to-man stuff gets old after a while."

Roddy laughed and patted her on the back. "Ah, come on. Relax. Stevens is strictly old school, and you look young enough to be a student instead of a teacher. Besides, he didn't spill anything important. I guess Tori told Coleman that she was closing in on the suspect. Sounded like it was one of the kids though and that would make Coleman go nuts. Expulsion, lawsuits by aggrieved parents—the whole shebang." Roddy grinned. "I suspect it was definitely a two-Prozac night for our boss."

That comment intrigued me. "Does he take that? Poor man must be under a lot of pressure."

Roddy looked abashed. "Forget I said anything. I should have kept my mouth shut. It's just that I saw a bottle of the stuff on his desk one day and it made sense. This school is his life, and any kind of scandal would sink him not to mention damage his marriage."

That made me wonder. Suppose the headmaster took extreme measures to quell a scandal and Tori suffered the consequences. From everything I'd heard, Tori was implacable when faced with what she considered to be a moral dilemma. The Kaboom incident or any other impropriety fit the bill rather nicely.

"Despite what Stevens said, I gather that nobody ever found Tori's iPad or computer."

"Nah and that's a shame. She was meticulous about keeping notes and gathering evidence." Gin grimaced. "The stuff he said about cosmetics was probably a lie too. Trust me. Tori deplored that type of thing. Called it paint and implied it was more suited to doxies than serious professionals."

"Doxies?" Roddy burst out laughing. "Where in the world did you get that? Sounds more like something from a nineteenth-century melodrama than anything contemporary."

Gin flushed. "Sorry. It so happens that we're staging a play from that era and that dialogue just sprang to mind. Very common in the times of Sherlock Holmes and his contemporaries. You know, the fallen woman."

I bridled a bit with all the disparaging comments about cosmetics. After all, that was how I made my living. Poppet was billed as a temple of beauty that empowered women and enabled them to be their best self. Luckily Claire appeared and defended my position.

"I use cosmetics," she said. "Anything that helps and makes me feel good. No harm in it at all. In fact, I was going to ask Marky for advice on updating my look." She turned to Gin. "So there!"

Ever the diplomat, Roddy dissipated the tension by referencing our proposed seminar. "You know, that's the type of question that would fit right in during our session. "Cosmetics in Art and History." Let the kids debate the issue. Plenty of kings and pirates were heavily into jewelry and makeup, and the Egyptian pharaohs loved ringing their eyes with Kohl and using plenty of gold."

I got a sudden inspiration. "Not that different than the modern fascination for tattoos. And lots of guys wear an earring these days. Another type of adornment. If we take that field trip to the DIA, we can visit their Egyptian section. Plenty of examples there. Think of King Tut and Alexander the Great." We ended our discussion on that upbeat note and disbursed to return once again to the business of teaching.

My group of aspiring artists was noticeably silent after Stevens' performance. They focused on their paintings with an intensity that surprised and alarmed me. Except for Priscilla Sayers, of course. Her constant array of smirks and smiles was at variance with the general solemnity in the classroom, so much so that the normally placid Ru Peterson called her out.

"Do you have something to say, Priscilla, or is this another pointless bid for attention."

Priscilla ignored his question and applied an additional layer of acrylic to her painting. The vivid hues and texture were intriguing, and I had to admit that despite her many deficiencies the girl had talent if only she chose to apply herself.

"Maybe you should answer him," Natalie said. "After all, you had plenty to tell that detective."

Priscilla arched a brow and dropped her paintbrush. "My oh my. Look who's finally coming out of her shell. By the way, Stevens was only a sergeant. This little hamlet doesn't rate a real detective. Get your terms straight, Natalie." She boldly eyed her fellow students and took center stage. "Everything I said was true. Your Ms. Aaron was no saint. She was a snoop who couldn't mind her own business. Curiosity and the cat—so true."

Tomas folded his arms and confronted her.

"You know something you're not telling. Were you the one Ms. Aaron was supposed to meet that night? I bet you did that Kaboom stuff, and she found out."

"Try again, town boy. I was with you stiffs watching Jeopardy. Remember?"

"Not so fast." For once, Abigail, courteous, polite Abigail Jenkins, fired back. "You followed Mr. Park when he left the room. We all noticed that because he's not interested, but you can't take a hint."

Priscilla's cheeks turned crimson. "I was only gone for a few minutes. Using the restroom isn't a crime in most places. And I didn't follow Mr. Park. He went down the corridor and disappeared."

I clapped my hands to restore order, all the while wondering where Roddy had gone the evening of Tori's murder. He hadn't mentioned anything about it, but there must be an innocent explanation for his absence. Good looks and easy manners didn't absolve Roddy as a suspect, but they made it harder to cast him as the villain. How much easier to blame Harrison Putnam, an unpleasant man who openly despised Tori and most of humanity.

When class ended for the day, I put Fantasia on her lead and wandered over to Claire's door. I'd grown to depend on her sound judgment and wry sense of humor to balance out the adolescent angst of the students. Besides, using the buddy system in the park had some advantages. If only Tori had availed herself of that she might still be alive. No one answered Claire's door, so I was forced to venture out alone. Perhaps she had already left with Raleigh, and we could catch up with them. I wasn't worried about it. There was still plenty of daylight to ward off any troublemakers and increase visibility. When we reached the poets' bench, I saw a familiar figure slumped over a book.

"Are you okay, Roddy?" He was normally so upbeat that this downtrodden version surprised me.

He raised his head and abruptly closed the book. When I saw the title, *Ariel*, by Sylvia Plath, I took a risk. "What was she really like? I've heard so many impressions of Tori that I'm confused."

At first, he stayed silent, but ultimately, Roddy Park spoke candidly about the woman he knew.

"Pretty obvious, aren't I? Sometimes I miss her so much that it helps to read the things she liked. Sylvia Plath was one of her idols, although suicide never appealed to Tori. You wouldn't catch her sticking her head in an oven like Plath. That seemed foolish to her and me too. I suppose I just don't understand the artistic temperament. Political science is my field, after all, not Confessional poetry. Guess I'm the one who's making the confession now." He took a deep breath but stayed unemotional. Thank goodness. Crying men totally unnerve me. I'm no fan of weepy women either.

"Were you a couple, you, and Tori? Forgive me for being so blunt." I felt uncomfortable invading his privacy but, in this instance, it was more than mere idle curiosity. He could have rebuffed me but Roddy Park, secret crush of hot-blooded females and probably a few males, unburdened himself. I suspect he longed to discuss her with someone, and a virtual stranger like me fit the bill.

"Tori was unique. Never met anyone like her before and probably won't ever again. Brilliant, talented, and genuinely kind. I guess you could say that I was in love with her. Would have married her in a flash, but she wasn't interested. Tori preferred a friend with benefits setup. Nothing permanent." Roddy reached down and stroked Fantasia's soft fur. "In some ways, I'm a traditional guy. You know, kids, pets, maybe even a picket fence. Not Tori. She saved her passion for social causes and her art. I hoped that if I just hung in there, she'd change her mind, but it didn't happen. The night she died, I decided to issue an ultimatum. Commit to me or let me go."

"And did you? Confront her, I mean." I prayed Roddy wouldn't confess to something unthinkable, like murder. "Each man kills the thing he loves." That's what the poet said, but it couldn't be true. Not in this case. I refused to believe that Professor Roddy Park, a bastion of intellect and rational thought, bashed the woman he loved in the head and left her to die alone.

"I never got the chance. I went looking for her when she didn't turn up for our game night, but I never found her. Then Raleigh showed up dragging his lead, and I knew something was very wrong." His voice was muffled as he continued. "I usually went with her when she walked him, but not that night. If I had, she'd be alive today."

How do you comfort a man in such pain? All I could do was pat his shoulder and give him a sisterly hug.

"Did Tori know who instigated that Kaboom thing? Maybe that's why she was killed." I pictured perfidious Priscilla Sayers whacking an enemy in the head if it suited her interests. Then again, I had to contain my prejudices against the girl. She was easy to dislike, and it distorted my judgment.

Roddy fumbled with his keys before answering. "Tori told me she'd found the culprit and was "handling it"—her words, not mine. Sometimes she got so close to those kids that she lost all objectivity. Teachers must maintain some distance even from the students we most like. Otherwise, you sacrifice your moral authority."

Easier said than done. Already I felt bonded to my little group, with the notable exception of Priscilla. Should I make a concerted effort to reach her or just accept my prejudices? Something told me that Priscilla had information about Tori's death. Information that I had to extract from the girl. It would be no easy task, but duplicity wasn't entirely foreign to me. Aunt Violet planned to visit on the weekend, and her advice on human relations was always spot on. Perhaps she'd have some techniques to share.

"Do you suppose that cop fabricated what he said? About having Tori's computer?" I didn't know Stevens, and he was a tough one to read. Surely if he had Tori's notes, he would already have arrested someone."

Roddy chuckled. "Probably. Anything to shake up those kids. I'm pretty sure one of them was the culprit. But that other stuff. About the makeup. How weird was that? Tori barely wore lipstick, let alone mascara. I have two sisters, so I'm used to seeing cosmetics lying around. Stevens might have been truthful about finding that."

I made a quick mental note to tackle the good sergeant about that. After all, who better to offer her expertise on cosmetics than yours truly, the proprietor and proud owner of Poppet? You can tell plenty about a woman by the brand and type of products she uses. One more question occurred to me.

"Weird what Gin overheard Coleman saying," I turned toward Roddy. "What do you suppose it could be?"

Roddy gave me a quizzical look. "You're really into this stuff, aren't you? It was probably nothing. Coleman overreacts to almost everything related to the school. Trust me, though, if any real scandal erupted, he'd be the first one on the firing line, or he'd jettison one of us in a hurry."

I realized that I had a decision to make. Roddy already suspected me of being a snoop or worse. Perhaps I could confide my real purpose to him and become an ally. After all, he had loved Tori. He couldn't be her killer, could he? Before I involved him, Claire and Raleigh appeared in the clearing. Roddy hastily concealed his book of poetry while I attempted to exude eau de innocence. Her eyes swept over us like a laser. "Okay. What are you guys up to? Come on. Spill it."

Roddy was far better than I at charming people, particularly those of the opposite sex. He shrugged his shoulders and moved over to give Claire a spot on the bench.

"No conspiracy. Just chatting."

I shrugged and beamed what I hoped was an innocent smile.

"I was curious about that stuff Gin heard. For all we know, this place is a powder keg ready to explode at any minute." Admittedly I dramatized things a bit, but it was necessary.

Claire laughed. In fact, she guffawed.

"Don't get your knickers in a twist, as my mama used to say. Gin exaggerates everything. Not deliberately. She just can't help it. Remember, her field is drama and stage. Coleman is an old worry wart, but nothing ever comes of it." She frowned. "Of course, that Kaboom fiasco was worrisome. If Tori got wind of that, it could be important. Adolescent emotions run high, and someone might have panicked and clobbered her without thinking."

We then switched the conversation to our proposed outing at the DIA. I promised to contact the headmaster the next day and seek his permission. Seemed like a great opportunity to probe for anything else that might be brewing at Sherborne.

Coleman Ross spooked rather easily for a man in his position. When I tapped at his door, he spun around as if he feared an imminent attack. Once again, I forced myself into non-threatening girl next-door mode. Fantasia, my constant companion, served as my wingman. The headmaster certainly didn't intimidate me. He puzzled me. I'm told that I have an engaging smile. To test that theory, I gave him a wide view of all my pearly whites and explained the proposal for a field trip.

He frowned, as though this was an issue equivalent to nuclear disarmament. I got the distinct impression that decision-making wasn't his strong suit. "I encourage cultural exchanges," he said, "but taking any group of students off campus comes with risks. Yes. Major risks."

"Naturally, we'd have supervision," I said. "Violet Davis has volunteered to join us and conduct the tour."

When he heard her name, Coleman brightened.

"Your aunt. Of course. Charming woman. Quite the artistic luminary."

"Several of her works are in the DIA's permanent collection," I said, trying hard not to brag.

I could tell that the headmaster was weakening. After several more inquiries, he agreed to our trip, provided of course that permission slips were obtained from the parents. "Absolutely imperative," he said. "Believe it or not, we've had a few students sneak off during outings. Some from good families too, if you can believe it. Fortunately, nothing came of it, but it was a near thing."

I vowed to remain vigilant and secure the necessary paperwork. Before leaving, I took a risk. That turned out to be a mistake.

"Claire told me about the Kaboom incident, headmaster. Perhaps the multicultural nature of the artwork would help to expand their horizons. You know, show them that genius comes from all types of people."

His eyes widened, and he leapt to his feet. "See here, Ms. Davis. We don't discuss that unfortunate incident at Sherborne. It was an abomination. Not typical of our students at all. Probably the work of some outside agitator."

Since that was foolish on the face of it, I gave Coleman props for holding his ground. He was unabashed even as he ranted about his conspiracy theory.

"Forgive me," I said. "It's just that the students mentioned it. They said Ms. Aaron was hot on the trail of the culprit."

His eyes bugged out as he sputtered a response.

"Tori Aaron! That woman still haunts me, even from the grave. I told her to mind her own business, but she refused. Can you believe it? She was insubordinate. Said she intended to rectify the situation. Deal with it her own way. The impertinence of that creature!"

I edged toward the door before I snatched defeat from the jaws of victory.

"You're right, of course. And thank you for agreeing to our trip." When I had escaped to the corridor, I leaned against the wall and heaved a sigh of relief. A man like Coleman Ross was difficult to deal with. He had so many insecurities that it was easy to alarm him. That's when I heard an unpleasant chuckle. Harrison Putnam stood opposite me, sorting his mail, or pretending to.

"Hard time with the headmaster," he sneered. "Not everyone can handle him. Of course, his family and mine go way back. I understand men like him and the importance of traditions."

His pomposity provoked me into an unwise move. "I suppose you'll want to join us on our field trip to the DIA. Lots of culture and tradition there. The students could really benefit from your wisdom."

Harrison folded his arms and stared me down.

"Don't think you fool me, Ms. Davis. Who sent you? I know about your degree from the Art Institute, but you have your own agenda. Were you one of her friends? An avenging angel?"

"What are you talking about?" I was genuinely perplexed by his outburst until I realized that it pertained to Tori. Harrison had a proverbial axe to grind when it came to her, almost a mania. That made me suspicious. What had she uncovered that threatened him? I doubted it was the Kaboom incident. Way too puerile for a pretentious twit like Harrison, and he probably considered mass media far beneath him. No. He might well be involved in something darker. If only Gin was a better snoop and had heard the full conversation in Coleman's office.

"Some secrets can't be buried," I said. "What's that old saying, 'Old sins cast long shadows.'? You seem obsessed with Tori Aaron. The woman's dead, for heaven's sake. Let her rest in peace."

He curled his lip as if I had blasphemed. "How dare you interfere in school matters. This is summer school. You're nothing but a camp counselor to a bunch of wannabe artists. A cosmetologist, for heaven's sake. Nothing more." His tone raised Fantasia's hackles, although Harrison did the snarling. "And keep that hairy beast away from me. Dogs have no place on school property."

His reaction was so extreme that it intrigued me.

"Maybe not. You raise an interesting point, though. I'm thinking of joining the faculty full-time. Not that I could ever take Tori's place, of course."

Harrison's response was comical. He was still sputtering nonsensically when I rounded the corner into the hallway and ran into a colleague.

Claire's grin was a mile wide.

"Poor old Harry. I can't believe you tortured him that way. Come to think of it; he deserved every bit of it, the big creep. If he wasn't such a coward, I'd suspect him of being Tori's killer."

"Why not? He certainly disliked her. Enough to murder her, perhaps."

Claire shook her head. "Here's something you don't know about our Harry. I've watched him for three years, and in my very humble opinion, the man didn't hate Tori at all."

"Huh?"

"He loved her. All that nonsense about opposing everything she said was just camouflage designed to make her notice him. The kind of behavior you see with little boys in grade school pulling pigtails. Trust me on that. I have no proof, of course. Just call it instinct."

I am seldom speechless, but on this occasion, I stayed mute. What was it about Tori that made both an irascible Brahmin like Harrison and an irresistible hunk like Roddy fall deeply in love? She was certainly no beauty queen, although Tori had a sort of energy that enlivened her. Her frame was petite but not spectacular. The woman didn't even wear makeup, for heaven's sake! As I pondered this, it suddenly occurred to me that my outrage had more to do with my own lackluster love life than hers. Objectively speaking, I ranked somewhere between wholesome and pretty. It sounds conceited, I know, but almost everyone agreed on that. Yet, in all my twenty-six years, I had failed to attract and keep any man worth having. What big character flaw handicapped me in the romance sweepstakes? Was I too spoiled or selfish to embrace a mature relationship? I'd had plenty of dates and more than a few admirers. Inevitably I let them drift away either through disinterest or some perceived deficiency. Was I too engrossed in finding Mr. Right to recognize him when he appeared? Perhaps I should rethink my priorities and stop defining success by my ability to bond with a man. That was such a pre-feminist concept, one that presumed a single woman was an anomaly. So, what if I remained a spinster forever. Spinster! Does anyone still use that term anymore? It was always a term of opprobrium, designed to isolate and shame the single woman who failed to bag a husband as an outcast. I knew Aunt Violet would have the answer. Trust me, no one would ever have used that term to describe her. She might be called a libertine, even a fallen woman by the more censorious people in town, but everyone I knew admired her. Aunt Violet had no problem administering tough love when it was warranted, and she knew me better than anyone besides my own mother.

Claire was staring at me as if I were in a fugue state. That made me return to the conundrum of a murdered artist and social warrior who tried to right wrongs. Focusing on the victim, not myself, made things much simpler.

"What was it about her," I asked Claire. "Tori was a magnet for men, yet she was no femme fatale. At least, I don't think so. You knew her, so you're a far better judge."

Claire gazed at the ceiling as if she were once again visualizing her lost friend. "Tori had passion. It suffused her entire being. That kind of damn the consequences commitment and bravery is so rare that it creates its own mystique. Some people call it integrity. It made her compelling to men and women as well. Most of us are too cowardly to behave that way."

"Don't sell yourself short," I said. "You infuse that passion into your writing. I read your novel last evening, and it captivated me. The characters were so real that I felt I knew them."

Claire grinned. "Sometimes writers save their courage for fiction. Much safer that way, and it doesn't get you fired."

While we were on the subject, I ventured another question. "Don't tell me Coleman was enthralled by her too. Our suspect pool has expanded wildly."

"Hardly! Our headmaster has only one true love, and it's Sherborne. Even his wife comes in a poor second. Tori was a thorn in his side, so if anything, he wanted to eliminate her. Bloodlessly, of course. He's simply not the type to be violent. That's way too vulgar for a cautious man like him."

I kept a thought to myself. If Tori threatened Sherborne school, then even Coleman Ross, patrician scholar, might well have resorted to violence. Would he mock her by placing cosmetics on her body? That kind of pettiness wouldn't occur to most men, especially one with his head in the clouds. No. I rejected that idea on the face of it and decided that there was only one thing to do. A confrontation with Sergeant Stevens was called for.

Chapter Six

The local police station, housed in the Department of Human Services Building, was an unprepossessing structure that resembled a relic from the thirties. Rather like a hastily constructed building from the WPA era. It looked incongruous in such an upscale community of brick and aggressive stone buildings that screamed of prosperity. Perhaps that was deliberate, intended to convey a message: We are not like big cities. Crime in this community is a minor annoyance. No big deal. Sergeant Stevens had been surprisingly gracious when I telephoned for an appointment. I had already determined that he was cagey and nobody's fool, so I opted for a low-key approach and vowed to keep up my guard. In preparation for our meeting, I dove into my cosmetics stash and retrieved every shadow, blush, and lipstick shade that projected innocence or a reasonable facsimile. Since pink suggested girlish innocence, it usually did the trick. This was no time for vamping the constabulary, so I wore my hair in a low ponytail and completed the effect with pearl stud earrings and a modest cotton shirtwaist. No one could accuse me of manipulation or using feminine wiles. No sir!

"Come in, Ms. Davis," Stevens said, showing a vulpine grin. "Sit down. Coffee?"

"No thanks. I've heard horror stories about cop coffee."

"Have you, now? Sorry, but you're way behind the times. Even police officers use a Keurig these days." He sipped his brew and waited for me to make the first move. That unnerved me and required supreme self-control to avoid babbling.

His voice was deep with just a tinge of irony. "Now. What can I do for you? No more trouble on campus I trust. Or have you come here to confess?"

That jolted me! "What? I wasn't even here when Tori was murdered."

He reared back in his chair and chortled. "Just kidding. I thought you were used to police stations and cop humor. Remember, I checked you out."

His bad manners alleviated all my queasiness. I knew he was teasing me, and it hurt my pride. "Okay. Cards on the table. Did you really find cosmetics with Tori's body? If so, maybe I can help you. I don't believe you found her computer or notes. Otherwise, you'd close in on her killer by now."

Stevens put his elbows on his desk and studied me. "I'm puzzled. How can you possibly help me? I always welcome citizen participation, but it does seem a bit out of your league."

Temper, temper. He's baiting you again. "You probably forgot that I own a cosmetics emporium. Quite frankly there's not much about products and brands that I don't know, and they tell you a lot about the purchaser."

"An emporium, huh? Impressive. Sounds much better than a makeup store."

"Show me what you found, and I'll evaluate it. You've got nothing to lose unless you're afraid a lowly civilian might solve this."

He mulled things over before deciding. "Okay. Wait here, and I'll bring it out. It's evidence remember, so don't touch anything."

I gave him a letter-perfect smile and nodded. It was true that the type and choice of cosmetics told a lot about a person. For instance, drugstore brands suggested someone who was tied financially or philosophically to economy purchases. Some women with enough money to buy the best felt guilty about spending cash on something they considered frivolous. Poppet featured only superior products from some of the finest houses, but I never touted the most expensive item if there was another alternative that would serve a customer just as well. Personally, I loved Kiehls, a mid-priced, no-nonsense brand with quality galore. I endorsed it to everyone. Some of my customers, however, insisted on purchasing only the most expensive things as if it reflected on them. Their choice, my profit. It told me however that those women were more focused on snob appeal than results or were suckers for a slick advertisement. Then again, manufacturers were selling a dream to each potential buyer. No harm in trying.

While I was musing, Stevens returned carrying a sealed plastic bag filled with cosmetics. He dangled it over my head, repeating once again, that I was not to touch anything. Chain of custody, blah, blah, blah. I carefully inspected the contents, noting the brand, shade, and condition of the cosmetics. Most of the items were available in drug stores or mass-market venues. Maybelline, L'Oréal, Revlon—although I wouldn't stock them for Poppet's customers, they were big sellers. Some makeup artists raved about Maybelline Great Lash mascara and insisted it was the best product available despite its down-market placement. Personally, I'd never had good results with it.

"Well?" Stevens hovered over me as if daring me to make a misstep.

I explained that most likely these items had been purchased at the town drug store, a favorite site for youngsters with limited spending money or expertise. Those brands were also used in school drama settings for plays and other onstage events. Cheap but effective. I planned to quiz Gin about that very thing as soon as I returned to campus.

"Someone smeared mascara on Tori's face. Her eyelashes, I presume."

Stevens nodded. "Yeah. Under her eyes too. They drew a funny smile on her lips as well. Kind of like a Kewpie doll with purple lips."

I steeled myself for rejection but soldiered on. "Don't suppose you'd let me see the crime scene photos. That may tell me a lot."

This time, he seemed really torn. "I don't know, Ms. Davis. They're hard to take."

After I assured him that I wouldn't faint or shriek, he shuffled over to a cabinet and removed a folder. On crime shows they called it the murder book, but I didn't dare mention that to Stevens. He already suspected that I was a voyeur or a murder groupie.

Seeing that last glimpse of Tori Aaron was difficult. I'll be the first to admit that. It wasn't the blood pooling around her head that affected me most. It was the shocking desecration of her face. Someone took a very personal pleasure in smearing cosmetics on the face of a woman who eschewed them. It was the ultimate act of contempt for a victim who couldn't fight back. Two bright spots of rouge also decorated her cheeks. I'd seen homeless or mentally challenged women roaming the streets of Chicago sporting just that look. Once again it was a cynical statement of hatred and impotent rage by the killer.

"Someone took time doing that." I forced my voice to remain monotone when in truth I was closer to hysteria than I'd ever expected. "This looks very personal, but I'm sure you already figured that out. No prints on any of those articles, I presume."

"Nope. Wiped clean. Ms. Aaron was a woman with set habits. Someone knew that and waited for his chance. It was obviously a local. Someone from the town or school. She clashed with a surprising number of people. Never backed down from a fight, or so they tell me."

If only her computer or notebook had been recovered. If Tori was the obsessive diarist her colleagues described, she would have left some clues. I was sure of that. "People say she knew who orchestrated that Kaboom caper and was planning on settling things. Would that be enough to incite such a vicious murder?"

Stevens closed his eyes. "Ms. Davis. I came here from the Detroit PD. You'd be surprised at the things that cause a murder. There it was usually money or drugs but here…prestige, position—all that's on the table, especially in those snooty schools like Sherborne."

I thanked him for his time and gathered my things. Before closing the door, Sergeant Stevens gave me a warning. "Stay clear of this, young lady. Whoever killed her won't stop doing it again, and I'd hate to see you in one of these photos."

* * *

Aunt Violet arrived bright and early that Friday afternoon looking perfectly self-possessed. After assuring me that Poppet was flourishing in the hands of Gemma, she immediately went to the heart of the issue. "Tell me. Everything you've learned and done about Tori's murder including any suspects."

I summarized everything, especially my visit with the authorities. Frankly, I was rather proud of my success with crusty Sergeant Stevens, so I bragged just a bit.

"Good job," Violet said. "Remember, though, with YouTube tutorials, every kid with a computer knows something about buying and applying products. Most of the brands touted by their "Social Influencers" aren't cheap, either. Social Influencers! How I loathe that term. The web allows relative nobodies to inflame gaggles of teenage girls with dreams of glamour and beauty while they pocket the endorsement money."

I hesitated to remind her that we did the same thing at Poppet, using a different, more subtle platform and targeting more sophisticated buyers. Everyone sold illusion. It was the basis of the entire advertising industry.

Violet grinned. "Okay. End of rant. Let's discuss your list of potential suspects."

I started with Coleman Ross. "He's obsessed with Sherborne and really didn't like Tori. Considered her some sort of infidel storming the gates."

"Interesting. I wonder what that discussion Gin heard was all about. Personally, I doubt that it was this Kaboom thing. That's obnoxious but hardly lethal enough to bring down the school, especially if it's dealt with firmly. Remember. They may be affluent, but these students are still kids with adolescent insecurities."

I saw her point, but Violet had never met Priscilla Sayers. That vixen was capable of almost anything and had an attitude of entitlement that astounded me. Why else would she pursue Roddy Park when it was evident that he had absolutely no interest in her?

"So, Roddy was in love with Tori. Hmm. I wonder if she felt the same way." My dear aunt looked away for a moment as if she were reliving a similar experience in her past. According to my mother, men trailed after Violet all her life, begging for even a crumb of affection. She had rebuffed all attempts to make relationships permanent, although she had what she termed "close friendships" with several suitors.

"Roddy would never hurt her," I said. "And he would never desecrate her face that way."

Violet gave me one of her knowing looks. "Sounds like you have a crush on the professor yourself, Marky. I admit he's handsome, but be cautious. All men have egos, especially the hot ones. They can feel very entitled when it comes to romance."

That led me to Harrison Putnam, the least attractive male on campus. I shared Claire's belief that he, too, was in love with Tori.

"Ugh. I can't imagine any woman even touching him. He probably has reptilian scales instead of skin. He's obsessed with class distinctions too. I'm sure if he could pin the murder on Tomas, he would. Harrison told me himself that Sherborne was no place for the lower orders. His words, not mine."

"Were his movements on that evening accounted for?"

A practical question, one I had considered too. I explained the "quiz night" challenge and the Jeopardy tournament gathering. "The show starts at 7:30, and potluck was served an hour before. Just for the record, Harrison never participated. He considered such activities too pedestrian and a distraction from their studies. Tori walked Raleigh at 6:15 each evening. Everyone knew that. I had to admit that between serving and eating the potluck and watching the show, someone could have easily slipped out and confronted Tori. The entire tragic episode wouldn't have taken that long. Suddenly another thought occurred to me. "Surely, the murderer would be covered with blood, and someone would have noticed it right away. You know how observant teenagers are."

My aunt looked me straight in the eye. "As I recall, it was a brisk night. You know how Spring can be in this part of Michigan. Was Tori wearing a coat by chance?"

I forced myself to visualize those dreadful crime scene photos once again. At first, I could only recall the blood and the garish face paint, but then I found the answer. "She was wearing a long thick sweater coat. You know, the kind that's oversized and usually made of wool. She was so petite that it almost swallowed her up." I shuddered. "Like a shroud."

I realized that I had answered her question. The killer's clothing had probably been protected from blood spatter by a coat or jacket as well. Thus, after disposing of it, he or she could slip back into the group without attracting any notice. Had Sergeant Stevens deduced the same thing. If so, had he mounted a search for a gore-soaked garment?

Violet then asked about Claire and Gin. They were closest to Tori and might have special insights into her. I assured her that both women were bereft by the loss of their friend, especially Claire, who had adopted Raleigh.

"That does show a good heart," Violet said, reaching down to hug Fantasia. "So many pets are cast aside when their owner dies. Raleigh was fortunate, and Fantasia was lucky also to find you."

I gulped. "I couldn't function without her. She's my rock."

Violet took notes as we discussed each person. "Remember. Just because someone mourns the loss of a friend, it doesn't mean she's innocent. Could be that either Gin or Claire killed Tori and bitterly regrets her crime. Don't automatically eliminate either one of them. Consider their motives. If either was involved in anything unethical, any hanky-panky involving money, or cheating, their livelihood was at stake. From what we've learned about Tori, she would have felt honor bound to report malfeasance no matter who it ruined. Think of the common motives for crime: money, love, hatred. I'm sure there are more, but that's a good start. Add young people into the mix, and things get even more volatile."

Violet saw the look of revulsion on my face and quickly shifted gears. "Let's evaluate the students. I presume that those in her art class are the most likely suspects."

I wrinkled my nose. Calling them suspects was distasteful, especially since most of the students trusted me. Was I a Quisling, a viper in the nest? If I had any courage, I would beg off this assignment and return to Poppet. Maybe Harrison was right, after all. I was a makeup saleswoman inadequate to the task and not a detective. Evaluating lipsticks and foundation was absolutely no problem for me, but singling out a murderer was another thing entirely.

Then I recalled those crime scene photos of Tori Aaron. The pool of blood, her disfigured face. She was a courageous woman committed to righting wrongs. Someone, most likely someone she trusted, had brutally extinguished that light. I couldn't refuse to do my part. Aunt Violet depended on me but so did Tori. I really had no alternative.

"Our core group consists of five students, two guys, and three girls. You met them the evening of that reception."

A patient nod by Violet spurred me on. I resisted the impulse to discuss Priscilla Sayers first. After all, even though she was my favorite suspect, we needed to discuss the students calmly and dispassionately. "Tomas Devereaux is an outsider. A townie. Naturally, both Coleman and Harrison Putnam consider him their prime suspect. He fits their prejudices perfectly and has no affluent parents to rush to his defense. I'm not quite sure where Stevens stands on the issue."

"How talented is Tomas?"

"Immensely. I understand that he was sort of Tori's pet project, too, since they came from similar backgrounds. Tomas takes pride in flaunting his differences. Sort of like a James Dean character if you get my drift."

Violet leaned back and closed her eyes.

"Ah, yes. One of those bad boys who always attract every little princess in their path. Like honey to a bee."

I felt compelled to defend him. "He's really very nice and more conventional than he's willing to admit. A scholarship student but an authentic talent too." I admit that I had wondered if Tori's interest in him was strictly platonic or something more. The age gap between them wasn't that much. Five years. The same thought must have occurred to Aunt Violet. She narrowed her eyes as if she were a hanging judge.

"How emotional is this young man? Would he react violently if Tori rebuffed his advances?"

"He idolized her. Still does. Tomas says she was the only adult who ever believed in him." Could Tomas have misinterpreted Tori's interest in him and have been devastated by rejection?" It was a possibility that even I recognized but refused to believe. Roddy said that Tori got too close to her students. Too involved in their lives. It was part of her passion for helping them. Did she step over the line? Claire would know.

I poured both of us another glass of wine. Violet had brought it with her, and as usual, it was exquisite. Alcohol didn't really interest me unless it was a fine vintage to be sipped and savored. My budget limited such choices, but Violet's did not.

"Okay," Violet said. "Who's next?"

I spent a few minutes describing Ru—his quirky sense of humor and genial manner. Not my idea of a killer by any stretch of the imagination. What motive could he possibly have? His family was wealthy and expected their son to do well, but by all accounts, he was a model student. Claire probably knew the particulars. None of the students, with one exception, exhibited antisocial tendencies. I reserved that name for last, toying with it like Fantasia with a bone. I banished my feelings of inadequacy and memories of another time when I'd seriously misjudged someone I liked, only to learn that he was indeed a merciless killer. After all, these were kids, barely old enough to drive. Everyone agreed that Tori's murder was well-planned and executed. Executed. What a strange verb to use in view of the situation. According to Sergeant Stevens, there had been no struggle, no defensive wounds. In detective shows, the pathologist always managed to find errant skin cells from the perpetrator, usually under the victim's fingernails. No such luck in this case. Tori's neatly clipped nails were innocent of polish and provided no trace of her killer. I suspected that the fatal blows had been struck quickly, ruthlessly, and without warning.

Violet already knew Abigail Jenkins and, of course, her father, far better than I did. When she asked about her, I was surprised.

"Abigail is another gentle soul who has been cosseted all her life. Could she have attacked Tori? Remember, she's been Daddy's little girl from birth. Not used to anyone telling her no and she lost her mother at a critical stage in her life."

I sputtered a quick denial. "No way. Abigail is another one who adored Tori. I think she regarded her almost like a mother figure or a big sister."

Violet gave me a quizzical look.

"Never heard of matricide, Marky? It's more common than you'd think. By getting so involved with her students, Tori made herself vulnerable. Sometimes, especially young people, don't always recognize that their idols

THE MASCARA MURDERS

have normal human frailties too. When confronted with reality, they can explode."

I wondered if my aunt spoke from experience. After all, she had mentored and inspired art students for decades. She knew all about the so-called artistic temperament. Painting requires both commitment and passion. Too much of either quality might prove lethal.

"You haven't met Natalie yet. Lovely girl. Another scholarship student but very different from Tomas. For one thing, she's more focused on art history than painting itself. Her aunt is one of the docents at the DIA who's arranging our tour. Natalie is shy at first but warms up when she gets to know you. No one has a bad word to say about her, and she idolized Tori."

I could never fool my aunt. Even as a child, she read me like a first-grade primer. "Okay," Violet said. "Now tell me about the one you do suspect. I think I can guess but surprise me."

Priscilla Sayers! How to describe the cunning creature I so disliked? In a larger group, she would lead the pack of mean girls preying on the weak and driving them to desperation. I had no proof that she killed Tori, just her own words of disdain for the dead teacher.

"Priscilla Sayers. No surprise there."

Violet laughed. "Oh, that precocious minx who elbowed her way into our conversation at the social. Long blonde hair and adept at using cosmetics to enhance her beauty. Am I right?"

I nodded. "I applaud her use of cosmetics. Quite expert, as it happens, although that doesn't excuse her other obnoxious traits. She's openly critical—vicious, actually—about anything related to Tori. Plus, she has an unrequited passion for Professor Park. Follows Roddy everywhere, trying to vamp him. If she knew for even one minute how he felt about Tori, Priscilla might well have become violent."

Dead silence as my aunt scrutinized my face. "How objective are you about her?"

There was that word again—objective. Honesty was the best policy, especially when cornered by someone like Violet, who knew me so well. "Not objective at all. She's an unlikeable creature. However, I must admit she has some artistic skill. Sort of in the Georgia O'Keefe mode."

"Hmm. Interesting. I agree with what you told the sergeant about cosmetics. More than likely, someone used school supplies or stole them from one of the kids. That element of hatred disturbs me. The killer made a statement by defiling Tori's face that way. Be careful around here." Violet glanced at her watch and jumped up. "Oops! I have a dinner engagement tonight. Must repair the ravages of time before leaving."

I couldn't resist asking. "Who's the lucky guy?"

She laughed. "Nothing special. The headmaster's hosting a party. Very intimate. Just five or six of us. With any luck, I might get some answers to our questions." She whisked away without another word leaving me curious and anxious for answers.

Chapter Seven

I fed Fantasia, grabbed her lead, and headed for the pathway. Violet had her own social life, and I had no reason to feel abandoned just because she'd made other arrangements. After all, I was an adult, capable of amusing myself. Truth be told, I felt a bit lonely since arriving at Sherborne. Everyone here was friendly but wary, and I missed Gemma's exuberance and the give and take of everyday life in Harbor Bay. Covert operatives could never feel totally at home especially when they were seeking a killer. Every kindness and act of friendship aroused my guilt and suspicion. I didn't really have the luxury of time to build a solid relationship with my colleagues and students. The summer session only lasted ten weeks and I'd already squandered two of them without much to show for my efforts. Time to buckle down and complete my mission. I suddenly heard footsteps behind me and immediately wheeled around to confront my stalker.

"Gee, Ms. Davis, I didn't mean to scare you." Ru Peterson gave his self-deprecating grin and patted Fantasia's head. I hadn't realized before just how tall the lad was. Ru towered over me. Tori was far shorter than my five feet seven and could have easily been overcome by him. I felt abashed for thinking that way and immediately overcompensated by inviting Ru to join me.

"You're sure you don't mind," he asked. "Sometimes I take walks just to be alone."

I assured Ru that his company was welcome, especially considering the uncertain climate at Sherborne. He bit his lip and looked troubled.

"Ms. Aaron knew who did that Kaboom stuff. Not sure how she found out, but she did."

"Oh?" I bit my tongue, fearful of spoiling the moment.

He nodded. "Yep. It was a mean trick doing that and hurting people's feelings. Most teachers would blow their top but not her. See, Ms. Aaron believed in second chances even for people who probably didn't deserve them."

His words puzzled me. If Tori knew who the culprit was, why in the world didn't she publicize it and end the charade? I studied Ru's face, so young and troubled.

"Do you know who played that prank? If you do, you must tell Sergeant Stevens immediately. That way, you'll be protected."

His reaction surprised me. "Sure, I know. All the kids do, but we won't Narc on anyone. That could ruin someone's chances for college or get him fired. Even old man Cole would have to do something then. See, Ms. Aaron spoke to everyone. She promised she wouldn't tell if it never happened again. As far as she was concerned, that ended it."

I debated whether Tori had acted wisely or foolishly. Perhaps the culprit didn't believe her and decided to make very sure that no one would find out. Although…if the kids already knew who was responsible, why bother. I had to believe that the crime had deeper roots. Tori's killer nursed a deep hatred for her, an emotion that defied rational thought. He or she had taken the time to spread cosmetics on the dead woman's face even though that increased the chances of being discovered. It wasn't enough to end her life. Oh no. That sicko had one final message to leave. It made no sense, but then murder rarely did.

"Are you okay?" Ru asked. I realized that I'd been so deep in thought that I had alarmed poor Ru.

"Ru, I want you to think about this. If you can't or won't tell me the name of the person involved in that fiasco at the assembly, at least inform the police. Send an anonymous note if you must or tell a teacher you trust. Professor Park or Ms. Claire."

He shrugged, and I realized that he had no intention of obliging me. That code of honor amongst teenagers was an age-old bond that I vividly recalled from my own high school days. Another thought suddenly jarred me. Suppose Ru, genial, gentle Ru, was himself the guilty party. I shivered and clutched Fantasia for reinforcement. Just then, a boisterous trio of teens carrying a football exploded around the corner. They urged Ru to join them in a game of touch football, and he readily obliged. I used that diversion to make my escape. Was I being foolish, suspecting the motives of every student in my group? Perhaps but that better safe than sorry maxim echoed in my brain. I pivoted and jogged back toward my lodgings with Fantasia hot on my heels.

When I arrived, dinner in the faculty dining room was in full swing. This was chicken pot pie night, and no one wanted to miss out. I accepted a generous portion of the yummy treat and found a seat between Claire and Gin. Roddy Park waved from across the table, but Harrison Putnam was too busy stuffing his face to acknowledge me. After sampling a bit of crust, I had to admit that his conduct was understandable. Most institutional fare was barely palatable, but this pot pie was the food of the gods.

"Ambrosia," Gin said, closing her eyes. "I skipped lunch just so I could pig out tonight."

Claire nodded her agreement. "This certainly hits the spot. By the way, Marky, didn't I see your aunt on campus this afternoon?"

"Yep. She's at some dinner party being hosted by the headmaster. Very select group."

We all exchanged looks, but Harrison curled his lip and spat out a reply. "Probably some fund-raising thing. Honestly, Coleman spends most of his time grubbing for dollars these days."

How odd for Harry to publicly criticize his boss. I flashed what I hoped was a look of admiration his way. "You're so connected with what's going on in the school. No wonder he trusts you."

Harry's chest swelled out like a pouter pigeon. "We think alike, you know. Both of us have the best interests of Sherborne at heart."

Roddy cast his eyes down, but Gin went on the attack. "What's this about a shortage in the scholarship fund? That could spell big trouble."

"Who told you that," Claire asked. "Any money issues are serious business best left to the finance committee."

Gin wrinkled her nose, undeterred by either probity or good manners.

Instead of answering, Harry sputtered something unintelligible and turned to Claire to rescue him. She obliged by adroitly changing the subject to the forthcoming community scholarship fair.

"I'm excited about it," she said. "We're including a writing competition along with the art exhibit and, of course, Gin's drama production." For a moment, her eyes filled as she recalled the genesis for the program. "Tori was the architect of the whole shebang. She had such big plans, such zeal."

Roddy crushed his napkin when he heard her name. His voice broke as he said, "There was no one quite like her." An awkward silence was broken by Gin's next remark.

"I heard you had a confab with Sergeant Stevens," Gin said, eyeing me. "Come on. Spill. We want details."

I tried without success to dissemble, but Gin had me pinned to the wall like a butterfly in a specimen case.

"I just thought I might be able to help. With the cosmetics angle. You know, an outsider's perspective can be useful sometimes."

Harrison, in a rare display of poor manners, planted both elbows on the table and stared.

"What did you learn, Ms. Davis? I believe all of us at this table can be trusted."

"Okay." The details still made me shudder, and discussing them in public was problematic, especially with those who cared for Tori present. "I examined the makeup they found and viewed the crime scene photos."

'Ugh!" Gin cried. "Ghoulish. I couldn't face that. How bad was it?"

Roddy swallowed twice as if the topic was too sensitive to discuss. He rose, quickly excused himself, and plunged out of the dining room without looking back.

"What's his problem?" Gin asked. "We've all watched those CSI shows ad nauseam."

For once, Claire lost patience with her younger colleague.

"Grow up, Gin. Roddy was in love with Tori, for heaven's sake. Talk about twisting the knife in his gut."

Harrison looked up and blinked. "Really? Park and Tori Amos. He certainly dodged a bullet there. Woman was nothing but trouble. She would have made his life a misery for sure." He primly wiped the corners of his mouth with one of Sherborne's monogrammed napkins. "Enough gossiping. Some of us have work to do."

No one stopped him from leaving. We didn't even try.

"Creep!" Gin spat. "No respect for anyone." She shrugged and turned my way, undeterred by the interruption. "Okay, Marky. Set the scene. After all, we're part of your truth squad. We need all the details no matter how hard it is to hear them."

Claire winced but nodded her approval.

I described the evidence photos, with particular emphasis on the cosmetics involved and my supposition that they might have come from the drama department or the local drug store.

"Anything missing from your stash, Gin?" Claire patted her colleague's shoulder.

"I dunno. Maybe. You know what a mess that place is." She scratched her head. "I do know we use that type of mascara. Everyone does. Cheap, but effective. The kids love to slap it on."

Claire joined in. "Have to admit I have some too. Not that I use cosmetics that much. Who's going to notice a forty-something novelist amongst all these fresh young faces anyway?"

I laughed. "You're missing the point, my dear. Makeup makes us feel and look our best. At least for some people if used judiciously." I pictured my Aunt Violet, a woman well into her fifties who turned heads wherever she went. "Besides, if everyone felt that way, Poppet would be bankrupt!"

That got a laugh from all three of us. Unfortunately, Gin hadn't finished her quest. "Did you look at her…. Tori, I mean?"

"Oh no. I can't bear to even think of it." Claire's distress was heartbreaking to witness.

"I did, but I don't want to discuss it." The look I gave Gin convinced her that the subject was closed. "You might be interested in a recent conversation

I had, though."

They were astonished to learn that Tori knew who caused the Kaboom kerfuffle. Claire's eyes widened, and Gin almost shrieked. "Well, who was it? Tell us, for heaven's sake."

I admitted that although most of the student body apparently knew, I did not. Not a clue.

Claire digested that bit of news before commenting.

"We can assume then, that Tori's killer had some other motive for eliminating her." She sighed. "I guess my friend was the keeper of many secrets, one of which may have been her undoing. She meant well, but Tori was stubborn as hell. When she decided to do something, nothing could change her mind."

Gin snorted at that remark. "Pshaw. Tori didn't have to right all the world's wrongs. Sometimes you must learn just to butt out and mind your own business."

I couldn't keep from giggling. "I never heard anyone use that word before. Pshaw! It's right out of an English grammar text. I recall our English grammar book had that in it. Something like, 'Pshaw, the boat is sinking.'"

Claire's good humor had been restored. "That's our Gin. Dialogue straight out of a nineteenth-century melodrama. Seriously though, someone should tell Sargent Stevens about that student conspiracy. He'll get to the bottom of things."

I didn't relish another session with the cops, so I kept my lips buttoned. When both Claire and Gin stared me down, I caved almost instantly.

"Okay. I'll call him, but I won't reveal my source no matter what he says."

Gin hooted a rude comment, and Claire grinned. I was spared further ridicule when the kitchen staff gathered our plates and cutlery, removed our cups, and indicated in the most genteel way possible that it was time for us to scoot. I hastened back to my lodgings, hoping that Aunt Violet would once again save the day.

Chapter Eight

Like Cinderella, Violet Davis returned home right at the stroke of midnight. I was waiting for her, paging through a novel I had read before. It was Claire's first published work about a young girl's journey through the academic wasteland. Once again, I marveled at her facility with language and ability to move her readers. As far as I knew, Claire had never married, but her main character endured a long and painful love affair with a married professor who ultimately rejected her. Was it autobiographical? I wondered. My aunt had read and admired the book and was also curious about its origins.

"Okay," I said after pouring both of us a cognac. "What dirt did you dig up tonight?"

Violet raised her eyebrows. "Dirt? Dig up? How déclassé. First, let me set the stage. In addition to Coleman and his wife, our party included Senator Jenkins and two members of the alumni association whose names escape me. Worthy souls, no doubt, but terminally boring."

She enjoyed teasing me by reciting the menu and drink options before discussing the substance of the meeting. Good thing I was satiated by that chicken pot pie because apparently the Coles had provided their guests with quite a feast. I resisted the temptation to interrupt her narrative, folded my hands, and waited patiently for the main act to begin.

Violet took a sip of her cognac. "Coleman is worried. Terrified. Not so much about that nonsense with Kaboom. I think he's over that. It's all related to money."

That got my interest immediately.

"You mean the scholarship fund?" I had no idea how much was involved but at a place like Sherborne, a six-figure sum was not unreasonable. Surely, they had checks and balances. Unannounced audits and co-signers. Any institution worth its salt would have those.

Violet nodded. "Their yearly haul astounded me, and Coleman admitted that he had been remiss. Lazy. Currently, they have a rotating committee comprised of teachers and at least one board member that oversees the fund. Basic accounting stuff. This year, everything changed when Tori Aaron was put in charge. She took it seriously, demanded accountability, and hired an outside auditor to check the books."

I knew where this was going, and it wasn't pretty. Tori, the social justice warrior, had a take-no-prisoners approach to almost everything. No way would she countenance malfeasance of any kind, particularly when a deserving student would be deprived of a scholarship as a result. Somehow, she must have tracked down the culprit and threatened to expose him or her.

"So, her murder was connected to Sherborne School. Does Coleman admit that now?"

Violet shook her head. "Nope. He still holds to the random mugging theory. Refuses to even mention it to the authorities. You know the drill. Scandal in the school, public outrage. Negative press coverage etc."

"How much is missing?"

The headmaster was vague, but after Senator Jenkins pinned him down, he admitted that the figure might well reach fifty thousand dollars. The scheme involved invoices issued to dummy corporations over several years for nonexistent services. Very professionally done. Sherborne had never lacked for funds, so nobody was especially vigilant about expenditures. Until Tori Aaron got involved.

"Who's part of this committee?" I asked.

The names didn't surprise me, although it pained me to even think of any of those people as thieves. Harrison Putnam had replaced Tori as the chair, assisted by Roddy, Claire, and Gin. The board member was a lawyer who lived in Manhattan and rarely attended any school functions. I recalled the banter between Claire and Gin about teachers' salaries and food stamps. No doubt, the culprit was convinced that squirreling away a personal slush fund was payback for an institution that took its scholars for granted. Tori would never have agreed to that.

"Why so pensive?" Violet asked. "Did you learn anything important?"

She gasped when I told her that the students knew who had engineered the Kaboom caper and refused to tell anyone. Maybe it didn't matter anymore, but I still believed it was linked to Tori's death. So many strands leading to that one fateful outcome.

"I haven't given up on it," I said. "Maybe Natalie will tell me. She's more vulnerable than the others and wants my approval. Stevens doesn't have to know, but for my own peace of mind, I need to track Tori's movements and contacts."

Violet and I discussed the forthcoming jaunt to the Detroit Institute of Art. It would provide a welcome diversion from the daily routine and give my kids the chance to compare their own efforts with some of the finest artists the world had ever known.

"Some of yours are in there. Right?"

She grinned. "A few. In the permanent collection of contemporary art, I'm proud and honored to say. But don't make a big deal about it. Wouldn't want those kids to think we're bragging."

Before we doused the lights, I had to ask. "Anything serious between you and Senator Jenkins? I've always wanted to be a bridesmaid, you know."

Violet always was very private about her personal life, and this was no exception. She merely shook her head and swatted me on the behind. "Still the curious little imp, I see."

I escorted my aunt to the bedroom, grabbed an extra pillow and some sheets, and with Fantasia as my pillow pal, bedded down for the evening on the sofa.

* * *

Violet left quite early the next morning. I was still bleary-eyed despite a double latte, but she emerged from the bedroom looking totally refreshed. Truth be told, I'd had a restless night. Sleep eluded me as I reviewed everything I'd learned about the embezzlement. It might be the key to Tori's murder. I was as positive of that as anyone could be absent a confession. But who amongst that list of educators and youngsters would have violated a trust. Moreover, who would then murder Tori Aaron to silence her?

None of the staff except for Harrison Putnam seemed especially flush with money. That didn't mean that a thief hadn't feathered a handsome nest out of sight of Sherborne. Fifty thousand dollars wasn't a fortune by any means. A comfortable cushion, perhaps. Roddy had expenses related to his Ph.D., and Claire had yet to produce a successful sequel to her first novel. Both could probably use some extra cash. It was hard to imagine Gin devising such an insidious plot although she had tons of creativity and talent aplenty. The biggest hurdle to overcome was picturing any of my colleagues taking Tori's life. I'd sooner believe it was one of the students. A fit of adolescent angst or temper. I pictured Claire's gentle face, contorted with grief for her lost friend. Would a killer give shelter to the beloved pet of the woman she had murdered? And Roddy. His emotion about Tori was genuine. I'd swear to that. If the woman he loved threatened his future, would he end her life? Impossible. And Gin. Blythe, auburn-haired Gin, more of a wood sprite than an adult, lived vicariously in the plays and dramas she staged with the students. Gin was certainly no Lady Macbeth. Far closer to Mary Poppins.

Today I had a special assignment, a workshop designed especially for teenagers entitled "Building your cosmetics IQ." Abigail and Natalie signed up first, as well as several girls from Roddy's history section and two of Claire's budding novelists. When Priscilla Sayers sauntered into the classroom with Ru, I was dumbfounded. That girl could probably teach me a few tricks, and not just about cosmetics. Ru's interest was theatrical makeup. He had won the lead in the Fall presentation of the Mikado and was keen to learn some basic techniques. I'd asked Gin to be my model, and she'd readily agreed. I started by screening images of various young celebrities and asking for feedback. Which look did they admire and seek to emulate? After an animated discussion, we went back to basics. Hygiene, skincare, and sound practices at any age. They balked at my lecture against sun damage and tanning, but fortunately, Gin backed me up. At their age, concepts like Melanoma or wrinkles seemed a lifetime away, but they were an unfortunate reality. Using Gin's bare face as a canvas, I illustrated proper cleansing, exfoliating, and moisturizing, followed by basic cosmetics. Thanks to Aunt Violet, I had a treasure trove of samples to distribute, a treat that thrilled the students. I circulated around the room as each of them used magnifying mirrors to practice their techniques and stopped in front of Natalie. Before I made my move, we spent a few minutes discussing products for women of color and how that arena had expanded in the past decade. During our morning break, I singled the girl out for more discussion and presented her with a list of companies that specialized in a variety of skin tones. Cautiously, stealthily, I then broached the topic of the Kaboom incident.

"That fuss at the assembly must have been tough for you," I said. "No one likes to be singled out for something that mean. It hurts too much."

Natalie nodded. "I tried not to cry, but it did hurt. Ms. Aaron said that kind of person didn't deserve my tears." She put her head down on her desk and covered her eyes. "I miss her so much."

I should have felt guilty, but I didn't, even though playing the compassionate counselor was a stretch.

"You kids know who did that. Why not tell someone? It might help us find Ms. Aaron's killer."

She gazed at me with tear-filled eyes and whispered.

"Really? I never thought of that. It was a prank. Nothing to do with Ms. Aaron's death. We all talked about it and decided not to tell."

At that moment, Priscilla strolled over and plopped down next to me. "What's this? Private coaching session. Some people must get special privileges, I suppose."

Natalie clammed up faster than a frightened mollusk, and I admitted defeat.

"Looks like you know all the trade secrets anyways," I told Priscilla. I had to admit that her skin was porcelain perfect, and her eyes were expertly shaded and lined. I suddenly got an inspiration. Flattery never hurt, especially when directed at a princess of privilege like her. She adored attention and admiration and considered it her due. Restraint was called for. I had to conceal my antipathy toward Priscilla, my number one suspect. Plus, as an adult, I felt a scintilla of guilt for singling out a teenager for blame.

"You've done a great smoky eye, Priscilla. What products do you use?"

Her expression made me yearn to slap the smirk right off her face, but criminal penalties and social conventions restrained me. Priscilla recited a lengthy list of high-end products that she favored, pausing to gauge the impact of each.

"I checked out your website," she smirked. "Looks like you carry the same things."

"Right, you are. Our customers are very particular. By the way, your lashes are perfect. Is that Great Lash mascara you're using?" I elicited just the response I had hoped for.

"That drug store junk?" Priscilla snorted. Her indignation threatened to derail our conversation right there. "I don't touch anything like that. Ever. Just ask Ms. Hastings. My complexion is far too sensitive. Even bring my own products when we do plays and all. That other stuff is for amateurs," she threw Natalie a venomous look, "or townies."

Gin frowned at the girl. "Cut it out, Priscilla. Your mean-girl act gets very tiresome. It just so happens that makeup artists use a variety of brands, including the ones you deem offensive. Check it out on the internet. You seem so attuned to social media." She put her arm around Natalie's shoulder. "Besides, lashes like Natalie's don't need enhancement. Anyone would envy them. I just keep a stash of products around for our shows. No sense in spending extra cash if it's not necessary."

Deterring a missile of malice from reaching her target wasn't easy. Priscilla pursed her lips and spat at Natalie. "That's what they found with Ms. Aaron's body, wasn't it? Drug store stuff. Didn't surprise me one bit. She knew nothing about beauty."

Her comment opened the floodgates as Natalie sobbed uncontrollably. Rue Peterson and Abigail came to the rescue and hugged their friend.

Rue's eyes smoldered with contempt.

"Don't let her get to you, Nat. Priscilla has a lot to answer for. What's that saying about putting lipstick on a pig?" His words had more impact than mine or Gin's could ever have. Priscilla shrugged and sauntered off to the other side of the classroom. Despite her attempt at nonchalance, I could see that his insult stung.

I decided to end our session on a high note. "For those of you who are interested, my colleague Gemma Watts will be here next weekend to discuss methods of releasing tension. She's a master masseuse and aesthetician, so you'll learn a lot from her. Students find university work stressful, so her tips have a practical advantage as well. You'll enjoy learning from her."

"Wow. Sign me up," Gin said. "We're having a dress rehearsal for SHAKESPEARE UNBOUND next week, and the stress is killing me."

Rue thumped his chest and announced that he had won the role of Romeo. The coveted role of the lovely Juliet had been awarded to Abigail. The students weren't staging the entire play, however. They'd picked famous scenes from several plays, including of course, Hamlet's soliloquy to showcase Shakespeare's masterpieces. It was a modern take on a classic that still respected his immortal words.

"Who else is involved?" I asked. Gin reached into her backpack and gave me a printout of the cast and characters. I quickly scanned the list and saw that both teachers and students participated in what looked like a fun event. Roddy Park would portray Hamlet, and in a surprise casting, Tomas Devereaux would appear as Othello, with Natalie as Desdemona. Priscilla's role as Lady Macbeth seemed closer to typecasting than even Gin would admit, but I had to say that choosing Harrison Putnam as Iago was also spot on. Claire had claimed the role of Portia, dispenser of wisdom, but oddly enough, Gin assigned herself the Ophelia spot. It was hard to envision Gin as that essentially passive young maiden considering her vivid mane of hair and general vivacity.

She shrugged when I mentioned that. "Oh well. Anything to get Roddy's hands on me. He can't mourn for Tori forever."

"I'd be glad to help," I said, ignoring that remark. No need to become entangled in a love triangle. Besides, most women would appreciate Gin's sentiments. Roddy was the complete package-smart, sexy, and sweet. "Maybe I could work backstage and do makeup and costumes."

"Terrific" Gin looked relieved to have some of the burden lifted off her shoulders. "We invite parents and community residents and charge a minimal fee. Everything goes into the scholarship fund, of course."

On that positive note, I dismissed the class and gathered up the remaining debris. Since it was lunchtime, the area quickly emptied out, leaving me isolated. I was deep in thought, so much so that I didn't sense anyone's presence until the classroom door slammed shut. Fortunately, my muse and guardian, Fantasia, was on alert. Her ears pricked up, and she emitted a low growl. Normally I'm no risk taker. I react sensibly to sounds and try not to panic. But Tori's murder had left me, like many others on campus, feeling anxious. When the lights suddenly switched off, I jumped.

"Who is it?" My voice quavered, but with Fantasia at my side, I was able to summon some dignity.

"What's wrong, Ms. Davis? Worried about the killer coming to get you?"

That taunting voice was all too familiar. Righteous anger replaced my fear as I turned to face Priscilla Sayers. "Not funny, Priscilla. What do you want?"

The girl confronted me without a hint of remorse or trepidation. On her lovely face, I detected sheer hatred with a dollop of contempt. "You don't like me, do you, teacher? Why not? Jealous?"

I was dumbfounded and, for just a moment, fearful. There was a psychotic streak in this little vixen that was truly amazing. Was she Tori's killer? It wouldn't have surprised me one bit. *Control, Marky. Be the adult in the room.*

"You try so hard to be noticed, Priscilla. Kindness works better than venom, you know."

My efforts went totally unnoticed. Instead of acting penitent, Priscilla sneered. "You don't know anything, do you? Snooping around. Acting like everyone's pal. The big detective. You don't fool me. You don't fool anyone. Of course, I know who freaked out the assembly. Everyone knows. You'll be surprised when you find out if you ever do." She fluffed out her hair and pirouetted. "But you're wrong if you think I did it. Not even close. That was strictly amateur hour."

Time to regain control. I smiled, just enough to show a few moves of my own.

"What about Ms. Aaron? I suppose you know who her killer was? Be very careful about that, Priscilla. Playing games with murderers is a dangerous proposition."

I couldn't dent that impermeable layer of conceit that surrounded her. Hard to believe that I was dealing with a teenager, seventeen years old, instead of a hardened criminal. Wait a moment. I couldn't be certain. Perhaps I was facing a killer after all.

Priscilla paused, and for once, I experienced a small victory over her. My triumph was short-lived, however. She folded her arms, faced me, and launched a final sally. "I know more than you think. It just so happens I took a little stroll myself that night. Maybe I saw something or someone. Maybe that someone owes me big time. Either way, I plan to collect."

I was gobsmacked. "Following Dr. Park, I presume. You always seem to trail him, although God knows why. He doesn't even know you exist. He loved Tori, Ms. Aaron."

That struck a nerve, and I felt ashamed of myself. Almost.

Priscilla tossed her head. Her cheeks grew flushed, although she remained composed. I had to admit that the kid was wise beyond her years. Too wise. I had to reassert myself. Reclaim my role as her teacher. That involved cleansing myself of all negative feelings and thinking of her welfare.

"Priscilla. Listen to me. If you saw anything—anything at all—contact Sergeant Stevens. He'll keep it confidential. It's too dangerous otherwise."

She sighed. "I'll consider it. Maybe." With that, she flounced out of the room. Not many girls can flounce, but I had to admit that Priscilla Sayers had style and an unsettling degree of self-confidence. Most teenagers were beset by self-doubt and insecurity. At least, they were when I was her age. Just my luck to confront one with more sangfroid than her years warranted or that I possessed. I was troubled. Way over my head in this abyss of teenage angst. I leaned down and hugged Fantasia, drawing comfort from the collie's presence and wisdom. Who could I turn to for a second opinion? Claire would know what to do. She could guide me. After all, she had been

Tori's best friend and the least likely one to be involved in the crime. If only Coleman Ross had substance instead of that fragile shell of authority. He wouldn't welcome interference from me, especially if it implicated an employee or student from Sherborne. Unless, of course, it was a scholarship student like Tomas. In his eyes, Tomas was merely a social experiment gone wrong. Coleman would gladly wash his hands of him if he could.

For the sake of my figure and peace of mind, I decided to forego lunch and instead take Fantasia for a long walk. Today was enchilada day at the cafeteria, and I knew that, given the opportunity, I would gorge on that luscious treat. After a bracing three-mile trek, both of us felt enlivened. I plopped down on a bench to fasten my shoelace and soon had company. I hadn't seen Tomas since yesterday, and his grim countenance surprised me.

"What's bothering you?" I asked. "Look at all that sunshine."

Tomas grumbled something inaudible and sat down beside me. Fantasia nudged his arm, angling for attention. That ploy worked far more effectively than my futile efforts. He smiled and gave the collie a hug. "It's nothing. Really. I was counting on some grant money that didn't come through. That's all."

Alarm bells clanged in my head. "It won't affect your scholarship at Sherborne, I hope. You're talented, Tomas. Keep up your grades, and you have a chance for the Art Institute or another great program. I'll help any way I can, and I know my aunt will too. She was impressed by your paintings."

His expression was puzzled as he glanced at me. "Why would you do that for someone you hardly know? You remind me of Ms. Aaron." He turned away.

"You really miss her, don't you? She must have been very special."

Tomas suddenly put his arm around me and pulled me close. Obviously, he had misinterpreted my interest. I quickly jerked away from him.

"Don't do that, Tomas. I want to help you, but there are no strings attached…. Absolutely none."

His face fell, making me wonder just what tradeoffs had been expected of this young man in the past. As luck would have it, we were then joined by a most unwelcome third party. Harrison Putnam assessed the situation and immediately jumped to the wrong conclusion.

"Is this a private party, or can anyone join in?" His tone suggested that he already knew the answer.

Tomas hastily jumped up, straightened his shirt, and excused himself. "See you later, Ms. Davis."

Harrison gave me a world-class smirk. "Providing some after-hours coaching, Ms. Davis? I wouldn't advise you to get too close. Not to someone like that. Rough trade has its attractions, but it can be dangerous. Besides, unless I miss my guess, young Mr. Devereaux won't be staying here much longer."

I tried not to sputter, but outrage overcame me.

"See here, Harry. I don't know what you thought you saw but forget it. Tomas is merely a student, but a very talented one. Someone who needs some guidance. Isn't that what we're here for?"

He wasn't fazed one bit. "Hmm. Guidance, is it? You sound just like your predecessor. Tori Aaron stepped over the line and look where it got her. I'd hate to see the same thing happen to you."

It took some effort, but I calmed myself enough to ask him. "Do you seriously think that Tomas Devereaux murdered Tori? That's absurd. Or were you threatening me?"

When it came to superior scorn, Harrison was a real champ. "Of course not. Merely a warning. I hear that Sergeant Stevens is closing in on a suspect. Someone who needs money…. We've had some financial shortages recently, you know. Maybe Tori found out more than was healthy for her. She was forever poking her nose where it didn't belong."

I was speechless. So angry that I felt almost faint. Before I could act, he patted my shoulder and rose. "Be careful, Marky. Things can get out of hand so easily."

Good thing I hadn't eaten. The taste of bile roiled my stomach and stirred my digestive juices. I flashed him my most innocent smile and changed directions. "Hey. I found out that you're joining us for the Shakespeare Fest. Very cool."

That surprised him. Harrison expected me to fold after being confronted.

"I've always been a fan of the Bard," he said loftily. "About time they injected some culture into the curriculum."

"And what a role to play. Iago—such an interesting character! A combination of guile and treachery. Almost typecast."

Once he digested my remark, Harrison got huffy. "Watch your step, Ms. Davis. Remember who you're talking to."

I patted his arm in an act of faux penitence. "Don't mind me, Harry. I'm such a Shakespeare buff that I get carried away. Good thing I'll be backstage. Cosmetics suit me much better than acting."

He curled his lip and turned away. "No offense taken."

That was the exit cue for Fantasia and me. I was in serious need of conversation, and Claire was my designated confidant. She had an air about her that inspired trust, not unlike my Aunt Violet. That one-two combo of Priscilla and Harrison had sapped my strength and filled me with self-doubt. Not to mention fending off romantic overtures from the talented Tomas Devereaux. Had I really sent mixed signals to the boy? If so, it was certainly unintentional, not to mention unforgivable. Roddy told me that Tomas had lost his mother at an early age and had been raised by his dad. Perhaps that explained his reaction.

After feeding Fantasia, I returned to my classroom for an afternoon focused on painting. My students were already assembled, bending over their easels with a look of determination. I was pleased to see that Natalie and Ru had made real progress. They'd never be serious artists, but to appreciate those who were, they needed to expend some effort themselves. After this morning's encounter, I was prepared for sulking and more histrionics from Priscilla. She surprised me, however, by focusing on her painting and ignoring other distractions, including me. Tomas avoided me by hunching over his canvas with his back to the group. I deliberately approached him and marveled at the power and raw emotion in his art.

"You have such promise, Tomas. Don't let anything or anyone deter you. I mean that."

He was embarrassed, I could see that, but to his credit, Tomas merely nodded and soldiered on. Our session continued in relative tranquility, broken only by the hum of the landscapers outdoors. I hurried out when class concluded since I was eager to corral Claire and get her take on my adventures. Moreover, I resolved to visit Sergeant Stevens and update him on my findings once again. If Harrison was correct, Stevens might be zeroing in on the wrong suspect, a move that could stigmatize Tomas for life. I admit that his talent had biased me, but I still refused to consider Tomas as a thief or, worse still, a murderer. Tori would have helped him if he was desperate enough to steal. He had no need to hurt her.

When I knocked at Claire's door, the only response I got was a bark from Raleigh.

"Looking for Claire?" Gin asked, coming up behind me. "Sorry. You're out of luck. Tonight, her literary group meets. Poor thing. She's never been able to replicate the success of her first novel, and this gaggle is sort of a support group. Lots of submissions but no takers. Coleman keeps bugging her about it, which doesn't help. You know how he loves to brag. His captive best-selling author. Puts pressure on Claire and gives her writer's block. Guess you're stuck with me at least until dinner time." She looped her arm in mine and led me to her door. "Stop in and have a drink. We can dream up dreadful things to say about Harrison and the headmaster."

I'd never visited Gin's place before, and I was curious. Home décor says a lot about an individual. In her case, the living room resembled a movie set. Framed posters from her favorite films decorated the walls, and a glamorous velvet sofa in flame red dominated most of the room. Cashmere throws on the loveseat and wing chairs added a luscious, opulent touch.

"Wow," I said. "This is really nice."

"Don't sound so surprised." She'd bristled at my comment, even though it was innocuous, or so I thought. "Not everyone lives for austerity like Tori." Gin fluffed her hair. "She thought any type of comfort was shameful. I mean, I adored her, but that social warrior crap got tedious after a while. She wanted to change everything. Even Columbus Day didn't pass muster. Had to be Indigenous Peoples Day."

I understood and sympathized with Gin. Saints or their modern equivalent were admirable, but they would be awfully difficult to be around. Constantly guilt-tripping others could stir up resentment.

"Was she really like that?" I asked. "Doesn't sound like much fun, but apparently Roddy thought so."

Gin poured Chablis into exquisite Baccarat wine glasses and slowly sipped her drink. "Take these, for example. Got them for a song at an auction, but Tori thought it was decadent. In her world, using empty jelly jars was just fine. Roddy Park is such a class act. It's hard to envision those two as a couple."

"Opposites attract, as the old saying goes. I must admit though, that he is quite a specimen. No wonder Priscilla makes such a play for him. Poor Roddy. He seems bereft without Tori."

"Huh!" Gin curled her lip. "What that boy needs is cash and plenty of it. A thorough shagging wouldn't hurt him, either. He lost a grant from Michigan for the final leg of his Ph.D., and desperation reigns. At least, it used to. Then the other day, he was all smiles saying that his money woes were finally over." She narrowed her eyes. "Funny, isn't it?"

I could think of several paths to salvation for Roddy, but at the back of my mind, there was a niggling doubt. The scholarship fund had been bilked for fifty grand. That tidy sum would ease anyone's economic pain. "I heard about the fund shortages," I said, testing the waters. "Aunt Violet got the story the other night at Coleman's little soirée. Are things really that lax around here?"

She wasn't surprised, although Gin tried to put on a brave front.

"All our dirty laundry in the wash, huh? I suppose it's not that hard to cook the books over a couple of years if you're not too greedy. Trust is a big thing at a place like Sherborne School, and sometimes it lets you down."

"Shouldn't Coleman tell the cops? After all, that's grand larceny or theft or something equally bad."

Gin gave me a look that mixed disdain with a healthy dose of pity.

"Wake up, Marky. If word got out that the headmaster lost control, he'd be finished. Sherborne is Coleman's life. Bet you anything that he or his snooty wife pony up the money. They'll paper it over as a clerical error. Just you wait and see. Unless, of course, that can find some poor chump to pin it all on. Preferably one without money."

She was probably right. Those in charge would engage in a conspiracy of silence, and all would once more be well. But Tori Aaron wouldn't have agreed to that. No way. Her sense of justice would have demanded that the culprit be unmasked and punished no matter who the guilty party was or who was injured. Could it be? Was that the motive for Tori's murder, or was it something as simple as a juvenile prank at a school assembly? Both actions would have consequences for those involved. I sipped my wine, pondering how a web of lies so often led to destruction.

Gin filled my glass one more time. "Hey. Relax. Chill out. While you're here, how about doing a makeover on me? Nothing too drastic. Just spruce me up." Gin held up a mirror and made a face. "A touch of glamor never hurt anyone, right?"

She was right, of course. I've always believed in the healing power of cosmetics and have made it my mission in life to spread the gospel of transformation. Call me crazy, but I've witnessed first-hand the impact that a touch of lipstick or a hint of blush can have on a woman. I hurried back to my apartment and grabbed my makeup kit. It was equipped with a variety of products and samples from 's vendors. In Gin's case, I recommended a gentle exfoliant, honey gel masque, and hair pack as preliminary steps. She was a natural redhead, so her complexion was delicate and needed protection. While we waited for the products to work their magic, the conversation turned back to our students. I shared my little contretemps with Priscilla striving mightily to be fair to the girl.

"She was truly unpleasant," I said. "Made no secret of her contempt for Tori either."

Gin put her hands on her chin. "You don't think she's a suspect, do you? Head of the mean girls for sure, but a killer? I can't believe that." She gulped. "Maybe I just don't want to believe it."

She was probably right, but I'd felt uneasy being alone with Priscilla. Talk about that Spidey sense of danger I'd always read about. An entitled teen with a penchant for getting her own way...anything was possible.

"She really has a thing for Roddy," I said.

Gin combed the conditioner through her hair and peered into the mirror. "Roddy affects lots of women that way. Of course, he's totally oblivious to it. I invited him over to my lair early on, and guess what he spent the evening talking about?"

"Tori!"

She grinned. "You've got it. No other woman existed for that boy. I suppose I could try to vamp Harrison just to test my skills, but the thought repels me. What if I succeeded?"

"Eeh!" I couldn't remain neutral even though I knew she was joking. "Just the thought of seeing Harrison naked is enough to send me directly to a nunnery along with Ophelia."

We shared a hearty laugh about that and clinked glasses. While Gin slipped into the shower to rinse off her hair, I studied her book collection. Lots of classics, especially those with film adaptations. She even had several volumes that looked like pricey first additions.

Gin crept up behind me and touched my shoulder. I shrieked and jumped straight up in the air. Guilt will do that to you. "Uh-oh," she said. "I see you found my treasures."

I flushed. "Sorry. I didn't mean to pry. These look valuable."

With her hair wrapped in a towel, and a face innocent of makeup, Gin looked like a schoolgirl. "Don't sweat it. And yes, they are valuable. To me, at least. My aunt was a collector, and she bequeathed them to me. I've thought of selling them a time or two but can't bring myself to part with them. Claire offered to hook me up with some friend of hers who deals in rare books, but I've been too lazy to connect."

I understood and sympathized with Gin's need to retain a part of her heritage. My Aunt Violet's paintings were special to me, and I cherished them. They had appreciated in value, but to me, they were priceless.

Time was a-wasting, so we switched gears and discussed cosmetics. I applied a light serum, concealer, and a pale foundation to her skin, followed by some contouring with blush and a dab of powder. Then I focused on those bright green eyes, using a neutral shadow, liner, and plenty of mascara.

"Wow!" Gin exclaimed. "My lashes look a mile long. What'd you use on them."

"Lancôme is my favorite product, but there are several others just as good."

Gin shook her head. "Big difference between that and the drug store stuff we use for the kids.

We both grew silent for a moment thinking once again of Tori and the slash of cheap mascara someone had used to defile her face.

"Did everyone know how Tori felt about cosmetics?" I asked.

Gin nodded. "It was no big secret. She was a purist in every way. No half measures with Tori. It was annoying at times, but I'll tell you something. If you needed someone to watch your back, Tori was right there." She reached for a tissue and dabbed her eyes. "I miss her, Marky. Nothing's been the same around here since she died." She bit her lip. "No. Let's be honest, since she was murdered."

I'm not a hugger, but in this instance, it seemed appropriate. "Come on," I said. "We just have time to blow dry your hair and hustle over to dinner. Tonight is vegetarian lasagna, unless I miss my guess. "

The promise of food cheered Gin up right away. When I finished doing her hair, she pirouetted before the mirror and grinned. "I feel like a new woman. Do you think anyone will notice?"

"Who cares," I said. "You look marvelous, my dear. Even the headmaster might make a play for you tonight."

Her eyes widened with horror. "Surely you jest. Have you met that wife of his? She'd scratch your eyes out if she thought her husband even looked at another woman. Not that anyone would want him to."

I spent a moment picturing the headmaster in the throes of passion. Not a pretty sight. He'd probably have to consult the Sherborne School manual for the right steps to follow. Gin tugged my arm and herded me out the door. "Come on. I want to see if anyone notices my new look."

I was right, after all. Vegetarian Lasagna it was. When paired with garlic bread and Caesar Salad, the meal was more than satisfying. The reaction to Gin's new look was even more satisfying. Roddy Park openly stared at her and even Harrison felt the need to comment. "Someone must have a hot date tonight. Dare I ask who the lucky man is?" Gin ignored him but basked in the glow of attention even so. Students took turns serving at table during the week, and Tomas Devereaux gave Gin a second glance as he handed her a plate. He was far too mannerly to comment. However, Priscilla showed no such restraint.

"Been busy with the paintbox, I see, Ms. Davis."

"Ah, cut it out, Priscilla. I think she looks great." Tomas blushed as he said that.

Priscilla brushed off the criticism. "Hey. It's quite an improvement. About time."

Roddy looked up and frowned. "Enough of that nonsense. Clear the plates and get ready for Jeopardy. Tonight's the college competition. Save your energy for that."

I'd forgotten. The Sherborne School ritual hadn't varied even after Tori's death. Perhaps that was fortuitous. I'd get the chance to reenact the scene without the grisly aftermath, of course. Most of the same cast of characters were assembled. I saw Ru, Abigail, and Natalie busily cleaning tables and chatting.

"Oops! I need to give Fantasia a comfort break before the program starts." I pushed back my chair and headed for the door.

"Want some company?" Roddy surprised me, but I readily agreed. He was somewhat of a puzzle, a man with the looks of an Adonis and the temperament of a medieval scholar. I suspected that he was lonely, still mourning for his lost love, and eager to hear her name just once more. As a stranger, I represented a sort of haven for him and most of the summer staff and students. No worry that I would linger when the summer term ended, and autumn arrived.

Fantasia bounded joyfully up the path as we followed behind at a more sedate pace. It didn't take long for Roddy to broach his favorite subject.

"Now that you know us a bit, do you have any theories?"

Play innocent, I told myself. "Theories? About what?"

"Her murder. Come on, Marky. I know you're poking around, asking questions. What have you learned?"

"Not much. Everything points to an insider, though. Tori rocked a lot of

THE MASCARA MURDERS

boats at Sherborne. Someone made her death very personal. That random mugging theory just doesn't wash."

He put his arms on my shoulders. "Maybe I can help. Who are your suspects?" There was an intensity to his plea that gave me pause. After all, Professor Park was right there, front and center, on my hit parade.

I called Fantasia to my side. The big dog's presence was comforting, not to mention a safety factor. Unlike Raleigh, if I were threatened, Fantasia wouldn't run. Herding dogs were bred to defend their flocks against enemies. Roddy probably wasn't a threat, but he was a big guy who could pulverize me in a minute if he chose to.

"You've got this all wrong," I told him. "True, I am curious about Tori's murder but my one and only encounter with danger was more than enough. It was scary, and I only stumbled upon the solution by chance. Aunt Violet was devastated when Tori died, and she asked me to nose around a bit." I shrugged. "As far as I can see, Sergeant Stevens has everything in hand."

I'm a dreadfully inept liar, and Roddy saw through me immediately. He was a gentleman. However, so rather than call me out, he changed the subject to politics, a topic rife with enough skullduggery and death to occupy us for the rest of our walk. When we reached the common room, students and faculty had formed a ring around the 90-inch television screen, poised to watch their favorite quiz show. It was an informal event, although I noted that no one was using Kahoot to record their answers. Too many unfortunate memories, I'd guess. There was a festive atmosphere in the air, and everyone felt free to shout out a response even when their guesses were woefully inadequate. I noticed that Abigail and Rue were good, able to cover numerous categories with aplomb. Frankly, they were far superior to the three contestants on the television show. To my surprise, the big winner in our audience was someone entirely different. Tomas Devereaux aced the Final Jeopardy question and by risking the highest amount of money, he surpassed Ru by several hundred dollars.

"Wow," Abigail wailed. "I thought I was a shoo-in tonight."

Gin gave the girl a smile. "Remember. Strategy is key in this game. Kind of like life."

94

"When you have nothing to lose, it's easy to gamble. Right, Tomas?" Priscilla's mean-spirited comment annoyed everyone. The girl seemed unable to let anyone else be happy.

"You all were awesome," Claire said. "It's fun to stretch those intellectual muscles. Now, how about straightening your chairs and heading about to your dorms."

Afterwards, as we adjourned to the faculty lounge, Priscilla's antics still rankled many of us.

"The girl is troubled," Claire said. "Clearly, she wants attention at any cost."

"Troubled? Is that what you call it?" Harrison snorted a vulgar word. "Someone should kick her privileged ass right out of this school. I don't care how much her guardian pledges each year."

His reaction surprised me. I expected him to side with Priscilla, especially since she had targeted Tomas. Was that a streak of humanity in the Putnam genes emerging? His next comment put paid to that thought.

"Why don't you counsel her, Roddy? She'd like that, I know." Back to the same old Harry, snide and sinister.

"Huh? Go soak your head, Harrison. Let's discuss something worthwhile for a change. How about that trip to the DIA, Marky? Are we all set?" Roddy chose the high road in dealing with his colleague, something that staved off conflict and restored equanimity to the group.

"Yep. My aunt plans to join us and conduct the tour. I guess we'll rent a bus unless anyone has a better idea." A sea of blank faces greeted me. "The museum can provide box lunches if we want, and Natalie's aunt offered to help. She's a docent there."

Gin leaned back and yawned.

"Don't forget. Next weekend is our Shakespeare Unbound program. Coleman is really jazzed about that. Culture for the masses and all."

We bantered back and forth, weighing the merits of the performing arts versus the written or physical. Everything seemed so normal in that staid academic environment. I never imagined that danger lurked so near and that a vicious murderer was poised to strike again.

Chapter Nine

I made an early visit to police headquarters that next day, hoping to catch Sergeant Stevens before his schedule got too hectic. My first class wasn't until 10 a.m., and that afternoon, Gemma would arrive for our spa event. Stevens wasn't thrilled to see me but at least he was polite. He sat at his desk, elbows up, and favored me with a grin that barely masked the cynicism he no doubt felt at yet another civilian incursion.

"Miss Davis. Or should I say, Ms. Davis? Wouldn't want to ruffle any politically correct feathers at Sherborne School. What can I do for you?"

I displayed all thirty-two of my teeth in a girlish grin. After all, my parents had paid a fortune to straighten and perfect those pearly whites. Why not use them to advantage? "Oh, it doesn't matter what you call me, Sergeant. Either will do. I'm not overly sensitive." I leaned forward, displaying just a hint of cleavage. Stevens didn't strike me as the lecherous type, but he was still a man. I was willing to use my assets to my advantage if need be. "I have some information to share. About Tori's murder. At least I think it could be helpful."

His antennas went up immediately. Stevens was wily enough to appreciate information from any reliable source, even a blundering amateur.

"Okay. Let's hear it. As you know, I can't promise to keep anything you tell me confidential."

Once we got that settled, I spilled everything, using every arrow in my quiver. Information gushed forth like a torrent of water from the Trevi Fountain. I mentioned the missing scholarship funds, the fact that all the kids knew the identity of the Kahoot culprit, and my certainty that the mascara used on Tori came from the drama society's stash. He kept quiet the entire time, using that most effective technique of all-dead silence. Before I realized it, I had sketched a thumbnail portrait of my prime suspects, complete with possible motives, means, and opportunity. I was officially a NARC, stoolie, or blabbermouth. Take your pick. Personally, I preferred the term 'responsible citizen,' even though it was a tad awkward. To his credit, Stevens did take notes. He even asked a few rather perceptive questions, particularly about the students involved.

"This Priscilla Sayers. Sounds like a mean little minx, but most of those snooty girls are. Do you really think she's capable of violence?" He squinted when he asked that, as if I had fabricated the entire thing.

"She loathed Tori Aaron and made no secret of it," I said. "Priscilla has an aura of menace surrounding her. Trust me on that. It's almost visceral."

My description elicited the first real sign of emotion in him. Stevens laughed. Correction. He snorted rather loudly. "Sounds kind of personal, Ms. Davis. I'm certain we questioned that girl already. Funny, no hint about that aura of menace. But then again, I'm just a local yokel."

I ignored the dig and focused on the main prize. "Yeah, but she could have easily slipped out of the room that night. Everyone was milling around, waiting for the television show to start."

This time Stevens sneered. "Ah, yes. *Jeopardy*, as I recall. All you really smart types love that show. Us common folk favor *Wheel of Fortune*, but I guess that says it all. Town versus gown. Isn't that the term?"

Do not let him get to you and distract you, Marky. I forced myself to ignore the sarcasm and soldier on. "Okay. Forget Priscilla. I think we should focus on Tori. I've learned a lot about her, and I think it's the key to the entire crime." Study the character of the victim. I'd gotten that piece of detective wisdom straight from the works of the great Hercule Poirot, but I'd never ever admit that to Stevens. His reaction would probably dwarf eruptions from Mount Vesuvius.

Stevens raised his eyebrows. "And what did your exhaustive study conclude?"

"Tori was uncompromising, especially when it concerned an injustice.

Nothing would stop her from exposing wrongdoing, even if it destroyed someone's life. If we uncover everyone's secrets, we'll find the murderer."

Stevens leapt up from his chair as if he'd been nudged by a cattle prod. "Hold on! There Is no we involved in this investigation. Get it? If you interfere in an official investigation, I swear I'll charge you. Get it, Miss Davis? Now go back to your painting and leave this to the professionals."

I can take a hint, although in this instance, it was more of a threat than a hint. What I couldn't do was resist taking one parting shot. "Have it your way, Sergeant. After all, you're doing such a bang-up job without my help." I squared my shoulders and strode out the door while Stevens sputtered and muttered something truly rude.

Gemma's arrival that afternoon brightened my day. I hadn't realized just how much I'd missed her lively chatter and camaraderie. Plus, she was a great sounding board, not timid at all about calling me out when I went astray. After hearing about my session with Stevens, she glared at me and heaved one gigantic sigh. "Nothing ever changes with you, Marky. No wonder that cop reamed you out. When will you ever learn?"

Not an auspicious start to our weekend, especially since Gemma was doing me a favor. I'd been deluged with requests for both massages and facials ever since posting a sign-up sheet on the board. That evening she'd agreed to conduct a free seminar on facials and massage, but despite my protests, the Saturday sessions were strictly pay-as-you-go.

"They can afford it," Gemma said, "Or at least their parents can. Don't let these rich brats fool you." She tossed her russet curls, daring me to challenge her. "Besides, I can help you size up potential suspects. I assume you're still nosing around hunting for the murderer despite your run-in with that cop."

I tried to protest but to no avail. Gemma simply knew me too well. Accompanied by Fantasia, we then joined Claire for drinks at her place before the communal dinner. Gemma took one look at Raleigh and started cooing. "What a good boy. I've always loved Goldens. Where'd you get him?"

Naturally, that resurrected the tale of Tori Aaron and her sad demise. Gemma was crafty when the need arose, and I believe that was a deliberate tactic. If so, it worked. Claire, prodded by Gemma, reminisced about her friend and the impact she'd had on everyone.

"What's wrong with the cops"? Gemma asked. "I mean, it's obvious this was an inside job. How many suspects can there be in a joint like this?"

Claire gasped. "I can't believe any of these kids would resort to violence. They loved Tori."

Nothing fazed Gemma when she was on a roll. "What about the teachers—your colleagues? She must have rubbed one of them the wrong way a time or two. Those self-righteous types aren't much fun."

"No. She could be stubborn when a matter of principle was concerned, but Tori was kind too. She knew more about me than my own mother, and she was compassionate." Tears formed in the corner of Claire's eyes. She blinked, as if she might wish away Gemma's remarks or maybe Gemma herself. Fortunately, time was our ally, and I hustled my two pals off to the dining hall while Fantasia and Raleigh settled into crates, happily munching marrow bones. The faculty table was at full strength, an unusual occurrence for a Friday. Even though she was in a supposedly serious relationship with the dreadful Deputy Soto, Gemma still had eyes. She stared pointedly at Roddy Park, holding his hand just a fraction too long when they were introduced. "Have you signed up for a massage," she asked him. "I sense tension in between your shoulder blades."

Roddy flushed and shook his head. "Missed the signup sheet, I guess."

Gemma brushed that excuse aside. "Don't worry. I'll make sure to squeeze you in. What time works best for you?"

He was trapped, and he knew it. Before dinner was served, Roddy had signed up for a neck and shoulder massage on Saturday morning. When Gemma was on a mission, very little could deter her, and she had zeroed in on poor Roddy as her prey.

Friday evening dinner was my favorite. The chef had a flair for preparing white fish with a delicacy that I'd seldom tasted before. Student servers that night were Natalie and Ru. I'd rather hoped that either Tomas or Priscilla would be conscripted, but such was the luck of the draw. When Harrison Putnam pulled up a chair and joined us, I was astonished. Mrs. Putnam was nowhere to be seen, and according to Gin, she only appeared twice a year, at the holiday party and graduation. Considering her husband's dour nature, the poor woman, if indeed she existed, probably encouraged him to attend outings alone whenever possible.

"Harry, meet Gemma Watts," Gin said. "She's Marky's business partner and our guest of honor."

He lowered his glasses and surveyed Gemma as if she were a prize heifer at the county fair or a particularly rare variety of insect. Naturally, that only encouraged my friend to act out.

"Harry, is it? And what do you teach, Harry? Something terribly intellectual, I bet." Gemma gave him a wide grin.

"Actually, I prefer to be called Harrison." I'd seen cardboard that was less stiff than Harry.

She squeezed his arm. "Oh, but that's so stuffy. And you seem like such a fun guy."

He looked so perturbed that Gin burst out laughing. "Our Harry is a math and science whiz straight from Dartmouth. Keeps the kids on their toes. Calculus, algebra, you name it. He's your guy. No wonder they get high SAT scores."

Harrison flushed and concentrated on his white fish. By the time dessert arrived, he had recovered enough to quiz Gemma on her background and credentials. From his reaction, it was obvious that certified massage therapist and aesthetician failed to impress him.

It was time for Gemma's presentation, so I excused both of us and headed for the largest of our classrooms. We assembled her massage table, adjusted the microphone, and readied the flip chart in preparation for an expected audience of thirty. Most of my students planned to attend, and I was eager to get Gemma's impressions of them. Promptly at eight o'clock, I introduced my partner and friend to the Sherborne school crowd. She wasn't awed by them, but she spent the session informing and illustrating the value of the body/ mind connection and getting it synchronized. When Gemma asked for volunteers, Priscilla Sayers's hand shot up first. I'd warned Gemma about her, but there was no way to avoid the girl without being obvious. Gemma handled the situation perfectly. She did an analysis of Priscilla's skin, pronounced it in perfect shape, then suggested that because of tension in her neck and back, an occasional hot stone massage might be helpful. When Claire rather timidly volunteered, Gemma repeated the process. During a lengthy question-and-answer segment, she fielded all types of questions, including an impudent one about salacious massage parlors and their scandals. At the conclusion of her presentation, Gemma received a hearty and well-deserved ovation from the group.

"You were terrific," Claire said as we walked back to her apartment. "I loved your points about the mind/body link. They gave me something to consider." After collecting Fantasia, Gemma and I headed back to my digs for conversation and cocoa.

"Well," I asked her, "Did you get any impressions of the group? Anyone stick out as a potential suspect?"

She laughed. "I'd like to frisk Dr. Roddy Park for weapons. Bet he has some awesome ones."

"Gemma! You're outrageous. Poor Roddy is still mourning for Tori. Besides, I don't think he ever gets his nose out of a textbook long enough to date."

"Oh, don't be so sure. I saw him sneak a few glances at you." Gemma smirked. "You could use some romance, my girl, and that professor fits the bill."

I sipped my drink and ignored her. "I'm taking a break from relationships for a while. Maybe then my luck will improve."

"You know what they say. You can't hit a home run if you're not in the game."

Platitudes annoyed me even when there was a grain of truth in them. "I've been officially benched for the season, and besides, who is this magical "they" who always know so much?"

"Wow! Touchy. Guess I struck a nerve." Gemma wisely switched subjects. "Claire and Gin seem like pretty solid citizens. I liked both." She rolled her eyes. "Of course. That doesn't mean they couldn't kill. Same goes for ravishing Roddy. Men have killed for jealousy plenty of times. Your Tori Aaron sounded like Mother Theresa with a paintbrush and a stick up her rear. Full of good works. Ugh!"

"Aunt Violet adored her. Admired her talent." I'd learned a lot about Tori since coming to Sherborne School, and I had to admit that Gemma made a good point. Everyone—well almost everyone—had some unsavory episode in their lives that they'd like to forget. If Tori felt compelled to expose it, that might have sealed her fate. Most murders had a direct link to the character of the victim. Of course, I was no expert, but I truly believed that. I'd read enough mystery novels to support my theory.

"Okay, spill it." Ignoring Gemma was a waste of effort. She simply wouldn't allow it. "You must have a theory. You always do. Lay your cards out on the table, Marky."

We spent some time reconstructing the crime and possible motives. If Tori's murder was indeed an inside job, I could think of only a few motives strong enough to elicit violence: the Kahoot incident, admittedly a childish bid for attention, or, the missing scholarship funds. The former might have ruined someone's academic prospects, but the latter would surely have landed the culprit in jail. Gemma listened to my theory without interrupting. That alone was a rarity. She stroked her chin before venturing an opinion. "If those kids know who did the Kahoot caper, you can find out. No problem. They crack like an egg at their age, especially when a trusted teacher like you puts the squeeze on them." Her eyes had an almost evil gleam to them. "The money scam might be tough to unravel. Hard to believe that they're so loosey goosy with big bucks." She paused. "At least fifty thousand is a lot to people like me."

Claire and Gin had said the same thing. On a teacher's salary, they had to pinch pennies. That money represented a year's salary, tax-free. Quite a temptation.

I admitted that Sherborne's lax approach surprised me too. Even the books for our little business were handled by a CPA. Big donors would explode if they knew how remiss Sherborne's policies were. That gave me pause. How far would Coleman Ross go to shield the school and save himself? Tori would have notified him as soon as she identified the problem. Perhaps he asked—no begged—her to keep quiet. Perhaps she refused. They quarreled, and things got out of hand. After all, the headmaster never attended those evening quiz sessions. No one knew or even asked his whereabouts, even Sergeant Stevens. When I mentioned that to Gemma, she laughed. "Well then. It's up to you to brace the big boss. You can do it. I've seen you charm the socks off old guys like him."

I agreed to tackle Coleman as soon as possible. Perhaps I could pretend to brief him on our trip to the DIA or, better still, ask for his advice. I hated to be sexist, but most men fell for that immediately.

Before we turned out the lights, Gemma wagged her finger at me. "And don't forget what I said. Roddy still ranks right up there on our list of suspects. Wasn't there a famous play about that? Shakespeare or one of those guys?"

Gemma could still astonish me at times. She was no scholar, but her mind was razor-sharp.

"Othello. That focused on jealousy and thwarted love. Roddy's playing that part in our drama presentation but believe me, it doesn't imply anything evil. No type casting."

Her expression told me that Gemma wasn't convinced. Suddenly the murder for jealousy plot gave me an entirely new insight. If Claire was right, Harrison Putnam also yearned for Tori. Had his advances been spurned, resulting in a fit of violence? Admittedly, Harrison didn't seem to be the passionate type unless the subject was either mathematics or his distinguished pedigree. And yet…if Tori rejected him for another suitor, a man Harrison considered his social inferior, who could predict his reaction?

"I really missed you," I said. "You see things so clearly."

She grinned. "As they say, it's a gift and a curse. Benny's mom thinks so anyway."

I visualized the mountainous Josephine Soto confronting Gemma, and it wasn't a pretty picture. "She's jealous. Afraid you're going to steal her little boy from her."

"Maybe. But trust me, I have no intention of doing so. At least not right away." Gemma's eyes sparkled with mischief. "I'll wait until you're ready. Double wedding. The works."

On that auspicious note, we said good night.

Between Gemma's massage schedules and the rehearsals for the Shakespeare pageant, Saturday was one hot mess. We skipped breakfast, a mistake I later regretted —and spent the time arranging Gemma's treatment room, towels, and products. A line of students and instructors was milling about when we threw open the door, and a festive mood permeated the air. Roddy was up first. He arrived promptly at eight a.m., clad in a University of Michigan sweatsuit that had seen better days. He managed a curt greeting to me and a nod to the gaggle of students enjoying the summer sunshine, but otherwise said very little. Perhaps he felt shy or was troubled by something else going on in his life. Gin had mentioned money troubles related to his Ph.D. program, a pricey undertaking at the best of times. That thought comforted me. After all, it suggested that he was not responsible for misappropriating those scholarship funds. *Don't be so sure,* I told myself. *Guilt can eat away at an otherwise decent person. And you have no business taking sides, Marketta Davis.*

Gemma ushered him into her cubbyhole and soon allayed any concerns he had. She was an old hand at assessing the needs and idiosyncrasies of her customers and could banish the blues like no one else I'd ever met. I heard Roddy's deep voice relaxing as Gemma chatted with him about his studies and the challenges of motivating students. That gave me time to dash back to my apartment and grab another latte. Fantasia stood by patiently, sending me that poignant plea that dogs excel at. As usual, I capitulated, tossed her a treat, and hitched up her harness. A bit of exercise would benefit both of us, besides that gave me a chance to read more of Claire's novel. Family sagas usually didn't interest me, but this one, a combination of romance and tragedy, was so beautifully crafted that I was thoroughly captivated. Small wonder Claire had won several literary prizes and had been hailed as a major talent. Too bad that she hadn't produced a sequel in the decade that followed. Writer's block must impose an almost intolerable burden on a creative artist. I perched on a nearby bench and vowed to limit my reading to thirty minutes. After all, I had challenges of my own to confront. Aunt Violet would arrive next week and despite my efforts, I had made very little progress. Only four weeks remained in the summer term, and Tori's murderer was still very much at large.

"I've been looking for you, Ms. Davis." Coleman Ross bent down, wearing a frown as big as Texas. His attire, a bespoke tweed suit, starched white shirt, and rep tie, made no concession to the weekend, nor did his frosty manner. I chose to ignore that and play the adoring acolyte, Innocence personified. It's scarcely my strong suit, but in a pinch, I can produce a plausible imitation.

"Good morning, Dr. Ross. What a lovely day."

He immediately dispensed with social niceties and went for the jugular. "I just ended a session with Sergeant Stevens. Apparently, you filled his ears with lies and innuendos about Sherborne School. I'm shocked and saddened by that disloyalty, Ms. Davis. Even though you're not really one of us, you must realize how harmful that sort of behavior can be." His outraged tone left no doubt that Stevens had given the headmaster a thorough shellacking. *Kudos to the local constabulary!*

"I'm puzzled, Dr. Ross. What did I do wrong? Sergeant Stevens asked me a few questions, and I responded."

Ross plowed on as if he hadn't heard a thing I'd said. "To think we have a Quisling on our faculty, a viper in our own nest. It's beyond outrageous."

She who stays composed retains the upper hand. Despite that realization, I responded in kind. "What's truly outrageous, sir, is that you are harboring a thief and potentially a murderer at Sherborne. Tori Aaron deserved better than your attempts to sweep her death under the rug."

Ross sputtered and stuttered as his complexion grew almost puce. A revolt by a serf was unthinkable and not on his agenda. I said a silent prayer that his heart was able to sustain the shock. When he regained his composure, Coleman Ross, headmaster of Sherborne School, lowered his voice and addressed me not as a lackey but as a reasonably intelligent being. "Don't tell me you believe that. What's your proof?"

I took a deep breath, certain that this was a pivotal moment. "Think about it. Someone knew Tori's schedule. That says insider all the way. Tori herself was famous or infamous, as you choose, for truth-telling. If she uncovered any type of malfeasance, she was sure to spill the proverbial beans no matter who it destroyed. Your missing funds, for instance—"

Coleman quickly interrupted. "Just an accounting error. Nothing criminal."

"Right." I continued my narrative as if he had never spoken. "She investigated that Kahoot scandal and promised not to create a fuss if it never happened again. Still, since most of the student body knows the score, the culprit might well have feared exposure."

"A childish prank," Coleman said. "Hardly worth killing for."

Only steely self-control enabled me to continue without shaking him or kicking his shins. Violence solves nothing, but it can feel so good at times. "By adult standards, it was nothing devastating, but kids have an exaggerated sense of doom. Why else would you have so many teen suicides?" Another deep breath. "The embezzlement—let's call it what it was—now that's a more serious matter. Careers could shatter, and someone could end up in jail or barred from teaching."

His eyes glazed over as if he were in a fugue state. Still, I soldiered on. "Then there's the personal angle. Tori had admirers, both students, and faculty, and passions can run amuck. Her murder was very personal. The killer showed real animus by using those cheap cosmetics to deface her body. Only an insider would know how much Tori loathed makeup. He or she was making quite a statement."

"Anything else?" Coleman braced himself, but instead of tough talk, I gave him a sunny smile. "Nope. I just felt Sergeant Stevens needed to consider those points."

He stood, once again in control. "Thank you for your insights, Ms. Davis. I'd appreciate it if you'd keep any further observations to yourself or discuss them with me first before notifying the authorities." Then, Coleman Ross pivoted, squared his shoulders, and marched down the path toward his school with military precision.

* * *

I felt guilty about scampering off to lunch without Gemma but justified it by the demands of raw hunger. The menu wasn't terrific—just sandwiches and soup—but it tasted like manna from heaven to me. The lunchroom was humming with conversation, much of it centering around Gemma's magical massages and the upcoming dress rehearsal for our play. Roddy sat next to me; a pleasant surprise made even more so by his unusually gregarious manner. "Wow," I said. "You seem on top of the world. Don't tell me that massage did that for you?"

"Nah. I just got some good news from Michigan. They're offering to fund the final leg of my dissertation if I teach a few classes for them. Not a fortune but a decent stipend. I can do that and still fulfill my commitments to Sherborne too."

We spent some time discussing the progress of his dissertation, "Non-Verbal Communication in Cold War Geopolitics." Quite a crowd-pleaser.

"It sounds deadly dull, I know, and probably no one will ever read it once it's finished." Roddy shrugged. "But the topic is fascinating and timely even today."

Time for me to take a risk. "I'd love to read it, even though that wasn't my field."

"Really?" His smile transformed those handsome features into superstardom. "You know, Tori always reviewed each chapter. Gave me a hard time about some of my conclusions too."

Warning signs flashed before my eyes. Had Tori's critiques wounded his ego or punctured his vanity enough for Roddy to strike out at her? "How did you feel about that? After all, you've devoted your life to that dissertation."

"You've got it all wrong, Marky. That only made things better, having to argue with Tori. Remember, I'll have to defend that manuscript in front of a panel of professors who'll be out for my blood. Convincing Tori was great preparation."

His eyes glazed over with a dreamy look. Was he remembering or regretting?

"You really loved her, didn't you?"

"Yeah, but she saw things differently. Marriage just wasn't in the cards for us. Tori made that clear. In some ways, I'm a traditional Korean guy. Family is important to me, you know, passing down my heritage to my kids someday. That was a bridge too far for Tori."

"How did you end things?" I knew I was being way too intrusive, but time was running out. Already Claire and Gin were filling their plates and heading our way. Despite my questions, Roddy didn't seem to mind. "We didn't really end things. Our friendship never ended. It just shifted to a different level. Sometimes being friends is better than being lovers."

I wasn't so sure about that, but Roddy made a valid point. Friends, male or female, were invaluable to most of us. It sounded plausible, and I longed to believe him. The cynical side of me wondered, though, if he was being candid or merely reciting a well-rehearsed alibi for Tori's murder.

Chapter Ten

The afternoon was packed full between Gemma's final customers and the dress rehearsal. While I immersed myself in my backstage duties, applying stage makeup for the performers, I had no time to ponder what Roddy had said. Objectivity flew out the window where he was concerned, and at least I was honest enough to recognize that. There was no proof that he meekly agreed to Tori's new world order. In fact, most men would have been devastated if the woman they loved dismissed them so cavalierly. Some men might have reacted badly. It was far easier to believe that a toad-like Harry Putnam had done the foul deed. I recalled that quote from the *Duchess* of *Malfi,* something about other sins only speak, but murder shrieks out. Theft and racist taunts were indeed sinful but murder, Tori's murder, was unforgivable. It did cry to the heavens for justice and perhaps I was the instrument of retribution.

Gemma joined me later that afternoon and soon pitched in, fitting and adjusting costumes and applying the occasional touch of glitter. Unlike me, she was a wizard with a needle and thread, a skill that we badly needed. With one exception, most of the actors were grateful for her help. That naysayer was Priscilla, who insisted that the bodice on her dress should be lowered several inches to expose more cleavage. Gin intervened and swiftly settled the issue. "Not going to happen, Priscilla. You're playing Lady Macbeth, not some strumpet. Get over it and stop complaining." The girl huffed and puffed and calmed down but not before she shot a look of pure malice Gin's way.

When I applied Abigail's makeup, I saw that she was close to tears. A galloping case of pre-performance jitters, or so I thought. Senator Jenkins was among the select preview audience and I was positive that his daughter hoped to shine in the role of Juliet.

"Don't worry, Abby. You look amazing, and you know your lines perfectly."

She hung her head. "That's not it. I have something to tell you, Ms. Davis." She turned around to assess the landscape. "It's private."

Before she could continue, Ru Peterson bounced over wearing a Hamlet costume. "How do I look? Professor Park traded roles with me." He struck a pose." To be or not to be, that is the question." He bowed and accepted our hearty applause. "Ah, if only I were playing Romeo. Then I could sweep this lovely maiden into my arms." Abby squealed with pleasure and raced off with Ru. No more tears for that young lady although I was curious about the secret she hadn't shared with me. Was it something about Tori, or merely another instance of teenage angst?

Gin shrugged when I asked about the role changes. "You know how mercurial these kids are. Tomas wanted to play Romeo, Ru begged to be cast as Hamlet, and Roddy didn't really care. I think he's perfect for Othello, anyway." She winked. "Good thing Sergeant Stevens won't be here. He might get ideas about Roddy killing the leading lady."

Claire edged over to our group. "Hush, Gin. Everyone's jumpy enough as it is." She pirouetted and asked. "Am I wise enough to be Portia, dispensing punishment? That was something I saw Tori playing. She was so intense about meting out justice."

Gin rolled her eyes. "Too bad she didn't fit the entire part. Can't exactly see Tori on that 'quality of mercy' stuff. She would have sawed off that pound of flesh from Shylock herself if it suited her."

"Oh Gin, what a terrible thing to say." Claire's eyes teared up. "You know better than that."

Gin put her hands on her hips and faced Claire down. "Sorry, hon, but that social justice warrior stuff got old at times. Not everything is worth a big battle. I got a headache at faculty meetings when she and Harrison would go at it. Over little things. Such drama made me'think I was back at Julliard."

I watched the two friends closely. Each had a different view of Tori, but both were probably accurate. Despite everything, I still believed that the key to the murder rested with Tori and her uncompromising sense of fair play. Each of us had our secrets. They shaped our lives and limited our futures. Even good souls like Gemma chose to shield certain parts of their lives. They demanded and deserved a zone of privacy. When I had been banished from the Art Institute of Chicago, I was ashamed. My first instinct was to hide and avoid the truth. Ultimately with the help of Gemma and Aunt Violet, I faced my demons and admitted that painting was no longer an option for me. At least not on the level I had hoped to achieve. How would I have reacted if someone like Tori publicized that very painful episode to the world? Violence has always been foreign to me but in a moment of heat, even an avowed pacifist can lose control. No. Tori's murder was carefully planned. The killer had studied her habits and spread a signature mark of disdain on her face. According to the police report, there were no defensive wounds on Tori. She apparently had known and not feared her assailant. So much for the initial theory of a random street crime. A woman who carried pepper spray wouldn't hesitate to use it if she were threatened. If only I could reconstruct that evening more precisely. Students and teachers were moving about quite freely between the dining area and the Jeopardy gang. Coleman Ross was not present, Roddy admitted that he had left the area looking for Tori, and Priscilla harbored a secret about that evening. Now I had another thing to consider, Was Abigail being overly dramatic, or did she indeed have something important to impart? My head ached just considering the possibility.

"Hey girl, wake up?" Gemma brandished a needle in one hand and a pair of wicked-looking scissors in the other. "Whew! Got to say I'm exhausted." She flopped down in a rather disreputable wing chair that had seen better days. "I got some hot tips for you, though. Surprising what people spill when they're on a massage table."

I sat patiently, knowing that's Gemma couldn't wait to share her news. It was a little game we'd played over the years that I always won. After a few seconds, she launched into a full, colorful description of her so-called hot tips. Since Roddy had been her first customer, I hoped and feared that he had said something meaningful. Thirty uninterrupted minutes with Gemma had pulverized many hearty souls.

"Okay. Your professor was shy at first, although plenty of women had probably offered him a massage before. Goodness, that man was tense! Lots of muscle cramps in his lower back." Although I enjoyed the anatomy lesson, I was eager for more substantive information. When Gemma finally obliged, it was worth the wait.

"He spent at least ten minutes describing his project. Called it a dissertation or something like that. I pretended to be interested even though he lost me after about five minutes. Finally, I was able to steer the conversation over to Tori. Roddy told me he'd proposed and everything, but she just wasn't interested." Gemma winked. "Seems she walked the 'friends with benefits' trail, but that wasn't enough for him."

"Did you ask how he reacted to that?"

"Oh yeah. He said at first, he was crushed but later realized it was for the best. And get this, Ms. Marky, he said he's interested in someone new but isn't sure how she feels about him."

I felt the heat rising to my cheeks but tried to play it cool. "Interesting. I know Gin Hastings and probably half the female students in the school would welcome his attention."

"Huh!" I never could fool Gemma. Don't know why I even bothered to try. "Roddy asked plenty of questions about you, girlfriend. Naturally, I gave you a glowing report. Told him you weren't married or engaged because of your art career but that I expected that to change."

"Did he say anything about the night Tori died?"

"Funny thing. He said she was worried about something she'd just found out that day by accident."

I held my breath and slowly exhaled. "What? Did he tell you?"

Gemma shook her head. "He never found out. Tori told him she wanted to check out whatever it was before she went public with it. Called it dynamite that could ruin someone's life."

That was indeed a bombshell. In under an hour, Gemma had managed to extract more information from Roddy Park than I had in a month.

"Anything else?" If Tori uncovered something incriminating, she would have felt honor bound to discuss it first with the person in question before alerting the authorities. Could it be that she had learned the identity of the embezzler?

"Most of the kids talked about school things. You know, teachers, college plans. Routine kind of boring stuff."

"Even Priscilla Sayers?"

Gemma's response was a cackle. "Oh no. That little madam had plenty to say, all of it about herself and her big career on the stage. She said she's going to...Julliard, is it? I asked if it was all set, and she said no, but she expected to wrap everything up soon. Some teacher at the school is pushing her." Gemma frowned. "You know that girl has a real nasty streak. When I said something like lucky you, or good for you, she laughed and talked said luck had nothing to do with it. Talked about some bargaining chip like it was gold plated."

She must have meant Gin as her ace in the hole, but I very much doubted if Gin was actively sponsoring the girl. Priscilla certainly had the ego and self-assurance for the stage, but her talent was a big question mark. I'd have to verify that when the dress rehearsal was over.

"I really liked Claire. She could be a nice friend. Funny thing though, she seems kind of sad." Gemma's assignment had been to mention Tori whenever possible, and she must have done so quite adroitly.

"Did she say anything about Tori? They were awfully close, you know."

"Not really. Most of the time, she talked about her sister who died. Clara or some name like that. She really adored her. Called her brilliant."

"Clara was a writer too. I think that death spurred Claire on to finish her novel. Of course, she's had trouble since then with her follow-up work. Writers' block. Not uncommon, or so I'm told."

Gemma yawned. "There's more, of course, but right now, I'd like to take a little break."

I checked my watch. "Yikes! The show is about ready to start. Let's move our chairs closer to the curtain so that we can watch them." I patted her shoulder. "You did a great job. Thanks for the hard work."

"No big deal. I've always wanted to be a sleuth. When people shed their clothes, they tend to open right up."

I considered that a warning. Keep your clothes on if you have anything to hide from Gemma.

We heard Gin welcome everyone and explain the purpose of Shakespeare Unbound. The audience consisted of other students and a sprinkling of proud parents whose broad grins and enthusiastic clapping instantly gave them away. I noticed Senator Jenkins, seated front row center, and accompanied by Coleman Ross. No surprise there. The headmaster was always eager to curry favor with the bigwigs, although, to be fair, it was an important part of his job. The woman next to him had to be Mrs. Ross, she of the comfortable family fortune. She was exquisitely dressed and perfectly groomed, with expertly styled brunette locks and understated but handsome jewelry. Aunt Violet would heartily approve of her taste. She always emphasized that in France, whether a woman was a socialite or a shop girl, she was expected to be stylish. Claire mentioned that Mrs. Ross kept close watch over her husband, and I did note a predatory look in her eagle eyes as she surveyed the landscape. Coleman was no big prize in my book, but with teens like Priscilla out and about, it was probably wise for a wife to be wary.

The first act was the famous balcony scene from Romeo and Juliet. Tomas entered the stage with swagger. Although he was closer in age to the title character than many of the famous actors who had played Romeo, Tomas was certainly a more muscular, earthy rendition of the love-struck Montague. When Abigail leaned over the flower-covered balcony we had constructed, I must admit that her delicacy and innate sweetness captivated me. Such a well-known passage can sometimes seem like a cliché, but seeing two passionate youngsters reenact the Bard's immortal words was truly moving. I watched Senator Jenkins' face, looking for any sign that he disapproved. Gemma elbowed me so hard that I yelped. "Hmm. Seems like those two have been rehearsing after hours. Trust me on this; they've played that love scene before."

It shocked me at first. They were just kids, but swirling hormones had no age limit. No wonder the headmaster appeared to target Tomas! He couldn't risk alienating Senator Jenkins over the fumbling of a lovestruck townie. Suddenly a sickening sensation lurched in my stomach. Oh, Lord! Please don't let Abby tell me she's pregnant! I'm not equipped to deal with that. Both those kids were way too young to even consider the repercussions.

Gemma elbowed me in the ribs yet again. I'd need surgery before the night was out if she kept that up. "What's wrong with you?" I grumbled. "Cool your jets before they call the paramedics."

"Hey, kid, you're the deep breather. Settle down and enjoy the show."

I nodded and forced myself to relax. No need to panic until I assessed the situation. Besides, the next presentation was *Othello*, with dashing Roddy Park fending off the insidious Iago. If Gin had typecasting in mind, she nailed it with Harrison Putnam as Iago. Snide remarks and poisonous asides were Harry's stock in trade much as they were for Iago. The narrative aligned perfectly with the story of Tori Aaron, a woman desired by both men. When Natalie came on stage, her fragility and innocence mirrored that of Desdemona. I gasped when Roddy enacted the death scene. Was fiction imitating life in front of my eyes? Had Roddy confronted the woman he loved in the same tragic way?

I tamped down my suspicions to enjoy the Macbeth segment. Imagination is a sterling quality, but an excess can be downright destructive. In my case, watching Priscilla Sayers as Lady Macbeth was almost anticlimactic. The girl embodied every invidious trait of her namesake, including the propensity to do harm. Frankly, I found it difficult to separate reality from fiction when Priscilla took the stage. She'd told Gemma that she had a bargaining chip that would ensure her success at Julliard. How far would Priscilla go to achieve her ends? I honestly believed that she might eliminate any obstacle, including Tori, if necessary. My thoughts were so jumbled that I couldn't focus on Ru's performance as Hamlet or any of the other scenes that followed. Afterwards, the audience gave a rousing ovation to all the actors and demanded a curtain call. This was merely a dress rehearsal, but by the vigor of the reaction, one would never know it. Gin took a well-deserved bow for her work, and everyone repaired to the reception hall for snacks and more kudos. To my surprise, one unexpected member of the audience emerged when Sergeant Stevens, looking rather dapper in a crisp summer suit, tapped me on the shoulder.

"Some event," he said. "Guess you know I followed up on your suggestions, or should I say accusations?"

Deception was not my strong suit, but when the occasion demanded, I could muster some semblance of it. "I beg your pardon. Since when is doing one's civic duty a crime? Pardon me for being a good citizen."

Gemma edged into our conversation and introduced herself. Since she had started dating the odious Benny Soto, she seemed to consider herself part of the law enforcement fraternity. I could only pray that the fad would soon pass.

"What's your take on the murder, Sergeant? Are you here officially?" Her friendly grin didn't deceive Stevens for a minute. He backed up and glowered. "I heard all about you, Ms. Watts, from the guys in your town. Another amateur detective. Just what I needed."

Nothing deters Gemma when she's on the hunt. She leaned closer and whispered. "I got to know your suspects today. Maybe I can help."

Stevens's glare was a thing of beauty. "Mind your own business, young woman. That's the way you can help me most. You and your friend need to keep your noses out of police business before you get hurt."

Further hostilities were averted by the arrival of Claire and Gin. They accepted our congratulations and watched as Stevens made a hasty escape. "Wow!" Gin laughed. "The case of the vanishing man. Was it something we did?"

"Forget it. He's probably just a disciple of the Bard." None of us believed that, but as a temporary measure, it would do. I heaped well-deserved praise upon my friends and ambled over to the other side of the room where most of the students had congregated. Their spirits were buoyed by the success of the play, and they kept re-enacting the triumph. I noted Abby's flushed cheeks as Tomas bent down to adjust the rose in her hair. Not comforting. The arrival of Senator Jenkins put paid to that behavior. He nodded courteously to Tomas and gently led his daughter away. I was startled when Roddy joined us and complimented Gemma on her massage program. Perhaps I had missed signals in our previous conversations. Gemma had mad instincts about men and their intentions. I did not. Before I could reciprocate, Priscilla wedged herself in between us, making fatuous comments about Roddy's performance.

"You were so intense, professor. I really thought you might strangle poor Natalie." She glanced at Gin and Claire. "Of course, some things aren't quite what they seem to be. It's surprising how often people who appear innocent deceive others."

Roddy turned his back and dismissed her, saying, "Run along now, Priscilla. Your classmates are waiting for you."

"Ooh, that girl," Gin grimaced. "She could drive a saint to violence."

Claire laughed. "True, but you must admit she nailed the part of Lady Macbeth."

"Type casting," I said, adding my touch of vinegar to the mix. "Sort of like Harrison as Iago."

Roddy chortled at that, and we turned our attention to more constructive matters. The final performance would be staged in three weeks to coincide with the charity art show. Gin was determined to perfect everyone's performance before then, even if it drove us to distraction. It would be challenging since our schedule was crammed with activities before the end of summer term. Next Saturday was the scheduled tour of the Detroit Institute of Art, something I was particularly keen on. Seeing Aunt Violet was another plus, even though Gemma assured me that Poppet was flourishing in my absence. Her attempt to reassure me fell flat. Instead of being comforted, it made me feel expendable and unneeded in my own store. I chided myself for being childish and ungrateful. After all, I had far more things to be thankful for than many of my contemporaries, even talented folks like Claire and Gin. Neither one complained about being trapped in the claustrophobic academic womb of Sherborne School. Still...Claire was one novel away from regaining fame, and Gin was still young enough to launch an acting career if she so chose. As for Roddy—that man would be a supernova once his dissertation was finished. I envisioned him as a sought-after guest on the many cable news programs and think tanks. With his looks and brains, it made sense.

"Hey, Marky," Gemma said. "You're a million miles away. Come down to earth, girl."

"Sorry. I was just thinking how lucky I am. Sometimes a different setting gives you perspective."

"I'm not sure what you mean, but you've always had your head in the clouds. Not me. I'm satisfied with life in Harbor Bay and running our business. Small towns suit me just fine."

I didn't ask if Deputy Benny Soto was part of that equation. I didn't dare. Gemma was my closest friend, and I wanted only the best for her. I cringed at the thought that Benny might become a permanent part of her life. *None of your business Marky.* True, he was no intellectual giant, but even I admitted that Benny had stable employment and no obvious bad habits. Not everyone wanted or needed to reach for the stars. That made me recall Abby and her attempt to confide in me. Now was not the time with her dad on the scene, but I would see her soon. Fingers crossed, her issue was some minor tempest in a teenage teapot and nothing earth-shaking.

Gemma joined me in a final walk with Fantasia before we bedded down for the evening. It was a lovely night, clear with a bright, star-filled sky and mild wind. We trod carefully past the site of Tori's demise, not wanting to desecrate it by idle chatter. The students had erected a small memorial to her, filled with flowers but thankfully not teddy bears or the like. I've never understood the compulsion to litter an area with that type of sodden shrine. Besides, even I knew that Tori was no sentimentalist. She would scoff at the idea of stuffed toys marking her final resting place.

"That's where it happened, isn't it?" Gemma's voice was quiet, almost reverent.

"Yeah. The school installed more lighting now that it's too late." My comment was unfair, and I admitted it. Until Tori's awful end, there had never been any violent incident to mar the area. Ironically, the park had always gone by the name Peaceful Meadow, although delicacy required that the sign be removed. We settled down on a bench that bore a brass plaque with Tori's name on it. Despite the ghoulish association, the area was serene and inviting. It was open space with nowhere for an assailant to crouch or conceal himself. Tori must have known her killer. At the very least, the person didn't arouse her suspicion. That argued for someone—either a student, colleague, or tradesperson—whose presence wasn't unusual. Not Roddy. I refused to even consider it. Tori had been found very near this bench that we now perched on. Perhaps she had spoken with the killer, tried to reason with him or her. From what I now knew of Tori Aaron, she was neither a coward nor a fool. The assault must have been unprovoked and sudden. Fantasia stayed alert, perhaps sensing that this place had been the scene of a tragedy. Even Gemma was uncharacteristically quiet at first, until she swallowed and blurted out her thoughts.

"I've been thinking. Someone who cozied up to my massage table was probably the murderer. It's weird. Scary."

She was trembling. That had to be first for the normally combative friend I knew so well.

"Okay," I said. "Finish your observations, Dr. Watson."

She closed her eyes and grimaced. "Okay. Let's finish with the kids. Abigail is a sweet kid with something on her mind. Probably not murder, but who knows with teenagers. Then, Tomas. Lots of swagger, but essentially a decent guy. Another sweet kid. Capable of violence based on those muscles, I felt, but that might just be the effect of manual labor. His dad is a mechanic or something like that. By the way, he's another one who had a crush on Tori Aaron. My Lord. That woman made her mark on this school! You'd think she was some sort of femme fatale."

Ru and Natalie hadn't left any vivid impression on Gemma, and she'd already shared her views on Priscilla. Harrison Putnam had refused to participate, although I believed that was an unintentional act of mercy for Gemma. Touching him, even in that most professional, clinical manner, might be a grisly experience that could scar her for life.

Suddenly Fantasia's ears pricked up, and she emitted a low growl. I couldn't see anything in the dark, but her eyesight and hearing put ours to shame.

Was someone listening to our conversation, hoping to overhear something? Gemma leapt up from the bench and craned her neck. "I don't see anyone, but I feel something. This place is spooky."

When Roddy appeared out of the shadows, I didn't know whether to be relieved or outraged. "Sorry, ladies," he said. "I assure you my intentions were honorable. I saw you leave and thought I'd escort you back." He peered over the bench toward the shrubbery. "Funny. I thought I heard someone there. Guess not. It's tough at night, especially in this place."

We weren't alone there. I'm not usually fanciful, but I could feel Tori's spirit permeating the air. Nothing threatening, sort of a benign presence urging us on. Maybe Fantasia had sensed it too. When it came to the spirit world, I pled neutral, being neither a believer nor a skeptic. Gemma regularly attended seances, but I'd never joined her. Dealing with corporal beings was more than enough for me. Either way, after the rigors of the day, we were all too ready to leave Peaceful Meadow and return to our rooms.

Chapter Eleven

Gemma's departure the next morning left me feeling both glum and ravenously hungry. Sunday brunch seemed like the perfect antidote to both conditions, and I could taste those pancakes as soon as I opened the cafeteria door. Others must have felt the same way. Claire waved at me from a table in the center of the room where most of the staff had congregated. Very few students had arrived yet but after the rush of Saturday's activities, I supposed they were still recuperating. At their age, I had burrowed under my bed covers and slept for hours every chance I got.

Roddy looked exceptionally handsome in a taupe linen jacket, crisp blue shirt, and navy tie. I tried unsuccessfully not to stare or otherwise disgrace myself, but Gin immediately caught me out.

"He looks spectacular, doesn't he?" she said. "Not that anyone noticed."

Roddy flushed and stared down at his plate. "I'm meeting with my academic advisor this afternoon. Final dissertation conference. Keep your fingers crossed and wish me luck."

I didn't ask if the advisor was male or female, but I had my suspicions.

Claire took pity on him and changed the subject. "Are we all set for our jaunt to the DIA next week? I'm not sure I mentioned that Natalie's aunt is a former classmate of mine from Wellesley. Of course, she switched to Juilliard after sophomore year, but we kept in touch. Carolyn was so talented. We were all in awe of her. I can't wait to see her again."

I recalled the Gin was also a Juilliard alum. "That must have been a wonderful experience. Did you know her, Gin? You were both in the Drama department."

"Nope. Before my time, I'm afraid. I was kind of an introvert anyway. Hunkered down and studied the entire time."

"Carolyn was very close to my sister," Claire said. "Practically inseparable." She sighed. "We had such dreams in those days. Clara and I were poised for the National Book Awards, and Caro was a sure shot for Broadway. At least, that's what we fantasized about. Funny how things turned out."

Gemma was right. Claire seemed dejected despite her considerable accomplishments. Perhaps it was the loss of her sister that marred her life as much as the loss of a dream.

"You won plenty of honors, though," I said. "Your novel was amazing."

She patted my hand. "You're too kind. But living on past glory gets harder every year. Coleman never fails to remind me of that."

Gin poured blueberry syrup on her pancakes and took a mighty forkful. "Phooey! I bet plenty of people envy us. Teaching at Sherborne is nothing to sneeze at, after all. It's the highlight of my young life."

"Hear, hear," Roddy said. "Let's cheer for the halls of Ivy!" His smile was dazzling, even more so because he was quite indifferent to the effect he had on others, particularly females. "I'll miss this place when I leave someday."

"You're leaving?" Gin's shock was palpable.

"Not right away. Some day. After I graduate. University life is pretty cushy, too, and a Ph.D. from Michigan is a great calling card. I've done some preliminary checking and had a few bites from other institutions." He held up his hands. "Nothing definite, so don't hold me to it, and please don't mention it to Coleman."

I'd had my own dreams of artistic acclaim. They'd been dashed for the worst possible reason—I simply wasn't good enough. That's what they told me at the Art Institute of Chicago, anyway. Aunt Violet urged me not to give up, but I'd finally come to terms with it. Painting was now an avocation rather than my obsession. From now on, I was officially a purveyor of beauty products and proud of it.

At that moment a gaggle of students straggled into the room, led by Ru and Tomas. By the looks on their faces and the food heaped on their plates, it appeared that their appetites for sustenance and life, in general, were in full force. Abigail was not present, but I suspected that she was spending some quality time with her dad. We caught their eye and waved at them before our group dispersed. Roddy left for his appointment, Claire headed for the library, and Gin declared that she planned to spend the day watching the Turner Classic Movie Channel. My plans were far more pedestrian. Fantasia needed her exercise and frankly so did I. Nothing banished the blues like the cheery grin of my beautiful collie along with a romp in the woods. Perhaps I could reconnect with the spirit of Tori Aaron and derive some inspiration from her.

That didn't happen, but I returned to my apartment with flushed cheeks and elevated spirits. I also felt inspired to paint. After feeding Fantasia, I fastened her harness, and we trotted off to my classroom studio to sketch out some concepts. No one else was about on a sunny Sunday afternoon, but I felt no sense of foreboding. If only I could recapture some of that passion that had consumed me in my student days. I seldom painted portraits and preferred to use oils. That day, however, I was driven to try a charcoal sketch of a woman in the throes of chaos. I immersed myself in the project, creating a series of slashing lines and figures that virtually jumped from the easel. Nothing distracts me when I am in the zone. It took Fantasia's urgent movements to alert me to a visitor at the door. A reasonable person would have hesitated to unlock that door, realizing how vulnerable she was in a deserted building on a Sunday afternoon. I acted on impulse and thrust open the door without hesitation. Fortunately, my visitor was no one to fear. The sweet face of Abigail Jenkins greeted me with a tentative smile.

"Ms. Davis. I'm sorry to disturb you, but I saw the light." She peered around the corner at my easel. "Oh. You're working. I'm so sorry. I can come back."

"Nonsense. Come and sit down. I was just fooling around."

Abby gasped. "It's Ms. Aaron, isn't it? I can see her in your sketch."

I couldn't seem to escape Tori no matter where I roamed. Abby saw it straight away, but I hadn't realized that the figure on my pad was eerily like the murdered teacher. Gemma would have immediately demanded a séance. I preferred a less dramatic interpretation. Tori Aaron was much on my mind, and it was only natural that her presence would be felt in my work.

"Did your dad leave for DC," I asked. "He really liked your performance last night. I could tell."

Abby nodded. She was working up to some revelation, and I steeled myself for it.

"I need to tell you something," she said. "I'm in trouble, and I need help."

Oh no! Here it comes. Just what I've been afraid of. She's either pregnant, or she's going to confess to killing Tori. Not certain which would be worse. Remain calm, Marky. Put on your wise teacher hat.

She was trembling, as fragile as a newborn pup. I put my arms around Abby and guided her to a chair. "Come on, now. How bad can it be?"

It might be bad, but I preferred to take the high road.

Tears seeped out of her eyes as she faced me. "I did it. I don't know why Ms. Davis, but I did it. Tomas said you'd understand and know what to do."

My throat felt so dry that I could hardly speak. "Calm down and tell me. What did you do?"

"Kahoot. I'm the one who did that. I put those mean sayings on the blackboards too." Abby covered her face with her hands and sobbed. "I'm so ashamed. My father doesn't know. I couldn't tell him even though I tried."

Fortunately, I found a package of tissues in my back pocket and handed it to her.

"What should I do, Ms. Davis? I'll be expelled." A fresh spate of tears flooded her eyes.

I'm considered a fast thinker, and this occasion certainly called for it. "Who else knows about this? Most of the other kids?"

Abby shook her head. "Just Tomas. And Ru and Natalie. They said they wouldn't tell."

"Ms. Aaron found out, didn't she?"

More nods from Abby. "She told me not to confess but never to do that again. And she made me see Dr. Stone. That's the school psychologist."

"Did it help?" I was faced with a difficult choice but decided to make a Solomon-like decision. "I think we should honor Ms. Aaron's wishes, don't you?" I tilted Abby's chin up and faced her. "You're a good person,

Abigail Jenkins. I know you're sorry for what you did. Now, maybe you can donate some time or money to the groups you offended. You know, like the Anti-defamation League or the minority tutoring program. Move on from this but learn from it too."

I saw the ghost of a smile appear on her face. "I'll do that. I knew you'd understand." She threw her arms around me in such a tight hug that I could barely breathe. After thanking me yet again, Abby skipped out the door with her head held high. Upon reflection, perhaps she didn't skip, but she certainly showed some spring in her step.

I fastened the door latch and returned to my easel. Was I dreaming, or did the image in that charcoal sketch glance back at me and smile? Was Tori giving me her special seal of approval? Who could tell? I had learned something important about her today. Tori's passion for justice had been tempered by an equally compelling sense of compassion. She was a social justice warrior with heart, and that suggested that whatever misdeed she had uncovered was a serious one, not an example of adolescent idiocy. The missing scholarship funds loomed in my mind, but there might have been something else that triggered the tragedy. One way or another, I was making progress. My time at Sherborne was growing short, but with tenacity and just a pinch of luck, I might still find the answer.

Chapter Twelve

Harrison Putnam cornered me at my mail slot. I didn't feel frightened, although any contact with that reptile was an unsavory experience. Fortunately, I have sharp elbows that I used to advantage, forcing him to back up and give me more space.

"Can I help you, Harry?" My smile was inviting; my expression impossible to read. That reaction surprised Harry and left him flustered. The Putnam playbook dictated that all lesser beings, especially women, must falter in his august presence.

"We need to talk, Ms. Davis. Now."

I placed a folder between us and moved to the side. "Okay. What's so urgent?"

His frown deepened. "You've been playing detective again and I don't like it. Asking about me."

I laughed. "Don't flatter yourself. No one seems to take you seriously as a murder suspect anyway. Why do you suppose that is?" My response was the height of insolence, but it was incredibly satisfying. Men like Harrison brought out the bully girl in me. In another life, I might have been a Valkyrie striding through life making death-defying decisions. Luckily for him, I was merely a purveyor of beauty products with a first-class art degree.

"You've been trouble from the minute you arrived here. I told Coleman it was a mistake to take you on. This school has traditions to uphold. Poking around in a murder case only cheapens our reputation." That harangue left him breathless and gave me an opportunity to speak.

"Unsolved murders don't enhance a reputation either. Besides I understand you were quite smitten with Tori Aaron. Surely you want her death to be avenged."

"Smitten! How dare you. I'll have you know I'm a happily divorced man. Tori Aaron was a nuisance and a troublemaker. Nothing more." His normally pale complexion grew red as he huffed and puffed. "I insist that you stop this nonsense immediately."

Our tête-à-tête ended with Gin's arrival on the scene. She breezed over to her mail slot after eyeing the two of us and giving a cheery greeting. "

Morning, all. Such a lovely day." She paused and addressed Harrison. "By the way, Harry, you're still getting accolades about your performance on Saturday. Seems Iago fit you like a glove."

That thinly veiled insult wrapped around a compliment left him bloodied and befuddled. Harrison took the coward's way out by retreating without saying another word.

"What's up with him?" Gin asked. "Face like a thundercloud. Might be indigestion, or did you spurn his advances?"

Easily known that Gin taught Drama. 'Spurning advances' was an expression worthy of a Victorian melodrama.

"Nothing so exciting, I'm afraid. Harry warned me about mixing in a murder investigation. Tori's to be exact."

Gin scoffed. "He's such a fusspot. But he has a point. You didn't really know Tori so why the interest?"

I explained about Aunt Violet and my promise to nose about. "Funny thing. I feel like I knew Tori after all. Plenty of layers to her personality."

Gin lowered her voice. "Any luck? We'd all feel safer if someone solved her murder. Sergeant Stevens doesn't seem up to the task."

We chatted a while, exchanging theories about the crime. Gin found it hard to believe that it was an inside job. "We're such a dull lot around here. What could be worth killing for?"

I considered how passionately artists felt about their work. Most would shrug off a slight but for some, it might provoke violence. All a matter of perspective. Prestige, position, or self-esteem were such individual things. For some, teaching at Sherborne School was the pinnacle of their career. Coleman Ross certainly felt that way. I had no doubt that he would vigorously defend his turf if it were threatened. But would he take another's life? That was the real question.

After checking my watch, I scurried across campus to my classroom. They were all there waiting for me with the glow of youthful optimism I had once shared not so long ago. Even Priscilla seemed more affable although that might have been an optical illusion. After revisiting the triumphs of Saturday's play, we hunkered down to our discussion topic: great artists and the forces that shaped them. The exchanges were lively and diverse. Ru was confident that Gauguin's intensity fueled his incredible array of work, and that Van Gogh's mental instability freed his creativity.

"Tough way to get creative," Tomas said. "Cutting off part of his ear, then killing himself. Not me brother. I'd like to live to see my success."

So many great artists never achieved success in their lifetime. I mentioned that a Van Gogh painting recently topped one hundred million dollars at auction. Quite a measure of success by anyone's standard, yet the artist died impoverished and disheartened at an early age.

Natalie raised her hand and timidly offered a remark. "Ms. Aaron always said that we should strive for excellence and not worry about getting recognition. You know, perfect our craft, and try our best."

Priscilla couldn't hide the sneer in her voice. "What if your work doesn't cut it? You understand what that's like Ms. Davis, don't you?"

I fought hard to contain my emotions. Several years ago, her comments would have crushed my spirit and left me devastated. Now I could take them in stride. "Interesting question, Priscilla. We all need an occasional reality check. Then there's a need to balance criticism with self-confidence. Getting a frank, honest assessment from someone you trust can be very helpful."

Tomas threw her a look of disgust, but Priscilla was undeterred and persistent. "How did you deal with it?"

Time for a candid response. Kids can separate the wheat from the chaff quite readily. "I always believed in my talent and still do. As a painter though, my instructor told me I'd never be top-flight. Not in the way I wanted to be anyway." I looked her straight in the eye. "It was painful. I won't deny it, but I was also able to sort out my priorities without having false hopes. There are so many fine painters and writers yet not everyone becomes famous. That's probably what Ms. Aaron meant."

Despite glares from the other students, Priscilla didn't retreat. She doubled down. "Some people's entire life is a lie. They're all around us pretending to be something they're not. Some of them might even kill to keep their secret."

Abigail gasped and covered her mouth, but Tomas responded angrily. "Cool it, Priscilla. You're such a drama queen. No one cares what you say anyway."

The girl was truly obnoxious, and I reminded myself to ignore her antics. She was but one bad apple in a very fine bushel of students.

"Ms. Aaron was a fine artist," I said, changing the subject. "She studied under my Aunt Violet Davis in Paris and had several exhibits. You were all lucky to have known her."

Nods from Tomas, Ru, and Abigail affirmed my statement. "She tried to help us be the best we could," Natalie said. "And she was kind, even when we screwed things up."

That drew laughter from her classmates and inspired them to contribute anecdotes about Tori and her impact on their lives. Despite Priscilla's refusal to join in we ended the session on a positive note. In preparation for our visit to the DIA, I assigned each participant the life of one of the artists who figured prominently in the museum's exhibits. Aunt Violet's story I reserved for myself.

I roused Fantasia from her dog bed and set out for a jog with Priscilla's comments ringing in my ears. Most likely the girl was sowing discord and inflating her own ego without any proof. Still. I intended to warn her to be cautious. A murderer was roaming about, and any unwise remark might put her in danger. Unless of course, she herself was guilty.

When we encountered Claire and Raleigh, I shared my misgivings. Her strong reaction surprised me.

"That girl is always running her mouth. I swear she has no common sense at all. Priscilla is a snoop, plain and simple. Thinks it's cool, I suppose. Some day she may learn to regret it."

"Could it be true?" I asked. Who knew what secrets lay beyond the bland façade most people presented to the world? Perhaps Harrison had lied about his family pedigree. He flaunted his patrician roots and disparaged those with lesser backgrounds. Might he lash out to protect his reputation? If Coleman embezzled those scholarship funds, he would conceal his crime at any cost, even murder. He was in an ideal position to cook the books if he so chose and was no supporter of Tori. I couldn't picture either Claire or Gin assaulting their friend and quite frankly I refused to consider Roddy as the culprit even though anything that threatened his dissertation might provoke him.

Claire gave me a puzzled look, and I realized that I had been woolgathering instead of speaking. "Don't mind me," I said. "Fact is, I'm a lousy detective. It's easy to implicate people I don't like but those I'm fond of get a free pass."

She laughed. "Like a certain Political Scientist, we both know. I've watched sparks fly between you two. Can't say that I blame you either."

I turned away. "Aw, forget it. My luck with men is even worse than my sleuthing skills. Maybe I'll take a cue from Ophelia and hie myself to a nunnery if they still exist."

"Remember, Marky. Ophelia had a bad ending. Living alone is certainly preferable to death. Just ask me." The look in her eyes suggested that, once again, Claire was remembering her sister. I decided to lighten the mood by discussing our forthcoming trip to the DIA.

"Hey, look at those two pups." I pointed at Raleigh and Fantasia. "They've got the right attitude."

Instead of moping, our dogs chased each other around the park, fetching sticks and barking lustily. Claire smiled as she watched them and explained the school's routine for class outings. Sherborne used a special bus service that featured a well-maintained vehicle and a skillful, patient driver. A local caterer supplied brown bag lunches bearing in mind the allergies, ethical preferences, and taste requirements of our charges.

"So many choices," Claire said. "You wouldn't believe how fussy these kids are. Gluten-free, vegan, lactose-free...wow! When I was a kid, we ate whatever our parents slapped together. Usually something pedestrian like tuna fish or peanut butter and jelly."

"Same here," I said. "Still, I must admit that I rebelled every time my mother fixed tuna casserole or the dreaded frozen fish sticks. Ugh!"

Claire reached into her bag and checked her phone. "Looks like we'll have a full house counting teachers and students. Remember to put their names on each lunch bag. God forbid we should mix up Ru's sushi with Priscilla's chicken salad. World War Three would erupt." She rubbed her tummy. "Fortunately, I eat almost anything except red meat. Guess it shows, doesn't it?" She made a sad face. "Believe it or not, at one time, I was a sylph. Clara and I drove my mom wild, refusing to eat." She bit her lip. "If only I'd realized what that led to."

Gin told me that Clara had died of cancer soon after finishing college. Such a cruel disease especially since loved ones often watched the victim literally wasting away before their eyes.

"My weight's never been a problem for me," I said, "but I admit that I love food. Too much at times. Aunt Violet taught me the technique that French women use—sample, don't gorge. That way, you don't deprive yourself of something you love."

"Makes sense," Claire said with a wry grin. "I'll have to keep that in mind next time they serve blueberry pancakes. Meanwhile, I have some good news to share." Her face lit up as she turned toward me. "I've started to write again. Really write. Good stuff that I'm proud of. At least, I think it's good."

"Wow! Is it a new novel?"

She nodded. "A sequel to the first one. If you're willing, I'd like you to review it. No strings and any critique are gratefully accepted. Gin agreed to help too."

I'm not normally a hugger, but this time, I couldn't resist. "Terrific! I'd be honored to join in." We locked arms and trotted back to the residence hall with the dogs prancing in our wake.

Aunt Violet arrived in time for dinner on Friday evening. Raindrops dotted the landscape, but predictably they did nothing to dampen her spirits or style. Her red hooded cape with matching high-heeled boots would have crippled any normal woman. Then again, where my aunt's concerned, I've learned to expect the extraordinary.

"I'm excited about our jaunt to the museum," she said. "The curator already discussed our schedule with me, and it promises to be fantastic. One glimpse of that Diego Rivera mural still floors me. Such genius."

"They're featuring several Freda Kahlo works as well. I've been trying to interest the kids in women artists, not just the better-known names like Violet Davis."

She grunted. "You're teasing me, but I don't care. Such an honor to be featured in a museum of that caliber. Someday, they'll save a space for abstracts by Marketta Davis. Just you wait."

I could always count on my aunt to elevate my spirits even when they had sunk to new depths. We chatted briefly about Gemma and the status of Poppet before broaching the topic of interest to us both—Tori Aaron.

"I'm afraid I've struck out, at least about finding the killer. Plenty of theories, and ample suspects but no real clues. Gemma did better during her massage sessions than I've done snooping around campus. Not to mention that Sergeant Stevens read me the riot act on two occasions."

Violet leaned back and sipped the champagne she'd brought with her. Krug Grand Cuvee if you can believe it. I loved the stuff, but the hefty price tag put it way beyond my means.

"Sounds like Tori was more complex than I had imagined. Justice tempered by mercy. A great combination but tricky, as Portia found out. What guilty secrets could a bunch of kids or academics harbor? Any hint about sexual hijinks? That's always a temptation in places like this?"

By all accounts, the staff had been wise enough to avoid romantic entanglements with their students. Thank Heaven for small favors. Other than normal kid stuff, I hadn't found any impropriety like that at Sherborne School. Had Tori uncovered that type of situation, she would have alerted the authorities. Besides, Sherborne was due for a state accreditation review next term and could ill afford any kind of adverse publicity. I shared Abigail's confession with my aunt but noted Tori had handled the situation deftly.

No need for Abby to strike out and silence her.

"Her Dad would be mortified if he found out," Violet said, "But he wouldn't overreact." She rolled her eyes when she saw the expression on my face. "He's a fine man, and I've grown very fond of him. But we're friends. Period. Forget the wedding bells, missy. Focus on your own love life."

I mentioned my belief that Coleman Ross would do anything to protect the school and his own position. If Tori threatened to publicize the embezzlement, he might have panicked.

"Maybe," Violet said. "Although Coleman would likely deny the whole thing. Cover it up. I suspect that he'd try bribery or something less violent to satisfy Tori. Increase scholarships for the locals, something like that. On the other hand, his wife wouldn't hesitate for a minute. In my book, she'd bash Tori or anyone else who got in her way. That is one tough woman."

Violet agreed to chat up some of the guests at dinner and see where that led. We were still puzzled by the killer's use of cosmetics to deface Tori. Such a mean-spirited gesture of contempt seemed more feminine than masculine to me. OOPS. I checked myself for such a sexist assumption. Plenty of males were willing to humiliate a woman, dead or alive, but they tended toward violent gestures rather than contemptuous ones. Then again, anyone who knew Tori and her preferences might enjoy adding a final macabre touch to her corpse.

Since Friday was fish fry night at Sherborne, we once again had a full house. Even the headmaster, accompanied by his wife, graced us with his presence. He immediately invited Violet to sit at the head table, although I was relegated to the peanut gallery with the rest of the staff. Gin patted my shoulder in mock sympathy. "So sorry you were banished, Marky. Don't despair. This table will be more fun anyway."

"Right, you are." Roddy was ebullient. His grin was a mile wide, and his eyes blazed with fervor, a sure sign that his discussion with his advisor had gone well. Naturally, Gin couldn't resist asking.

"Okay. Out with it. How did your conference go?"

At first, he demurred, but ultimately those high spirits gave him away. "Fantastic! We'll be presenting my dissertation to the committee next month, and I'll prepare to defend it in January."

After congratulating him, Claire shared her news. "It's early days, of course, but I feel really encouraged. My goal is one thousand words per day until it's finished." She ducked her head. "I've contacted my former agent too. Just in case."

I was elated for my colleagues, although I noted that Gin seemed a bit glum. She shrugged it off, but I could tell that she'd hoped for good news about her own career. That *Shakespeare Unbound* concept was vying for a national award that would elevate Sherborne's prestige and Gin's as well.

Natalie was our assigned waiter that evening, and she, too, bubbled over with excitement. "Don't mind her," Ru said, gathering up our plates. "Nat can't wait for our excursion tomorrow. Remember, her auntie is a big deal there. A play-write or so she claims."

Claire swatted at Ru with her napkin. "Don't mind him, Nat. Your aunt is phenomenal. Julliard always produces the best, right Gin?"

Before Gin responded, Ru jumped in. "Oh yeah? So why is Priscilla going there?"

"Is she?" Roddy asked. "I hadn't heard that. What's the scoop?"

Claire shooed Ru away to avoid the topic. Gossiping about other students was strictly forbidden and very unprofessional. When he left, Roddy repeated his question. Gin shook her head and dismissed it. "That girl has been bragging to everyone about Julliard. She's only a junior, and it's way too soon for anyone to get acceptance letters. You know Priscilla. Always pushing the envelope."

I watched Aunt Violet at the head table sipping her tea and absorbing everyone's comments. The woman had charm to spare, a gift that enabled her to extract all sorts of information from her victims without their knowledge. Coleman Ross was all smiles while his wife appeared to focus her energy exclusively on my aunt. I could hardly wait for dinner to end so that I could learn what nuggets of gossip Violet had unearthed.

Instead of meeting in the teachers' lounge, we decided to adjourn for the evening. Our excursion to the DIA would require plenty of energy and a sharp eye to keep our exuberant charges in line. They were basically good kids, but I reminded myself that they were also teenagers. The potential for mischief was ever present in that age group. I knew that from personal experience. While we gave Fantasia her final stroll for the evening, Violet reported her findings. Coleman Ross had been in high spirits, as was his wife. No hint of concern about the upcoming state review or the missing scholarship funds.

"What gives?" I asked. "I figured the headmaster would be freaked out at the prospect."

"Nope." Violet laughed as she quoted him. "There was no embezzlement. Merely an accounting error. All is well, and the books are in perfect harmony. That's the official story, and they're sticking to it."

We exchanged knowing looks. As predicted, Coleman must have dipped into his bountiful checking account to correct the problem. That meant that a crime had been papered over and a criminal allowed to go unpunished. Kind of like the miscreant who had so ruthlessly taken Tori's life. Sometimes I felt that life at Sherborne School was more reminiscent of a 1950s sitcom than life in the new millennium. Sort of a *Leave it to Beaver* world with a touch of *Father Knows Best.* I enjoyed watching those old re-runs about a world that had never truly existed. It insulated me from the harsh realities of murder, mayhem, and evildoers and provided a temporary respite from fear. No one in those mythical towns ever clobbered a well-intentioned teacher to death. Women wore pearls and a tidy shirtwaist to breakfast. Men wore sober suits, and no one used foul language or abused the police.

"Hey, girl," Aunt Violet said, pinching my arm. "Looks like you're dreaming. I was wrong to involve you in Tori's death. Relax and let the police handle everything while we enjoy our outing tomorrow. We'll be surrounded by beauty. Remember, Picasso said that art washes away the everyday dust from the soul. That man knew a thing or two worth remembering."

Fantasia nuzzled my hand as if to affirm the sentiment. Perhaps immersing myself in a world of beauty was just the prescription I needed. Nothing could be amiss within the sacred confines of a museum. In that temple of tranquility, I might reconnect with the important elements of life.

* * *

The weather cooperated with us, and we bundled into our coach without mishap. Claire stationed herself at the front of the bus, clipboard in hand, and ticked off names from her list as each student entered. Gin staffed the rear door, and Roddy handled the middle. To avoid any scenes, we reserved four rows exclusively for our teachers. Otherwise, Priscilla might stage a revolt to sit next to Roddy, or even worse; everyone might ignore Harrison and leave his seat unoccupied. Aunt Violet winked at me and claimed that spot for herself. Predictably Tomas and Abigail chose adjoining seats, as did Ru and Natalie. Priscilla fumed as she headed for the rear of the coach and sat alone in the farthest and least desirable seat adjacent to the restroom.

"Hey, Marky," Roddy said as I edged up the aisle, "Will you join me?"

I was raised to be courteous, so naturally, I made the supreme sacrifice and slid into the seat adjoining him. "Our adventure begins," I said. "Museums feel like a sacred spot to me. Cathedrals of beauty. Does that sound strange?"

"Not at all. I feel that way in a library. So much accumulated wisdom." He suddenly whirled around and glared at a student as a spitball sailed through the air. "Hey. Cool it unless you plan to spend the rest of the term in detention."

I reminded myself anew that despite their privileged lives and talent, these kids were still teenagers whose high spirits could quickly turn to mischief if left unchecked.

Roddy held up the brochure from the DIA. "Tori and I spent the day here last December. I had to practically drag her out of the place before it closed." He lowered his eyes. "Good times."

Tori again. Would her spirit never be exorcised? She seemed to inhabit everything, especially the mind of one Roddy Park. Hard to believe that he had accepted her refusal so calmly when the man obviously still loved her. An uneasy feeling assailed me. Throughout history, spurned lovers sometimes turned to murder. Shakespeare portrayed this in Othello, but there were plenty of real-life examples too. Perhaps the only remedy was to find Tori's killer and finally give her the justice she deserved. Then she might rest in peace, and those who were still in her thrall could move on with their lives.

Our excursion took longer than I had planned. Detroit traffic, with the inevitable rollover accidents that accompanied it, slowed our progress to a crawl. The students' chatter increased, and they became restless by the time we arrived at the visitors' entrance to the DIA. Claire stood up before anyone charged the exit and laid down the rules. "Remember. No unruly behavior or loud talking. Be courteous and absorb the beauty around us. Our guide is Natalie's aunt Carolyn, a distinguished play-write, and my friend, so be on your best behavior."

Aunt Violet then stepped to the front of the bus and introduced herself. She offered to answer any questions that arose during our tour. Although she was too modest to mention it, Claire quickly remarked that Violet Davis was a listed artist whose work appeared in the DIA. "We're honored to have her with us."

Carolyn Peters, Natalie's aunt, stood at the entrance waiting for us. She was an adult replica of her lovely niece with a petite frame encased in a flame-colored dress and complemented by a striking Hermes scarf. Loved that scarf, but the prohibitive price kept me at bay. Besides, I could never master the technique of artfully draping the material. Aunt Violet said it was a French thing, but whatever it eluded me completely. Carolyn Peters fit my mental image of a dramatist. I was especially struck by her eyes, beautiful hazel orbs that were alight with enthusiasm. In another setting, I would have longed to paint her portrait and try to capture that exuberance and glow. She explained the agenda for the day, asked for any questions, and led our charges through the visitors' entrance. "Just spend a few seconds absorbing the Diego Rivera murals on the walls," she said. "They're one of our prize possessions and deserve your reverence."

By prior agreement, we separated into three groups, with two adults leading each. The Museum is a cavernous space with over one-hundred galleries and 65,000 works. We had no desire to lose one of our young scholars in its confines.

I joined Harrison and shepherded a small group to the theater area, where a lecture on modern dramatists was being held. Priscilla immediately sidled up to us, wearing a triumphant grin. "They're discussing detective films this afternoon," she said, giving me a slight sneer. "Maybe you can give everyone some tips. Who knows, maybe you can learn some yourself."

Harrison gave her a vaguely puzzled look. "Mind your manners, Missy. Remember where you are, and don't be tiresome."

Priscilla affected a look of injured innocence. "But Mr. Putnam, I thought she planned to solve Ms. Aaron's murder. Everyone says so."

Harrison was no admirer of mine, but he stamped out impertinence from students whenever it arose. "That's none of your business unless you know something about it. Do you?"

Her expression could only be described as sly. Priscilla flashed a half smile his way, saying, "Maybe I do. After all, Sherborne promotes honesty, doesn't it? Some secrets might be worth killing for." Having delivered that bombshell, she sashayed off toward the entrance to the theater.

Harrison's normally pale complexion grew even more ghostly as he tried to regain his composure.

Are you okay?" I asked. "Need some water or something?"

He shook his head. "Dreadful girl. Hard to believe Julliard would even consider having her."

That made me wonder. Was that yet another figment of Priscilla's fevered imagination, or had she some assurance that the famed institution would accept her? Gin had dismissed the idea as poppycock, but the girl seemed so certain. Someone like Senator Jenkins might sponsor her if Priscilla threatened his daughter's future, and Coleman Ross was certainly influential enough if the reputation of Sherborne were at stake. Priscilla wouldn't hesitate for a moment at blackmail if it suited her needs, but I struggled to link Tori's murder to those seemingly mundane actions like graffiti and embezzlement.

"She says she knows something about Tori's murder. Is that a bid for attention or something real?"

Harrison shrugged. "To use a good old British expression, balderdash. Ignore her."

"Maybe I should notify Sergeant Stevens. If she's telling the truth, Priscilla could be in danger."

He curled his lip as if I were something beneath contempt. "Mind your own business, Ms. Davis. We've had that discussion before, but it obviously didn't register with you."

Any warm feelings I might have had for him quickly evaporated as Harrison Putnam reclaimed his reptilian status. I straightened my shoulders and strode on into the theater without saying another word. Still, I couldn't forget Harrison's reaction to Priscilla's taunt. What secrets did he harbor, and what would he do to protect them? He and Tori were adversaries, but according to Gin, he wanted a very different relationship. Had spurned feelings led to something lethal? Maybe for once, Harrison was right. Minding my own business was sound advice worth considering. I shrugged it off and eased into one of the cushioned seats, allowing myself to absorb what turned out to be an excellent presentation. I failed to find any new inspiration, but reliving classics like *Laura, the Maltese Falcon, and The Thin Man* was always worthwhile.

Violet had to virtually drag me out of the Impressionist exhibit. Being among those timeless beauties reactivated every artistic bone in my body and carried me back to my days at the Art Institute of Chicago. Most of my students were as interested in the biographies of the artists as they were in their painting genius. Monet, Manet, Morisot—these teens begged for tidbits about the lives and loves of the greats, especially any salacious ones. Violet knew them all and selectively fed her audience bon mots that satisfied both of their appetites. By the time we gathered to eat, our entire group had earned their lunch. A set of picnic tables had been reserved for us, and Gin, with the help of Roddy distributed each meal to the appropriate recipient. Some squabbling was expected especially when it appeared that the menus had gotten mixed up.

"Hey," Ru griped, "I never asked for tuna salad. Hate the stuff. Roast Beef, rare. That's my choice." He made a muscle. "Real man's food."

Don't be a baby," Natalie teased. "Here. Trade with me. I don't eat red meat anyway. Besides you can eat my cookie."

Tomas rolled his eyes as if that meant something lewd, and Abigail blushed beet red. Their high spirits were quickly subdued by Harrison Putnam, who showed his talent for spreading gloom. "Enough of that smutty talk. Act like Sherborne students, not gutter snipes." I noticed that he glared at Tomas as he said that.

Priscilla, who discarded most of her lunch without eating it, sniffed at them, rose, and left the table. Claire immediately did the same, asking, "Are you okay, Priscilla? We need to stay together."

"I assume I'm allowed to use the restroom without a guard," Priscilla said in her most haughty manner. "We're not prisoners after all."

Claire ignored that comment and the attitude, choosing instead to ask if anyone else needed a comfort break. That woman had such class. I really admired her ability to rise above petty remarks and keep her eye on the prize.

Our final session was the climax of a memorable day. Aunt Violet and Natalie's aunt's team taught a presentation entitled "Cosmetic Touches, Using Gems and Artifice Throughout the Ages." Their excellent slide show illustrated famous paintings of both men and women in which jewels and cosmetics were used to advantage. In some cultures, males of rank proudly displayed jewels and touches of makeup, and since, in Shakespeare's day, male actors frequently portrayed female roles, they enhanced their faces with lavish displays of cosmetics. No one at the time considered this unmanly, although today, it might still raise a few eyebrows. Much of this was news to our students. They absorbed the information thoughtfully and asked intelligent questions that left me glowing with pride. Perhaps we were doing something right after all.

By the time we clambered into our coach, the group had exhausted some of its excess spirits and settled into quiet conversations. Claire remained vigilant and clutched her clipboard until each person occupied the same seat as before, and every name on her list was accounted for. Roddy and Gin also maintained their posts until everyone was aboard. I felt somewhat drowsy myself, but naturally, Aunt Violet was as fresh as her namesake blossom. As a special treat, Natalie's aunt provided each of us with a small box containing

French chocolates, a "ballotin," as my aunt reminded us, for our ride home. Gin distributed them to the delight of our students and, I must admit, the adults as well. A taste of fine chocolate was one of life's great gifts. Not enough to gorge on, just enough to sample.

"Everything went well," Roddy said. "You should be proud."

"Oh! It was a team effort," I said. "No false modesty here. I could never have managed it alone."

Tomas and Ru soon started a raucous sing-along that lasted for half our return trip to Sherborne. Roddy joined in, displaying a surprisingly fine baritone. Since I was cursed with a tin ear, I wisely abstained. Better to enjoy the skills of others rather than detract from the harmony. The line to the only bathroom was longer than I'd anticipated, so I forced myself to control my urges and wait my turn. Roddy and Claire kept the kids engaged by staging a mini-jeopardy quiz with small prizes. Tomas emerged as the winner after a close contest with Abigail and a spirited challenge by Ru.

That enlivened the group, and despite Claire's best efforts, as soon as the doors opened, the students surged off the bus en masse. "Don't forget your backpacks and other belongings," she cautioned, but very few heeded the warning or even appeared to hear her. Roddy helped me from my seat and chatted as we inched toward the door.

"I enjoyed your company today, Marky. Maybe we could stop for coffee tomorrow."

I was astonished. Pleasantly so. "Sure. I'd like that. I always walk Fantasia at noon. How about meeting in the park?"

Before we finalized arrangements, Claire staggered up to us, gasping for breath. "It's Priscilla," she said.

"What's that brat up to now?" Roddy asked.

Claire pointed to the rear seat where Priscilla still sat. "Something's wrong. I think she's ill."

Aunt Violet sped to the girl's side, calm as the proverbial cucumber. "Let me check. I have some medical training."

Roddy and I followed close behind her. It was probably another bid for attention by Priscilla, although I had a premonition of something far worse.

She'd made a point of publicly commenting on Tori's murder, and that type of action was never wise. Had Priscilla forced the hand of a determined killer?

My aunt turned toward us with a grave expression on her face. "Better call the police. I'm afraid she's dead."

Chapter Thirteen

"Impossible! She can't be dead." Harrison Putnam's voice was shrill with fear. Claire looked very near to collapsing, so I guided her to a seat several rows in front of the dead girl. Meanwhile, Gin clutched her phone and, after a few missteps, managed to call 911. Roddy planted himself in the doorway to shield the scene from any curious onlookers. His motion seemed mechanical, as if he were an automaton. I didn't hesitate for a moment. Sergeant Stevens' number was on my cell phone, and I called him immediately.

"What are you doing?" Harry shrieked.

"Alerting the authorities. What else?" I had no time to pamper hysterical males, especially that one.

He immediately launched a verbal assault, invoking the name of the headmaster as if he were a deity and threatening to unleash the furies upon me. It took Aunt Violet to calm the man down and restore some sense of sanity to the situation. Stevens was away from his desk, so I left what I hoped was a coherent account of our plight and asked for his help ASAP.

Meanwhile, when I glanced at Priscilla, I felt pity, not revulsion. She was a nasty specimen in life but death that great leveler had rendered her looking harmless and curiously vulnerable. Her gleaming blond curls were in disarray, although they effectively masked the contorted features of her face. Traces of vomit decorated her chin, and her once lovely blue eyes were open but glazed. Harrison, having recovered his wits, had hastened to contact Coleman Ross. I heard enough of the conversation to know that Coleman was on his way post haste to oversee the situation.

"He forbids you to contact the police," said Harry. "That's an order."

Once again, steely self-control was my saving grace. I patted Harry's arm in a gesture of womanly comfort. I would have preferred to throttle the pretentious prat, but one murder per day was my quota.

"We have no choice," I said. Aunt Violet nodded in agreement. "At the very least, this is an unexplained death, but I believe Priscilla was murdered."

"Oh no!" Claire's voice was more of a whimper than a cry. "Not another."

Aunt Violet added. "We can't be sure until an autopsy is conducted, of course, but circumstances strongly suggest that." The expression on her face said that she was very certain of the outcome.

"Autopsy!" Harrison bayed. "Her relatives won't allow that. Desecrating the poor girl's body. It's inhumane."

He wasn't very observant. Otherwise, he could have noticed the taut fabric that encircled Priscilla's neck in a garrote and the red streaks in those dreamy blue eyes. Petechiae hemorrhage, they call them on forensic shows. The girl had clearly been strangled. Even an amateur could tell that. Harrison must have had better things to do with his time than watch *CSI*. Alas, I did not. What concerned me even more was the murder weapon in question. I recognized that Hermes scarf. Natalie's aunt had worn either that garment or its twin, only this morning, a rouge lipstick and fuchsia confection in cashmere with an astronomical price tag. Come to think of it, Carolyn hadn't been wearing it when we departed the DIA. How like Priscilla to pilfer something valuable and consider it her due? How ironic if it proved to be her undoing.

A gaggle of students had converged outside our tour bus, but a determined effort by Roddy kept them at bay until all hell broke loose. Flashing lights from the coroner's van, the wail of sirens from a police cruiser, and the arrival of Coleman Ross exacerbated an already volatile situation and caused a near riot. I peered out the window and saw a variety of reactions from the crowd. They didn't yet know the particulars or who it involved, but no one seemed to doubt that something serious was afoot. Natalie was wide-eyed, almost shell-shocked, and Abby bit her lip as if holding back tears. Ru hunched over his cell phone, babbling to someone, but Tomas stood soldier-straight without showing any emotion at all. The moment Sergeant Stevens arrived, Coleman Ross leapt from his Mercedes and blocked his path.

"Wait a minute, Sergeant. I see no need for police presence. After all, we're dealing with a medical emergency here. Ms. Davis shouldn't have involved you."

Stevens threw a pitying glance his way and ignored him. Meanwhile, the medical examiner, a spare woman of indeterminate age and a no-nonsense manner, angled her way through the throng and onto the bus. Stevens followed close behind her. After telling us to be seated, he asked,

"Anyone in charge here? I'll need to interview everyone who joined you today, including the students."

Claire wiped her eyes and handed him her clipboard. "This list has all the names. Except the staff." She pointed to us. "We're all here, and I saw the headmaster arrive just now."

Stevens beckoned to me. "You. Ms. Davis. You're the one who called me. Give me the lowdown."

Before I could answer, Harrison pushed past me and took center stage. "I'm the senior staff member present. Ask me anything you want to know."

By arching his eyebrows, the cop managed to convey disbelief without showing disrespect. I recalled that he had met Harrison during the investigation of Tori's murder. Enough said!

"This bus is an official crime scene. Clear out and bring the students together. I'll need to interview them." He gestured toward Priscilla. "I presume the victim was a student also."

We all nodded and proceeded to file out and follow orders. "I'll brief the headmaster," Harrison said. "There are legal issues to consider when dealing with minors."

Stevens stood, hands on hips, and glared. "We've been through this drill before when Ms. Aaron was murdered. Just make sure that one of you is there when we interview them. In loco parentis, isn't that the fancy term you guys use?"

He was baiting us, and Harrison swallowed it hook, line, and sinker.

"See here, Sergeant. I insist that you consult with Coleman Ross before proceeding any further. He's probably already notified our attorney."

"No problem," Stevens said. "Seems simple enough. Someone snuffed the life out of that girl," he pointed to Priscilla, "while half a dozen supposedly responsible adults looked on. Simple."

"No need for sarcasm, Sergeant." Coleman Ross had managed to worm his way past the deputy guarding the door. "Ms. Sayers, the victim as you call her, was a beloved senior student at Sherborne. Surely this was some type of accident."

Beloved? Accident? Our esteemed leader was either delusional or duplicitous. An old hand like Stevens would unearth the truth about Priscilla the minute he cornered the first student. Plus, I was hard-pressed to imagine how a garrot, however elegant, could accidentally asphyxiate someone in full view of thirty others.

Stevens uttered a sound suspiciously like a snort. "Two murders within one year? What are you teaching them at this place? Should be called Homicide High."

The headmaster made an outraged squawk and turned away. As soon as I exited the bus, I gulped a breath of fresh air to forestall the unease I felt. Hard to believe that a murderer lurked within our jolly group of museumgoers. Violet and I exchanged glances as we approached the students. Although it was difficult, we deliberately suppressed all emotion and projected an image of calm. Roddy did the same, although I could see that Claire was teetering on the edge of collapse and Gin's hands were trembling. We all knew that Priscilla was a nasty piece of work who had probably provoked her own murder. That didn't excuse the crime. It merely explained it. She prided herself on unearthing secrets, slivers of gossip that could wound or destroy others. I also suspected that Priscilla indulged in an occasional spot of blackmail, not for financial gain but to assert control and amass power. That was dangerous, particularly if she knew or deduced the identity of Tori's killer. Coleman Ross's depiction of her as beloved was stretching the truth even by his very elastic standards.

"What's going on?" Tomas asked.

Other students soon joined the chorus. "Yeah, what's wrong?"

"There's been an accident," Roddy said. "We need you to assemble in the dining hall right away."

"Who's hurt?" Abigail's voice quivered.

"It's Priscilla, isn't it?" Natalie said nothing, but her entire body trembled.

Ru pushed toward the front of the crowd. "Is she okay? How come the medical examiner's here?"

"I bet she's dead." Tomas's voice lacked any trace of sorrow. "Probably an overdose."

"Enough!" Roddy held up his hand and silenced them. "Idle speculation won't help anyone. Let's regroup in the dining hall and wait to speak with the police. Spend your time reconstructing everything you recall from our trip back."

They grumbled but slowly ambled toward the main building with Gin and Roddy guiding them. Harrison accompanied the headmaster and followed a safe distance behind the group. Coleman's face was a study in despair. His furrowed brow and downturned mouth suggested that he was a dead man walking. Parents and the overseers of Sherborne were unlikely to accept yet another violent death, particularly of a student. As dexterous as he was, even Coleman couldn't label Priscilla's murder as a random act of violence. There would be consequences, and they would probably start at the top.

Violet and I waited for Claire to join us. She was still in a fugue state, almost inconsolable. "I can't believe it," she said. "How could something like that happen right in front of us? We had six adults on that bus, for heaven's sake!"

No sense mentioning that between the raucous sing-along and the spirited Jeopardy quiz, we simply weren't paying attention to the activity at the back of the bus. Besides, there was a long, loud line of teens waiting to use the restroom that adjoined Priscilla's seat. Not an excuse, merely an explanation, although it provided cold comfort to us all. Priscilla didn't cry out or otherwise fight for her life. That was odd. Perhaps her attacker had taken her by surprise.

I noted that a sad procession of forensic specialists had entered the bus, carrying with them an array of objects—tools of their ghoulish trade. With thirty people trampling through the area, I very much doubted if they could discover any viable trace evidence, but then again, the wonders of science had always eluded me. Priscilla's corpse remained in the bus, although I suspected that it would soon be removed. With any luck, our students would all be gone by then. That was one aspect of cruel reality that I hoped to spare them from.

"I feel guilty," Claire said. "She was hard to like but still very young. I should feel sorry, but instead, I only feel horrified."

Violet patted her shoulder and urged her toward the dining hall. "Hey. You're still in shock. Don't beat yourself up. Besides, from what I've heard, Priscilla angered plenty of people. That Sergeant Stevens looks very tough. Bet he'll get to the bottom of this right away."

I've learned never to correct my aunt, but this time, she was misguided. If we were dealing with a double murderer, that person was unlikely to confess in a *Perry Mason* moment. Stevens might sweat out damaging admissions from students or even the staff, but would he find the culprit? Not tonight.

They were waiting for us when we entered the dining hall. By the haunted looks on their faces, I knew that someone must have given them at least a preliminary heads up. Priscilla was not their friend, but she was one of them, and her death made them all feel vulnerable. The shock and pain etched on their faces reminded me that they were just kids unused to the slings and arrows of outrageous fortune. The adults were not faring much better. Roddy kept an inscrutable expression on his handsome features, but I believed that behind that wall was the pain of remembrance. Tori again. Would her memory ever leave him? Gin, on the other hand, looked ravaged. She laced her fingers together as if in prayer and kept her head down. No one spoke. After Claire, Aunt Violet, and I were seated, Stevens strode to the front of the room and surveyed the group. He was an imposing figure with his gun dangling from a shoulder holster and a grim set to his face. Harrison and Coleman Ross sat in the front row soldier-straight, never moving a muscle.

"As I mentioned, one of your group, Priscilla Sayers, was found dead this afternoon. It wasn't an accident. She was murdered."

A collective gasp filled the room. They were prepared for drug overdoses or heart ailments, but violent death was not on the menu.

"Murder?" Ru yelped. "That can't be true. We were all there." Natalie moved closer to him and clutched his hand. Shock kept her wide-eyed and pale.

Tomas bit his lip but remained stoic. He knew that as the townie, the low-rent outsider, he most likely had a target on his back. Coleman Ross would gladly sacrifice him if needs be. When Abigail put her arm around him, he brusquely shrugged it off, ignoring her crestfallen look.

Reinforcements from the police barracks soon arrived, allowing Stevens to separate us into groups of two before we were led away to interrogation rooms. Each student was assigned an adult to accompany him or her through the process. Abigail was put in my charge. The girl shivered despite the warmth of the hall and barely acknowledged my presence. Did she fear that her role in the Kaput scandal would be revealed? That was my guess. When Stevens wasn't listening, I bent down and whispered, "Just answer his questions. Tell the truth but don't volunteer anything." That advice was designed to protect Abby, not the authorities. I knew from personal experience that they would link any admission, however trivial, to Priscilla's murder and proceed to build their case. A young, uniformed officer sat at the back of the room, notebook in hand. After we were seated, Stevens aimed a faux grin our way and proceeded to read Abby her constitutional rights.

She gulped. "Just like on TV. Do I need a lawyer?"

Stevens spread out his hands. "You're not under arrest, Ms. Jenkins. This is merely an informal chat." He was a veteran, as cagey as they come. Although he didn't lie, Stevens didn't answer her question either. His colleague switched on a tape recorder, and I returned the favor by activating the record mode on my iPhone. What's sauce for the goose....

I knew that he would drop his avuncular act as soon as she relaxed her guard, so I tried a diversionary tactic. "She could get an attorney if she wanted to, I suppose. Her Dad, Senator Jenkins, is one."

Name-dropping was normally not my style, but this situation wasn't normal. Stevens curled his lip and shot me a venomous look. "Let's see how things go before we call in the cavalry. Now, Abigail, tell me this. Did you like Priscilla Sayers?"

She hesitated for only a moment. "No, sir."

"Why not? The headmaster said she was beloved. How would you describe her?"

That opened the floodgates as Abby listed the many sides of her fallen classmate. "She was mean. Always trying to hurt someone and snooping around. No one liked her."

Stevens kept his manner lowkey. "Didn't she have a boyfriend? She was awfully pretty."

Oh oh. I knew what was coming next.

Abby looked at me before responding, but I cast my eyes downward. "She wasn't interested in kids her age. Priscilla loved Dr. Park. She was crazy about him. Always trying to get him to notice her."

"Really?" Talk about the fox in the henhouse. Stevens inched forward for the kill. "Did Dr. Park reciprocate?"

Abby seemed shocked by the very suggestion. "Oh no. He avoided her. Besides he loved Ms. Aaron. Everyone knew that."

"Tori Aaron? The teacher who was murdered several months ago?"

I could almost see the wheels turning in his head. Had Priscilla killed Tori and been murdered in turn by Roddy Park? A twisted love triangle would wrap the case up nicely and explain two deaths.

Stevens then had Abby recite her every movement, from boarding the coach in the morning to exiting in the afternoon. "You sat near the front of the bus and stayed there? Never left your seat even once?"

Discussing bodily functions, especially their own, can cause embarrassment to youngsters. A flush spread over Abby's cheeks. "I used the bathroom once. There was a long line." She hadn't noticed Priscilla sitting directly across from the lavatory because they were all playing Jeopardy.

"Didn't Ms. Sayers participate?" Stevens asked. His honied words were spiced with cayenne pepper.

"Oh no. Priscilla wasn't smart enough. She only played games she could win." Abby smiled at that, never realizing where it was leading.

"Let me see," Stevens thumbed through a thick file folder filled with neatly clipped printouts. "Priscilla wasn't with you the evening Ms. Aaron was killed. That was game night, too, I believe." He showed his teeth in a fulsome grin. "You've been very helpful, Ms. Jenkins." Then in a Columbo touch, he added. "Just one more thing. What did Priscilla Sayers have on you?"

As Abby fell back in her chair and gasped for breath, I immediately called a timeout. "Hold on, Sergeant. This girl has asthma. Let me find her inhaler." I rooted around in her purse but came up empty. Fortunately, the school had supplied a pitcher of water, and I poured her a glass. "Here. Sip this and take a deep breath." For a second, I thought she might have fainted, but the liquid revived her. The asthma ruse had worked its charms and caused Stevens to lose his rhythm. Abby caught on right away and kept her eyes tightly closed. Her student health record hadn't mentioned asthma, and I had reviewed all of them as a precaution. Still, one never knew.

"Let's end this for now," Stevens said. He narrowed his eyes as he watched me but elected to yield the floor. It was only a temporary reprieve but better than nothing. "We'll continue this later, Ms. Jenkins."

I helped Abby out of the room and put my finger against my lips to denote silence. "Do me a favor. Here's the key to my apartment. Go get Fantasia and give her a walk. Feed her too. I don't know how long he'll keep me here."

She nodded and skipped away, thrilled to escape from the clutches of the law. When I turned around there was Stevens standing there with his arms folded.

"Nicely done, Ms. Davis. Withholding information in a murder case can get you in trouble, though."

I played the injured innocent. "I don't know what you mean. Believe me, if I knew anything about the murder, I would gladly spill my guts."

Stevens made a retching sound. "Not appealing, madam. No need to overdo things." He moved closer. "Listen. Despite everything, you have a good head on your shoulders, and you're an outsider here. Come see me tomorrow if you will. We need to talk. Bring that aunt of yours, too, if you can."

I was astonished. Was Stevens asking me for help? I leapt at the chance to become involved. "Sure. We'll swing by after chapel tomorrow."

Chapter Fourteen

I couldn't wait to tell my aunt the news. Unfortunately, it had to wait. When I arrived back at my apartment, she had a guest. Two guests, Claire, and Raleigh. One glance at Claire told me all was not well. Her face was tear-stained, and she clutched her brandy glass as if her life depended upon it. In contrast, Violet's manner was placid, a soothing tonic to a horrific day.

I walked up to Claire and gave her a hug. "You're not responsible for what happened. Don't think that for a moment. We were all there, and nobody noticed anything until it was too late."

"That's kind of you to say, but there's more to it." Claire took a mighty gulp of air and stroked Raleigh's golden fur. "The police are looking for motives. At least that's what Harrison said."

"Yeah. So what? Priscilla enjoyed making enemies. Nobody liked her."

Violet held out her arm to silence me. "Let her speak, Marky. Go on, Claire."

"She victimized everyone around her. I guess you could call it blackmail."

I thought of Abigail and her part in the Kahoot mess. No doubt Priscilla used that against her if she knew the story. Leverage with Senator Jenkins to influence Julliard. Who knew how many others had fallen prey to her schemes? I was still convinced that Priscilla's murder was linked to Tori Aaron. Priscilla had either seen or surmised the identity of the killer and tried to press her advantage. That had been her undoing.

Claire was speaking so softly that at first, I didn't hear her. When her words finally registered, I gasped. "You. She was blackmailing you, Claire?

Whatever for?"

Tears flowed once more as Claire shared her story. "I have no right to be here, Marky. None. You see, I'm a fraud. Phony. My great claim to success, my celebrated novel—-I didn't write it. Clara did."

I tried not to react, but it was impossible. "That can't be true. Surely, you're exaggerating." If Claire was telling the truth, however, it explained why she had never produced a sequel. It also suggested a Jim Dandy motive for murder. Tori Aaron had a strong ethical streak. Almost puritanical. If she learned Claire's secret, she would have felt honor bound to reveal it.

"Did Tori know?" I asked, praying that I was wrong.

Claire's smiled as she nodded. "I told her myself. Confessed the whole sorry tale. I knew I could trust her to do the right thing."

"What was her reaction?" Violet asked.

If Claire murdered Tori, I didn't think I could bear it. The thought of my gentle friend striking down another was unendurable.

"See, that was the thing about Tori. Ethics tempered with mercy. We spent an entire evening discussing things. Weighing all the factors. Clara and I had always worked together, sharing ideas and concepts. Sometimes it was hard to know where her work left off, and mine began. Tori called it collaboration, not plagiarism. She convinced me to keep my secret to myself."

I recalled that in the book's forward, Claire had included a lengthy tribute to her sister and the contributions she had made to the novel. At the time, I discounted that. Now I understood.

"Where did Priscilla come in?" I asked.

"She overheard something—probably a conversation between Tori and me—and pieced everything together."

"What concessions did she want?"

Claire laughed. "I'll never know. I told the little vixen to peddle her papers elsewhere and leave me alone. Believe it or not, it worked."

Violet explained Claire's dilemma. Should she tell her story to Sergeant Stevens or remain silent? It did explain at least partially why Priscilla was murdered. On the other hand, word would inevitably get out, and Claire's career would be ruined for no reason.

"I vote to honor Tori's wish. You didn't murder your friend, and you certainly didn't kill Priscilla. I know that for a fact. You stayed at the front of the bus the entire time. Not even a bathroom break, as I recall."

Violet agreed. "I can vouch for that too. We were seated together. Writing a sequel would be the best tribute to your sister and Tori." She scratched her chin. "I think the blackmail angle is worth pursuing, however. Someone may have killed twice to keep something secret."

After we toasted Tori and Clara, our gathering broke up. Claire and Raleigh returned home, and Violet and I plotted strategy for our session with Stevens.

"We need to be careful," Violet said. "He's wily. Don't fall for his hick cop act."

I focused on secrets, who had them, what they were, and who would kill to protect them. It was difficult to imagine Harrison as a murderer. He had the intellect but not the passion or creativity to plan and execute two deaths.

"Suppose someone found out something that would destroy his self-image," Violet said. "For most of us, it wouldn't matter, but your Mr. Putnam prizes his social position."

She had a point. For all we knew, Harrison might come from humble origins. His tales of family connections might be totally fabricated. Coleman Ross would certainly look askance at that, and Mrs. Ross would snub him royally. Priscilla would gladly spread the story around campus, but that still lacked a connection to Tori Aaron and her murder. Unless, of course, it was still a matter of thwarted love.

"It all comes back to Tori," Violet said. "Claire and Abby's cases showed that she used discretion. This social justice warrior pose had its limits. Someone must have had a secret that Tori felt compelled to report." She looked my way. "Unless love and passion fueled the crime. Then delicious Roddy Park needs to be re-examined. Sorry, Marky."

Time to change the subject. I asked Violet whose interview she had chaperoned, and it turned out to be Tomas Devereaux. She frowned as she recalled the conversation.

"He's a puzzle, isn't he? Brooding. Very Heathcliff-like, yet somehow quite sweet. He didn't volunteer much to the cops except that Priscilla wasn't liked by anyone. According to Tomas, almost everyone passed near her seat as they queued up to use the restroom. Between the singing and the Jeopardy quiz, he didn't notice much. Priscilla had her back turned to them, but he figured that was simply her way of snubbing them. When the coach reached Sherborne, it was bedlam. Flailing arms and legs and scrambling students. He never looked backwards again and forgot all about Priscilla."

"Odd, isn't it," I asked. "Someone managed to slip into the seat and strangle that girl without anyone even noticing. How did Priscilla get that Hermes scarf? I'm positive that it belonged to Carolyn. Priscilla must have swiped it when nobody was looking."

Violet yawned and gathered up her things. "My mind is too muddled to think anymore. Let's fix an omelet or something so that we can avoid the crowd. And don't bother answering the door. Some newshound will likely be prowling around looking for gossip."

She was right. How come my aunt always was right? We turned off our phones and cobbled together cheese and tomato omelets and cups of soothing cocoa before calling it a night. Despite my best efforts, however, sleep eluded me. I checked the doors and windows several times even though I knew that Fantasia was on guard. How disquieting to realize that a ruthless killer lurked somewhere on the campus and might strike again. Light snoring from my bedroom confirmed that Aunt Violet had risen above such concerns and was sleeping soundly. I crept to the kitchen, grabbed my iPad, and reconstructed, as best I could, a timeline for our journey home. It was inelegant, but it was thorough. While I was at it, I listed all the questions that remained outstanding. At least we now had a departure point for the next day's discussion with Sergeant Stevens. Finally, through the good offices of Hypnos and Morpheus, I fell into a deep and dreamless sleep.

I had to conduct a reality check the next morning. Had Priscilla really been murdered right before our eyes, or was it part of a gruesome nightmare? One look at my aunt's face gave me the answer. Violet was perfectly groomed of course, but strain was evident on her face. I shared the timeline I'd composed and asked for her reaction.

"Excellent departure point. Let's not forget the personal angle, though. I keep thinking of the mascara smeared all over Tori's face. She aroused a great deal of contempt from someone. It was different for Priscilla. She overplayed her hand and paid the price. I wonder if she kept a diary or some other record of her findings. Might be worth pursuing."

We had two hours before our meeting with Stevens. Enough time to walk Fantasia and peek at Priscilla's room. Naturally, we wouldn't tamper with evidence. Not really.

The entrance to the dorm presented a problem. A well-muscled, uniformed emissary of the law stood outside, staring pointedly at anyone who tried to enter. Violet and I exchanged looks and went into action. She gripped Fantasia's lead, strolled over to the deputy, and turned on the charm machine. Before long, they were chatting amicably, leaving me the chance to slip into the building undetected. Knowing that Priscilla's room was on the second floor, I elected to use the stairs rather than risk the elevator. Fortune favored me, and as soon as I reached the area, Natalie appeared.

"Ms. Davis!" She threw her arms around me and gave me a vigorous hug. "I'm so glad to see you."

I pried myself loose and walked with her down the hallway. "Listen, Nat. I want to scope out Priscilla's room. I don't suppose the police have been there yet."

She shook her head.

"Okay. I'll slip inside, and you play lookout. We need to help the authorities if we can." I was positive that Sergeant Stevens would dispute my definition of *help*, but with any luck, he would never find out. "Do you know if Priscilla kept a diary? So many girls do during high school. I know that I did."

Natalie thought for a moment. "She was always writing stuff down in a little red notebook. We thought it was weird. Kind of like the sayings of Chairman Mao during the cultural revolution."

High-end prep schools teach kids things like that. Things that are lost to most public-school students and several college students as well. I patted her arm and thanked her for the info. "I don't suppose the door is locked."

That possibility was something I hadn't considered. Some burglar I'd make!

Natalie giggled. "Sure. But that's no problem. All our keys work on each other's door. Dr. Ross would have a cow if he knew. Here." She handed me her key and danced from one foot to another. "Oh boy! This is just like a spy show."

She was right. That key worked like a charm. I tiptoed in and surveyed the carnage. Priscilla's room reminded me more of a dressing room in Neiman Marcus rather than a teenager's lair. Every article of clothing was strewn about, from shoes to lingerie. *Had that girl never heard of using a hanger?* Thousands of dollars of pricey garments had been heaped about the room in discarded mounds. I suddenly got a bright idea. Perhaps I was not the first one to search. Police would have been tidier, so I suspected that the killer had preceded me on this errand. If only I could locate that red notebook.

Stop. Think like a paranoid teen. This was Priscilla's insurance policy. She would have secreted it in some isolated space.

After searching under the mattress and poking about for loose floorboards, I lost my nerve. Every sound convinced me that Stevens or his minions were on my trail. On my final look around, I noticed something peculiar—an eight by ten framed snapshot of Priscilla beaming at Professor Roddy Park. It had obviously been photoshopped since Roddy's expression was one of complete indifference. Moreover, the gilt and leather frame had a slight bulge at the back. My hands trembled as I carefully removed the hinges and claimed the prize, a slender red notebook.

You can't take it with you, I reminded myself. No evidence tampering.

Agreed, but that didn't stop me from whipping out my iPhone and copying every page. Besides, it wasn't that difficult a task since Priscilla had only filled about a third of the book. Her writing was a girlish scrawl that would take some time to decipher, but I still emerged from the room feeling victorious.

"Did you find it?" Natalie's eyes had an almost maniacal glint to them. I'd seen that before in addicts, and it sobered me immediately. I recalled that old saying about loose lips and sinking ships.

"Hush. Don't tell anyone about this, Natalie. I'm counting on you. Promise?"

"What's going on? Are you two hatching some plot?" In my haste, I hadn't seen Gin motoring up the corridor. I'd probably share my find with her later, but now was not the time. Aunt Violet was waiting for me, and besides, we had our appointment with Stevens.

"We're trying to brainstorm," I said. "Trying to figure out why Priscilla was murdered."

Gin scoffed. "No big deal. Easier to figure out why she wasn't eliminated sooner. Let's face it the girl was a menace. I still think she may have killed Tori or, at the very least, that she knew who did."

Natalie hung her head. "She always bragged. Pretended to know everything. Ms. Aaron told her to mind her own business, but that didn't work. Priscilla always tried to get dirt on people. She said she knew things that could get them fired."

That comment puzzled me. Did Priscilla think the killer was a member of the faculty or staff? Who else could be fired by whatever dirt she had dug up? More likely, it was the taunt of an attention-seeking juvenile who was desperate for the limelight.

Gin narrowed her eyes. "Say. Wasn't that your Aunt Carolyn's scarf they found on Priscilla? Those things are beautiful but too rich for my blood or pocketbook." Thank goodness she didn't get more specific. Natalie was already nervous, and references to strangling might just tip her over.

"My aunt misplaced it. We searched but couldn't find it." Natalie's freckles stood out more vividly than ever. She twisted her hands together and seemed close to tears. "I never saw it again. Honest."

"Huh!" Gin smirked at that. "Now we know why. Ever heard the old saying hoist on her own petard? That fits perfectly. A thief supplies her own death weapon."

Poor Natalie shivered as she processed that little gem. I gave her a hug and distracted Gin by asking if she had spoken to Sergeant Stevens.

"Spoken—ha! He grilled me like a porterhouse steak. Even questioned those little boxes of candy everyone got. I don't know why. But boy oh boy, I was glad to leave before he slapped the cuffs on me."

I left them there and made my escape. Outside of the dorm, Aunt Violet and Fantasia were sitting placidly on a bench, enjoying the brisk summer breeze. The police guard glanced my way but made no attempt to stop me.

"Ready?" Guilt made me uneasy. I expected the long arm of the law to grab me at any moment.

Violet rose and called to Fantasia. "Come on, girl. Time to get going." She put her arm around me and whispered in my ear. "I presume you were successful."

"Maybe." I explained about the little red book whose pages now resided on my phone. "We have some time to decipher it before our meeting." I hoped that Sergeant Stevens wouldn't quiz me about my side visit to Priscilla's room or even know I was in the vicinity. He was the type of cop who wasn't easy to fool. Natalie was bound to crack like a lychee nut if she were questioned.

"Jump in my car," Violet said, "and we'll check it out." She unlocked the big Mercedes and settled into the driver's seat. I joined her and opened my phone. It took some time to decipher Priscilla's messages. She used a very elementary code that relied primarily on nicknames. Tori was obviously "wonder woman." There were plenty of snide comments about her but several that caught my eye.

Overheard Wonder Woman threatening to out one of our prissy little teachers. Big blowup followed by tears and pleas. Check the records and pedigree.

I recalled that Priscilla worked around the school's administrative office. It was her part of required service that was supposed to align Sherborne students with working stiffs. That gave her access to computer files on almost everyone and everything, including some very private information. Even medical records were available in those things. I suspected that, like many institutions, Sherborne was lax about cyber security and according to Claire, Priscilla possessed mad computer skills. In the hands of a demon like her, that could spell trouble and open the floodgates to damaging information.

Violet peered over my shoulder at another entry. "Oh no. That girl stalked Roddy Park like there was no tomorrow. Can you believe it? She hacked his emails and knew everything, especially where Tori was concerned. Dangerous and delusional. What a combination."

Our meeting time with Sergeant Stevens was fast approaching, so we deferred our deep dive into all things Priscilla until afterwards. Both of us resolved to be on our best behavior, cautious but courteous. As Violet stressed, we should be able to finagle a few nuggets of information from Stevens in exchange for giving him our help. That was our plan, at least. Too bad the sergeant had a different agenda. He greeted us with a formality that suggested less collaboration and more interrogation. After dispensing with the amenities, he quickly skipped to the main menu.

"You've been snooping around since you got to Sherborne," he said, eyeing me. "Time to come clean. What have you learned?"

His tough cop routine didn't frighten me, but it caused me to think carefully before responding. After all, I neither knew nor suspected much except that Tori's murder was linked to Priscilla's. I'd planned to be subtle and offer him a few leads. Instead, I blurted out the first thing that came to mind.

"Priscilla knew who killed Tori Aaron. I'm sure of it. Knowing her, she probably tried to get leverage and was killed for her pains." There. I'd said it. I stared Stevens down, daring him to disagree.

"How about you, Ms. Davis?" Naturally, he was deferential to Violet. She inspired that sort of respect from others. "Do you agree with your niece?" His tone was mild, and he was sweet as could be, although I sensed a trap.

Violet shrugged and gave him her most winsome smile. "Here's what I observed. That girl was an accident waiting to happen. Impulsive, unlikeable, and arrogant. I hate saying that about a child but in this case, it's true. Priscilla was obsessed with Dr. Park. Stalked him constantly. I believe she was equally focused on Tori because of her relationship with Roddy. It's quite likely that Priscilla saw or guessed something about Tori's murderer and used it to taunt him or her. I have no doubt that blackmail was within her skill set."

Stevens folded his arms and nodded. "Makes sense. Her killer got close enough to surprise her. Obviously, it was someone she didn't fear. And as I recall, Priscilla Sayers was roaming around the night Ms. Aaron was murdered. Blackmail is a tricky business, you know. The victim can turn on you before you realize a thing. In my experience. It usually doesn't end well for either party."

"The murder weapon was Carolyn's Hermes scarf, I presume." Violet sighed. "Quite a pricey item." She handed him the timeline we'd worked out the evening before. "This might answer some of your questions. I don't have any idea who the murderer is, but personally, I'd focus on the motive. Someone killed Tori to protect his secret and finished off Priscilla for the same reason. At least that's what we surmise."

Stevens twirled his mustache. It was a showy handlebar affair that gave him a faintly sinister, Snidely Whiplash kind of look. "Got any idea what kind of secret that might be? I checked out that embezzlement scheme that you mentioned, Marky. According to Dr. Ross, it was merely an accounting error. No harm, no foul."

Violet and I exchanged glances. What a surprise. Coleman once again running interference for his beloved institution.

"I've spoken to a lot of people," I said, "and I think that the answer rests with Tori Aaron. She was a very principled person, but she also was kind. She didn't indulge in mindless gossip, particularly the kind that could ruin a person's life or career. Whatever secret she uncovered was something big. Something she felt compelled to make public."

Stevens then recited a litany of potential acts that might sabotage a person's future. Cheating on exams, illicit love affairs, theft, bribery, or plagiarism among them. The list was endless. I grimaced when he mentioned several things, recalling Claire's situation and Abigail's ill-advised prank. Tori would never break her promise to them. I was positive of that.

He retrieved a printout and handed it to Violet. For some reason, he deliberately excluded me. That made me even more determined to insert myself into the discussion.

Stevens was unimpressed by my efforts. He continued to direct his comments to my aunt. "Priscilla Sayers had a hefty savings account for a kid. Regular deposits of one hundred dollars a week. Nothing spectacular but steady."

"But surely her parents sent her that. Most kids around here get whopping big allowances." I wasn't impressed by the sums, but they were suggestive.

He shook his head. "Nope. I spoke with her guardian this morning..."

"Guardian? What about her parents?" Interrupting was rude, but I couldn't help myself.

Stevens explained that Priscilla was an orphan. A very wealthy orphan, but still... A surge of guilt overwhelmed me. Unlike Priscilla, I'd been raised by loving, supportive parents. Perhaps that explained the girl's constant quest for attention and undesirable traits. It didn't make her more likable, but it helped to understand her better. Priscilla was financially secure but had no parents and no friends. It was a sad commentary on a young life.

"So, she had no need for money," Violet said. "Those payments must have been blackmail, a way of controlling her victims. Very dangerous. Not huge sums unless you're on a very limited budget."

My thoughts turned again to Claire. That money would be a stretch on a teacher's salary.

"This Roddy Park seems to be some kind of matinee idol around here," Stevens said. "Any chance he succumbed to temptation and paid the price? School girls throwing themselves at him and all. A man can only take so much." Stevens sighed as if he, too, had experienced that. I suddenly realized that he was making a dead set at my aunt, trying to impress her with a man-of-the-world manner. Dream on. Against my better judgment, I leapt to Roddy's defense.

"Absolutely not. He took pains to discourage their attention, particularly Priscilla's. Besides, he was in love with Tori."

Stevens' smirk said it all. "If Ms. Aaron rejected him, maybe he killed her, and Priscilla found out. After all, he discovered her body, and as I recall, he was standing close to Priscilla's seat on the bus too. Big guy like that. He could strangle a girl before she knew what was happening."

Neither Violet nor I responded to that taunt, and Stevens didn't seem to expect us to. He was on an obvious fishing expedition and wasn't above using Roddy as bait. Violet changed the subject. "I suppose you're checking bank records, Sergeant, although that wasn't a great deal of cash."

He nodded. "We're certain that we know where it came from. Another faculty member suggested that, too, by the way. Harrison Putnam. He's no fan of yours, Marky. Seems to think you're an agitator, not unlike Ms. Aaron."

"Me?" That was so unfair that I couldn't help reacting. "Any comparison to Tori is a compliment whether he realizes that or not. Harrison is the ultimate snob. Thinks he's descended from the Mayflower or perhaps Mount Olympus. I wouldn't believe a thing he said. Besides, he was smitten with Tori himself." I lifted my head high. "I have that on good authority."

Stevens proceeded to spring the trap he'd set. "I'm disappointed, Marky. You haven't been honest with me."

"Huh?"

"Why didn't you tell me about Abigail Jenkins and that Kahoot incident? Her attorney called me this morning at the Senator's behest. Seems she's the one who's been paying Priscilla that money. But you knew all about that, didn't you?"

I took a deep breath. Stevens was a slick article who wasn't above trickery. "I didn't know she was being extorted by that twit Priscilla. That other thing was just kid stuff. No big deal. They all seemed to know about it anyway. The kids, that is. I'm not sure the faculty knew the score."

He rubbed his mustache again. "I wonder. Teenagers blow lots of things out of proportion. Maybe Abigail thought she'd be expelled if it got out. Bad publicity for Daddy." He let the other shoe drop. "Of course, it's far more likely that her boyfriend stepped in."

I glared at him. "Tomas? You must be joking. Just because he's on scholarship doesn't make him a killer."

"He has a record, you know, and a temper. Mostly petty stuff but suggestive. Has a father in jail too. Aggravated assault. Almost killed some guy in a bar fight."

Violet intervened. "Surely you aren't targeting Tomas for his father's mistake. The boy is a talented artist with a fine career ahead of him. Besides, he was devoted to Tori."

Stevens snorted. "His mother had a sad ending, too, you know. Alcoholic dementia. Might have affected the boy having two parents with problems. Bad genes and all."

Our window of time was running short, and Stevens hadn't furnished us with much information. I decided to confront him on another matter. "Did Priscilla have any files on her computer? Incriminating ones?"

Stevens demurred. "That's confidential, Ms. Davis. But I will tell you we're looking for her diary. Some red notebook she carried around. It wasn't on her person when she died." He gave us the tough cop stare. "Know anything about that?"

I decided to be forthright—within reason. "Some of the kids mentioned that. You know, like Mao's little red book. It sounded like a joke."

He curled his lip. "I'm not laughing, Marky. That could be vital evidence. If you have it…"

I raised my hand. "I don't. I swear I don't. If it exists, it's probably in her room. You know how sloppy kids are."

My answer didn't satisfy him, but Stevens decided to back off. I'm positive it was only a temporary reprieve, but my caffeine-starved system screamed for relief. Time. I needed time to study those pages and try to piece together a theory. Knowing Priscilla, she had probably confronted her victim openly and fearlessly, never dreaming of the consequences. Stevens stood and dismissed us with a final warning. "We're dealing with a double murderer here. Stay out of it for your own good and those students you claim to care about."

Violet led me back to her car without saying a thing until we were blocks away from the police station. "That was quite an experience. Stevens is under a lot of pressure, and I worry about Tomas. Let's face it, no one really has an alibi for that afternoon apart from you, me, Clare, and the bus driver."

There was humor in that comment, but I failed to find it. We three had stayed in our seats, not even pausing for a comfort break. Everyone else had moved about, especially the instructors. I squeezed my eyes shut, hoping to banish the bad news. Oh, how I longed to be back in Harbor Bay, secure in my store, stocking the shelves of Poppet with beauty products and dealing with irascible customers. Sherborne School and all its inmates, including Roddy Park, had reduced me to a quivering mass of Jell-O. In three weeks, the summer term would end, and I would finally be free. Would the spirits of Tori Aaron and Priscilla ever leave me in peace?

Stop deluding yourself, Marky. You're no super sleuth. Cosmetics, not crime, are your bailiwick. Tori's killer will never be found by a bumbling amateur like you.

* * *

Aunt Violet left early the next morning after promising to return with Gemma for the charity art show. Despite my lethargy, I forced myself to crawl into the shower, attend to my hair and makeup, and head for the dining hall. No sense in abandoning good grooming just because a crazed killer roamed about, and every day might be my last. Fantasia licked my face in solidarity and went on an abbreviated walk without complaint. I hugged her with such vigor that she whined in protest. How could anyone dislike animals? They gave so much and asked so little in return. Ten minutes with Fantasia was more therapeutic than an hour spent with a shrink. I resolved to count my blessings, stop moping, and get moving.

Besides, one big positive motivated me: Sunday meant blueberry pancakes! I planned to stuff my face with that yummy treat, and calories be damned. Although the normal high spirits of the group were subdued, the demand for those hotcakes had intensified. Claire dove into her portion, and despite her diminutive size, Gin managed to handle a double stack. I sat alongside Roddy as he mechanically shoveled sausages into his mouth without appearing to taste them. I felt no shame at the fact that I matched his performance minus the meat. This was no time for feminine charades. I needed fuel to activate my brain cells, and blueberries were potent antioxidants. The syrup, not so much, but why quibble?

Roddy lay down his fork and smiled. "You're amazing. Despite everything that happened, you look as lovely as ever."

That took me by surprise. Compliments on appearance were simply not Roddy's style.

"I do? Gee, thanks." I pushed my plate aside as if eating was the last thing on my mind. "Who's arranging a memorial for Priscilla? Do you know, or is it too soon to ask?"

Roddy shrugged. His indifference was obvious and rather surprising. Most of the faculty had at least feigned sorrow at the girl's demise. "Gin probably is. She knew her best because of the Julliard link."

Claire and Gin stopped talking and looked my way.

"Dr. Ross wants a gathering in the chapel. Nothing fancy but, for propriety's sake, something to acknowledge her passing. His words, not mine." Gin groaned. "I drew the short straw, so I'm organizing it. The hard thing will be finding someone to give a eulogy."

"You met with Sergeant Stevens yesterday, I understand." Claire gave me a quizzical look. "Anything we should know?"

I hesitated. "He's searching for Priscilla's diary, but he's convinced she was blackmailing someone. Someone from Sherborne. Probably more than one victim."

No one displayed any reaction. That was curious. Finally, Roddy spoke. "He suspects one of us, I presume. If you ask me, the killer's desperate to strike in broad daylight like that."

"Of course, Stevens suspects one of us. Use your head, Roddy. Who else was on that bus? Besides, I'd call the killer audacious, not desperate." Gin looked carefully at each of us. "Seems like his plan worked too. No one was expecting any trouble, and we let down our guard. Let's face it, it was one slick move. Too sophisticated for most kids to pull off. That points the fickle finger of fate toward us."

Claire nibbled at her hot cake. "Ru Peterson told me something interesting. Priscilla bragged to him she had the "smoking gun" in Tori's murder. Something she found while prowling around the park where Tori died."

All eyes were glued to Claire's face waiting for her next words. Instead of speaking, she ignored us and slowly chewed her pancake. The suspense took its toll on everyone at the table. Roddy grimaced, Gin clenched her fists, and I yearned to shake my friend until she spilled the beans.

"What are you all up to?" a jarring voice asked. Harrison Putnam pulled out a chair and sat next to Claire. "I heard something about Priscilla and a smoking gun."

Claire discarded her napkin and pushed her plate away. "You'll have to ask

Ru yourself. It was really nothing significant. I should never have mentioned it." She excused herself and hurriedly left the table.

"Well," Harrison huffed. "Some welcome I got. The headmaster told me not to worry. He expects the police will nab the perpetrator by the end of the week."

"Really?" Gin tried to keep her voice neutral.

Harrison gave his trademark superior smirk. "Believe me, you won't be surprised. This person's been on their radar for quite some time. No great loss to the Sherborne community either."

My insides churned as I thought of Tomas. Based on Stevens' comments the prior day, I had no doubt that he was the prime suspect. There was no time for delicacy. I had to study Priscilla's notes and confront Ru and Tomas about their suspicions before it was too late.

Chapter Fifteen

I considered asking Roddy to help me decipher those notes but quickly rejected the idea. If we discovered anything incriminating, he might feel honor bound to notify the authorities and furthermore, it might prove dangerous. Suppose he was the killer? It was unthinkable and unlikely but still...I try to be honest with myself whenever possible and involving Roddy might also seem like a ploy to get closer to him. Totally unacceptable but tempting.

I chose an inviting alternative—basking outdoors in the warm summer sun. After a brisk walk with Fantasia, I spread a blanket on a grassy spot and got to work, notepad in hand. Priscilla's girlish scribble about "Prince Charming," aka Roddy, bordered on fantasy and was largely irrelevant. Only one thing of value emerged: Roddy spent most of his time either in the library or alone in his apartment. Tori occasionally stayed the night but even that spoke more of habit than passion. No other woman or coed appeared in the narrative. That pleased me for some obscure reason. Since Priscilla was obsessive about him, I dismissed Stevens' suggestion that Roddy had been lured by some campus Lolita into compromising situations. Priscilla would have hunted down the temptress in question, of that I had no doubt.

Another character was dubbed, "The Pretender." Her notes about this individual (gender unspecified) were sketchy. Suffice it to say, the Pretender was someone whose claims to glory were totally unfounded. Priscilla discovered proof of that and intended to use it at a time of her own choosing. I wondered if she knew about Claire and her famous novel. If so, Priscilla would have a potent bargaining chip at her disposal. Problem was Claire had no money to give her and no way to influence her career. Revealing that secret would be an act of pure malice something Priscilla was more than capable of. Coleman Ross also fit the Pretender description. If she had inside information about the embezzlement that could ignite a powder keg that would blow him right out of his precious position. Worth killing for? Perhaps.

I recognized Abigail, ("daddy's little girl") immediately. Priscilla had collected several thousand dollars in "Tribute" (her word) from Abby but apparently had no imminent plans to do anything else with the information. Having a Senator's daughter as her lackey must have fed Priscilla's ego and no doubt, she enjoyed holding that club over poor Abby's head.

Halfway into the notes, I tired of slogging through the malicious mud and took a break. Our charity art show, the culmination of the summer term was only two weeks away and several students were working diligently on their projects. I hoped to find Ru or Tomas among them. Tomas had created an impressionist oil that was truly masterful. Unlike so many aspiring artists, that boy had talent to spare and the desire to succeed. He hadn't harmed Tori or anyone else, I would bet my life on that. The phrase was particularly ill-suited to our present situation, so I mentally revised it. I would risk my career on the certainty that Tomas was innocent. Like most of the kids, he had roamed back and forth on the coach, but I hadn't seen him lurking near Priscilla's seat. Stevens' words about Tomas haunted me. Was he to suffer for the sins of the father? I felt compelled to do something but powerless to know what that was.

As I approached our studio, sounds of lively chatter wafted out. Sure enough, both Ru and Tomas were positioned at their easels, working diligently. I tackled Ru first. He had created a collage comprised of found materials, that he dubbed, "saving the planet." It wasn't a work of genius but there was a clever spin to it that would probably excite some bidders.

"Hey. You're making real progress," I said. "Someone will love this."

The lad laughed. "Don't worry. It's already sold. My parents donated in exchange for the masterpiece from the hands of their number one son." He bowed. "That's me, in case you're wondering."

Parental interference was contrary to the rules of the program but since fundraising was our goal, I couldn't object. Besides, I suspected that the headmaster had bowed to the bountiful checkbook of Li Peterson, Ru's well-heeled father. It was a win-win outcome as far as Sherborne was concerned.

"Let me ask you something." I bent over so that only Ru could hear me. "What was this smoking gun that Priscilla told you about? If it concerned Tori's murder it might be important."

Ru bit his lip as if he were under duress. "Gee, I'm not sure I should say. It probably was a lie anyway."

My small store of patience was rapidly evaporating, and I summoned my mean teacher voice. "Stop stalling. You might put yourself in danger too. Besides you owe it to Ms. Aaron."

He looked around at his comrades before answering. Tomas had stopped painting and was giving him a hard stare. Even Natalie and Abby were openly eavesdropping. "Priscilla said she found something in the bushes. Near where Ms. Aaron died."

Any more delay might cause me to shake this student back into his grade school days. "What was it, Ru?" I raised my voice only slightly.

The answer was anticlimactic. "She found some of that eyelash stuff. Mascara. Just the top of the tube."

"So?"

Ru stuttered and glanced around at his friends. "It's just that she thought it might have prints. You know, the killer's prints like on TV. She was going to have it tested by a lab."

It probably meant nothing. Lots of debris collected in bushes around the school. Tissues, plastic cups, and even condoms were plentiful. Students were constantly being cautioned about littering, destroying the environment, and general carelessness. Still, I couldn't afford to overlook any clue, however meaningless. "And did she? Did Priscilla have it tested?"

"That's the funny thing. She told me at the museum that some university nerd had done it for her." He held up his arms. "That's all I know. She didn't say whose it was or anything. Just smiled that the crazy way she had and called it her 'ticket to ride,' you know, like the old Beatles song."

I thanked him and stepped aside to process the information. If Priscilla was telling the truth—and that was a big if—she still needed someone to compare the prints against a database like NCIC. One of the universities might have access to that, but they were unlikely to allow just anyone to use it. More research was required, and that task was suited to the talents of our Ph.D. student, Roddy Park. A nagging doubt stopped me. That presumed, of course, that he was not the guilty party. It also caused me to examine my own desire to grow closer to Roddy. Of late, my track record in the romance department had been dismal. Another failure would probably doom me to permanent spinsterhood. Aunt Violet would scoff at that and tell me to go with my heart. At her core, she was quite the romantic, although, for some reason, she herself had never married.

I suspected that Priscilla had cast a wide net and bragged about her find to as many people as she could. Common sense had not been her strong suit. She had spooked the killer into acting quickly and efficiently to eliminate the threat.

Tomas was looking my way, so I joined him at his easel. I assessed his painting and was floored by the excellence and maturity of his work. He'd taken Impressionism to its heights and although he still had some techniques to improve, I believed there was no limit to his potential. That strengthened my resolve to keep Stevens, Harrison, and anyone else from ruining the boy's life.

"Excellent work, Tomas," I said. "You might consider blending a bit of crimson into the mix."

Ru jeered at him. "Teacher's pet." He was immediately shouted down by Abby and Natalie, who gathered 'round his easel and clapped. Abby's spirits seemed elevated, and I attributed that to finally confessing her misdeed to her father. Without Priscilla to taunt her, life was probably much improved. No one appeared to miss Priscilla Sayers and that was a sad commentary on her all too brief life. Someone had placed a covering over her work in progress, a thoughtful gesture that nevertheless reminded all of us of her absence. Tori was the one whose memory lingered most vividly in the hearts of her colleagues and students. I still maintained that her passion for justice was at the core of the murders.

Natalie crept up to me and whispered. "Did you ever find Priscilla's diary? The police combed through her room right after you left. They wouldn't tell us anything."

I try to be honest, but sometimes misdirection in pursuit of a goal was necessary. "I didn't take anything. That wouldn't be right. Wish I had found that mascara top, though. By the way, how is your aunt reacting to all this?"

Natalie grimaced. "Aunty freaked out when they told her how that shawl was used. She used to love it so much. It was a gift from a special friend. Now she can't bear to even think about wearing it. Priscilla admired the shawl when we were at the museum. Asked all kinds of questions like she couldn't believe my Aunt Caro would have a genuine Hermes scarf. Do you know she even asked if it was a knockoff!"

How like our dearly departed Priscilla to impugn something so beautiful. Small wonder she was barely missed. I was more curious about that mascara tube. Both Michigan State and the University of Michigan had thriving criminal justice programs. They probably had access to NCIC databases as well. Priscilla was an attractive girl who might have inveigled some lovesick swain into checking out those fingerprints. Time to come clean with Sergeant Stevens.

His voice was brusque when he finally answered my call. It appeared that he considered me a meddlesome pest rather than an ally. Maybe with this information, I could curry favor and change his mind. Dream on. His reaction was less than enthusiastic.

"Who told you about this so-called clue?" he barked. "Probably a fabrication. You know how kids love to make stuff up."

I powered down before responding. Stevens might be baiting me. "I'm not sure. Priscilla apparently told several people about it. I just thought you'd like to know. Full disclosure in case you found it in her room."

"Anything else? Keep this up and you could be a cop consultant with a badge and everything. No gun, though. We're strict about that." Sarcasm was not an effective weapon, although Stevens wielded it with great gusto. I didn't need his scorn, so I summoned my remaining shreds of dignity and rang off. Fantasia awaited my arrival, and I needed her furry presence to comfort me and put things into perspective. Besides, somewhere in Priscilla's scribblings, there might be a nugget of gold. The murderer certainly must have thought so.

The third page in her journal stopped me in my tracks. While prowling around in the Sherborne record system, she had apparently uncovered a bombshell. Priscilla ranted at length about an imposter, a two-faced, hydra-headed being who blinded others to reality. Her unabashed glee over the find was unsettling. Her direct quote was chilling: "I'm going to use this to my advantage." I had no clue about the identity of the imposter in question. Every personnel file was retained on the school's computer system and Priscilla was known as a computer wizard. Tomas called her a hacker who could access almost everything. I had no such skills, but I knew someone who did. That evening I called my business partner and best pal, Gemma Watts, and made a proposal to her. Her response was typical Gemma.

"Are you kidding? That cloak-and-dagger stuff is right up my alley. Most schools haven't a clue about cyber security. Piece of cake to burrow into their records. My nephew needed some help last year. Nothing major, just some disciplinary stuff he wanted to disappear. I hacked right into the high school database and puff...gone in a flash."

I was basically a goody-two-shoes who played by the rules and avoided any kind of trouble. Just considering this kind of caper made me queasy. Was computer hacking a federal offense or just a minor infraction? Gemma wasn't going to alter any records or steal anything. It was more like surveillance than stealing. At least, that was the rationale I gave myself. Besides my motive was pure. Something in those files might help to catch a killer. A double murderer. Surely that justified a spot of unauthorized peeking. Gemma rang off, eager to start our project. I'd given her the names of both students and faculty members who might be involved. In addition, she promised to conduct a thorough internet search of those same individuals. Private Eye.com was one of her favorite haunts, a revelation that made me shiver and agonize about the loss of privacy in the computer age. At her suggestion, I agreed to peruse social media accounts.

"You'd be surprised at the things people post," Gemma said. "Especially kids. They have no sense at all. Make sure you look at the photos too. And not just Facebook. That's passé for younger users." She proceeded to give me a list of platforms that I had never even heard of before. It heightened my fears that even at age twenty-six, I was an anachronism, a fuddy-duddy who was hopelessly behind the times. If only I could confide in someone at Sherborne. Claire's name came to mind, but I hesitated to share my activities. Suppose she disapproved? Claire was conservative about prying into the lives of others. She might feel obliged to alert her colleagues and potentially the killer. Roddy was another matter entirely. I valued his good opinion and feared that he would consider me a snoop or stalker if I confessed my plan. No, until further notice, I had to be the Lone Ranger, riding the range of Sherborne school in my quest for the silver bullet that would catch a killer. If only Tonto was with me!

At dinner that evening, I kept my own counsel, so much so that Claire feared I was ill. Gin wasn't so easily deceived, however. She gave me side-eye and demanded an explanation for my behavior.

"Love life a problem?" She asked.

"Huh! If only. I guess it's just the culmination of all that's happened. I'll be leaving soon, and there's so much left to do."

Roddy and Harrison were absent, so our conversation was much less restrained. "I spoke to Stevens today and got my head handed to me."

"Oh? How come?" Gin grinned as if she already knew the answer.

"He accused me of meddling and basically trying to be a cop groupie. It was humiliating."

Claire put her arm around me. "Don't fret. He's just afraid you'll solve the murders when he couldn't. I worry that you'll put yourself in danger."

I assured them both that I was officially out of the school snoop business. It was only a tiny lie, a minor prevarication, and I kept my fingers crossed so that it didn't count.

Our conversation turned to the charity art auction. Claire was exhilarated by the thought of it, but Gin was cautious. "What if something else happens? Sherborne can't withstand another tragedy."

"That won't happen." Claire said it with authority, as if she guaranteed a happy outcome. "Besides, we're doing this to honor Tori. I just feel she'll be watching over us and keeping us safe."

Gin rolled her eyes at that. She was probably an agnostic, although that was sheer speculation on my part. No one at Sherborne had ever discussed religious beliefs and that was fine with me. Academic debates were tedious enough, but theological ones would be unbearable.

"Too bad Tori wasn't watching over Priscilla. Someone should have, for heaven's sake." Gin folded her arms and scowled.

I sensed a vein of anger in her words. Priscilla, unlovable creature that she was had been Gin's protégé, at least in her quest to reach Juilliard. In fairness, the girl did have some talent if one overlooked her deficiencies.

"Guess who agreed to help judge our art auction?" Claire beamed as she said the name. "Carolyn! Why with her academic credentials and your Aunt Violet's fame, we'll have a first-class operation."

That boded well for our aspiring artists and thespians. Gin's version of Shakespeare Unleashed was sure to be a hit, and the offerings by my students should be snapped up. I declined their offer of drinks and a bridge match because I was eager to start my online sleuthing. Besides, Fantasia grew lonely if I left her to her own devices. I knew all about abandonment, and it was no fun.

My first foray into my colleagues' lives started with Harrison Putnam. I reasoned that a prominent family like his should be all over social media and search engines, and indeed I found numerous entries for Putnam Industries, and the good works it sponsored. Obituaries traced the lineage of the Putnams from old Elijah, a scion of the seafaring trade, to the current purveyors of a multifaceted food conglomerate. The images on the screen showed a strong family resemblance to my esteemed colleague with prominent noses and jutting chins on display. One thing puzzled me, however. Nowhere was there any mention of Harrison or his side of the family. Could it be? Was his line the impoverished branch of that family tree? I knew he had attended Exeter and Dartmouth, but a thought suddenly assailed me. What if Harrison Putnam, the ultimate snob, had been a scholarship student? That might explain his disdain toward Tomas and others who achieved success through sheer talent rather than trading on family connections. It made sense and suggested a wedge that an unscrupulous scamp like Priscilla might use to extract favors from an instructor. I devised a plan to test my theory without directly confronting Harrison. Although it seemed unlikely, I had to consider that he might have taken extreme measures to preserve the fiction he had created. Harrison had no desire to be one of the common herd. Anyone who threatened his status might suffer the consequences. I then checked the official CV he posted on the Sherborne school website. In it was the typical listing of academic credentials plus an inordinately long digression about his roots and the prominence of the Putnam family. Was he the imposter that Priscilla had inveighed against? More to the point, why would Tori have gotten involved in that? Her egalitarian instincts would have applauded Harrison's humble origins rather than decried them. Perhaps when Gemma did a deep dive into his background, she would uncover something interesting.

I circulated back to Priscilla's notes. She had written PLAGIARIST in big capital letters with a question mark. That made me gulp. Had she uncovered the truth about Claire's novel? It seemed unlikely, but still possible. Even more unlikely was the thought that Claire might have lied to me. I had only her word that Tori had agreed not to publicize the issue. Wasn't it just as likely that Tori would feel honor bound to alert the school authorities? Sherborne proudly touted Claire's achievements as a novelist and the benefits they conferred on students. There were monetary issues to consider as well. According to Claire, her novel still sold well and brought in enough royalties to supplement her rather meager earnings as a teacher. Had Priscilla muscled in on that as well, or had Tori recoiled at the thought of illicit gains? I couldn't believe it. I refused to believe that my gentle friend would ever resort to violence. Besides, as Aunt Violet observed, there was no proof that Clara and not Claire was the principal architect of the novel. Just to be sure, I scoured the internet for any mention of Claire. High praise abounded from Publishers Weekly, the *New York Times Book Review, the national book review committee,* and seemingly every reputable literary source in the nation, citing the sensitivity and precision of Claire's book. It was so like the author herself. I'd read her work with awe, inspired by the lucidity of its plot and the vivid depiction of the characters. One reviewer had likened it to Harper Lee's *To Kill a Mockingbird* and termed it a national treasure. High praise indeed, but right on track. No one should impugn Claire's talent or bring that work into disrepute, and I refused to believe that Tori would destroy her friend's legacy. Claire was a beloved teacher who had guided many young minds. Surely that was the ultimate test of any professional.

Before retiring for the evening, I made a quick pass at Claire's Facebook account. The photos it contained were more intriguing than the rather mundane posts that she shared. One especially caught my eye. It showed three young women, obviously Claire, her sister Clara, and Carolyn, with their arms entwined. They were laughing, exploring the sand dunes of a local beach with an exuberant Labrador at their side. Clara although painfully thin, looked almost identical to her sister. It was a sweet memory, a snapshot of yesterday captured for eternity. I realized then that I had no hope of objectivity. None. Claire was no killer, and I refused to even consider it again. Besides, Carolyn would have known the story. She would scarcely have condoned a literary fraud or remained Claire's close friend and ally if something unethical had occurred.

Fantasia nudged me and placed her lovely head on my knee. It was time for her final walk of the day. Like many dogs, she had an unerring sense of time and place and had no trouble reminding me of my obligations. Perhaps snooping had roused my insecurities because I grabbed my trusty torch before we left the house. A full moon illuminated the sky, but the presence of that truncheon steeled my nerves. Memories of Tori's battered head flashed across my mind, and I resolved to be extra vigilant. Sergeant Stevens had found an unused container of pepper spray in Tori's pocket. That suggested that she knew her assailant and was untroubled. Perhaps she had even arranged to meet the culprit. Priscilla, too, was unafraid of her killer. After all, she felt confident enough to blackmail someone she faced every day. That implied either guts or complete foolishness on her part. It might also point to a peer, someone from her own age group who seemed to pose no threat. I pictured the entire crew: Tomas, Ru, Natalie, and Abby. Good kids, all of them. I wouldn't fear any of them, and neither would Tori. Priscilla was arrogant enough to feel invulnerable, especially when she was on a public conveyance surrounded by Sherborne students.

A growl from Fantasia made me jump. My heartbeat accelerated, and that famous fight or flight response kicked in. I whirled around and clutched my torch like a weapon.

"Whoa, girl, what's your problem?" Gin gave me a puzzled look and bent down to pat my dog. '

"Nothing. Guess I'm just a bit jumpy."

"You think?" Gin laughed. She pointed to my torch. "Didn't know you were a warrior princess, Ms. Davis. On the other hand, this spot is very close to where Tori was attacked. I don't blame you for being cautious. It's kind of spooky. Almost like she still haunts the place."

I nodded. "One thing both Tori and Priscilla had in common: neither one feared her assailant. It had to be someone nonthreatening, although no one around here is exactly intimidating."

"What about Coleman? He's surprisingly fit for a guy his age. Watch him on the tennis court, and you'd see what I mean. He played on his college team and apparently was quite good."

The headmaster. I'd already assumed that he would do almost anything to salvage his own position and the reputation of Sherborne. But did that include a brutal murder? Besides, he hadn't been with us when Priscilla met her doom. But Harrison was. Shameless sycophant, he might be, but would his activities extend to murder? The thought sickened me and made me once again yearn for the comforts of my hometown and my little store.

"Hey. Earth to Marky." Gin elbowed me. "Are you okay?"

"Yeah. Just overwhelmed. No wonder Stevens told me to butt out. I'm no detective. It's far easier solving crimes in books or movies." Having said that, I asked Gin something. "How well do you know Harrison?"

She frowned. "Well enough. Not in the Biblical sense, thank goodness, but we've been colleagues for five years."

"Okay. Is his family as important as he says?"

Gin shrugged. "I don't know. Maybe. He talks about them enough. Always bemoaning the incursion of the lower classes. People like me, I guess."

We both knew she was joking. After all, America was a meritocracy where native talent and initiative counted more than family roots. Until it didn't. I thought of how easily Coleman and Harrison had turned on Tomas when trouble arose. One false move and he would be ushered right out of the door or made a scapegoat. It wasn't fair, yet it was reality. Perhaps that was why Harrison clung so desperately to his vaunted family roots.

I shook my head and called to Fantasia. "I can't think about it anymore tonight. Maybe I'll go back, take a bubble bath, and sip a glass of brandy. That should calm my nerves."

Gin bit her lip. "Maybe you should listen to Stevens after all. He gets paid to do this stuff, and he carries a gun. At least, I think he does. He strikes me as a guy who suspects everyone." She nodded. "Maybe Tori and even the dreadful Priscilla would still be alive if they did the same thing."

Her words surprised me. "Don't get me wrong," Gin said. "I loved Tori. But she was a meddler. Couldn't' leave other people's business alone. That history of Sherborne she was working on became almost an obsession. Seemed like Tori never let up doing research and interviewing us and people who knew us years ago. Lord, how I hated those interviews. More like interrogations. Even Roddy told her they were intrusive, and you know that in his eyes, Tori could do no wrong. Her motives were always good, unlike Priscilla's. I just wish Tori had backed off whatever crusade she was on. I miss her." Gin's eyes teared up, and she dabbed them with a crumbled tissue. "Oops. Now my mascara will be down to my chin. Oh well. That's what I get for wearing the cheap stuff."

"I can suggest some better brands if you like. Lancôme makes fantastic eye products. Worth the extra cost. My aunt can bring you some samples when she comes up next week."

Gin shrugged. 'Gee, I hate to be a moocher. It's so easy to raid the stash at the drama department that I got lazy. Oh well, sweet charity and all that. Sure, anything to upgrade my image."

I was glad to have company walking back to our rooms. I'm no alarmist, but two women and a sizable dog are a lot more formidable than just one person—namely me. Gin's comment about the history of Sherborne stayed in my mind long after we parted. I wondered who had taken responsibility for the project after Tori's death. Had she uncovered something incriminating that had led to her doom? It seemed unlikely, and yet there was no denying that a killer haunted the halls of Sherborne, shared our communal dinners, and even participated in Jeopardy game nights. It was only ten p.m., and Claire would still be awake. I dialed her number and asked about the Sherborne project. The question startled her, but she knew the answer immediately. "Roddy Park took over that project for Tori. A labor of love, I rather thought. Why?"

"Oh, no big deal. I just need to check something out with him. I'll just give him a call." I rang his number without considering that he might have company or be immersed in work. Afterwards, I realized that Roddy might consider it a pretext on my part or, heaven forbid, a romantic overture. He answered before my better instincts asserted themselves and said he'd come right over.

* * *

Roddy bounded into my living room, carrying his laptop and a bottle of wine. I'd never seen him in such casual clothes before and I marveled at what his supple form could do for a simple t-shirt and jeans.

WHOA, GIRL, I told myself. Get a grip! You've been single for too long, and it's beginning to show.

"I didn't mean to disturb you," I said suddenly, feeling shy and out of my depth. I was no ingenue, but I was acting like one.

"Hey, no problem. I needed to take a break." He glanced around the room and sighed. "You know I haven't been in this place for a long time. Since Tori died." The man was in the grip of nostalgia and had no intentions toward me despite what Claire thought. I opened the wine, poured both of us a glass, and motioned toward the small table that served as dining and desk space. "I'm not trying to intrude if you'd rather complete this yourself. I'll help any way that I can."

His smile was captivating. Small wonder that he had legions of female fans. "You don't realize this, but you're kind of an answer to a prayer. I've felt so guilty, but now I can confess."

A sudden chill swept through me. Was I once again closeted up with a killer? Roddy was a big guy who could crush me like a bug. If he confessed to two murders, even with the assistance of my brave Fantasia, I was doomed.

"Confess?" My voice sounded weak and quivery even to my ears. Fortunately, Roddy seemed oblivious to the change in climate.

"Yeah. I've been so focused on my dissertation that I ignored that stupid Sherborne Anthology. Tori had already done the preliminary research, but I kept procrastinating. The narrative just seemed like too much work."

"I've got some spare time. Let me give you a hand." Once again, I reproached myself since I wanted to give the man far more than a hand. When had I become so lecherous? Marketta Davis, ice princess, and all-around good girl was melting before my eyes.

"Great! How about if I send you the file, and you can see what you're getting into. Got to warn you though, it's kind of a mess. Tori had many talents, but writing wasn't one of them. What's your email?" Roddy took a swallow of wine and hunched over his computer. When I opened the file, I saw just what he meant. Tori had assembled her research according to the academic department and included both facts and tidbits on both staff and students. Most of it was general information culled from faculty CVs, although she had also inserted humorous anecdotes whenever possible. For instance, she gave plaudits to Harrison Putnam for his inspired portrayal of the hunchback of Notre Dame, and lauded Gin for her star turn as Evita during a stage production. A side comment gave a big hurrah to Juilliard for producing such a prodigy.

"Harrison as the hunchback," I asked Roddy. "Sorry, I missed that. No typecasting there."

He grinned as he replayed that scene. "It really was something. Hard to believe that our staff aristocrat lowered himself that way. I don't know if she mentioned it, but Priscilla was in that production of Evita. Must admit she was good, too. Girl could sing and act. Too bad she ended up like she did. Juilliard was really interested in her from what Gin said."

"Should a tribute to Priscilla be included?" I asked.

He thought about it for a bit, then shrugged. "Gee. Better ask Gin. I'm never sure about stuff like that, but she'll know. They always had their heads together."

That surprised me. Most of the faculty and students avoided Priscilla as if she were a noxious rash. Very likely, Gin was trying to mold the girl into an acceptable human being. No, an easy task no matter how hard she tried. I was getting nowhere using indirect methods. Time to go bold. "Hey, look it. You know these people better than I ever will. Who's your candidate for double murderer if you had to pick one?"

He was startled and dumbstruck, or so it seemed. Perhaps there was something to be said for subtlety over confrontation after all. Roddy finished his glass of wine and, after a brief pause, gave a halfhearted unhelpful response.

"Gosh. I never really thought about it that way. After we lost Tori, everyone just assumed it was some street thug. Now with Priscilla gone too..." The anguished look on his face told the tale. Roddy was a nice guy who wanted to avoid fingering his colleagues. There was another possibility, of course. If Roddy himself was the culprit, his reluctance to discuss the subject was understandable. "Why get involved, Marky? You'll be gone soon but the rest of us must face our coworkers. It's dangerous poking around people's private lives. Look what happened to Tori. She never knew when to quit. Always prodding and prying. Most people have some secrets they'd just as soon keep to themselves. Wouldn't you agree?"

I wondered what secrets this sultry stranger harbored. Probably something to do with sex. Just my luck. I tried to inject some humor into our discussion.

"And what are you trying to hide, Mr. Park? An obsession with Russian history?" His frown deepened, and he turned away.

Unfortunately, my own life was an open book. An essentially boring essay on a mundane existence. I had no titillating anecdotes to trade or fear. Still, persistence is one of my strong points.

"One more thing Roddy. Don't you feel any obligation to Tori and Priscilla too, I suppose to get justice for them?"

Roddy set his mouth in a harsh, firm line. No more mister nice guy...I had obviously gone too far.

"Look. If I knew something, if I could help, I'd do so, but I'm not a detective or a cop, and may I say once again, neither are you. What if you find out that someone you care about, like Tomas, committed those crimes? Would you turn him in?"

"He's just a kid," I protested. "An easy target because he's poor. He adored Tori. Why would he kill her?"

Roddy grabbed my shoulders and gave them a gentle shake. I admit that his touch felt rather pleasant, and I didn't resist.

"Tomas is passionate. Tempestuous. Even you described his painting that way. Speaking as a man, I can say that Tori could really get under a guy's skin. I think Tomas was in love with her. He misinterpreted her interest in him as something else. I saw that, and so did she." He grimaced. "If he made a play for Tori—and I mean if—and she resisted, yeah, I could see the situation getting ugly in a hurry."

"What about Priscilla? What sparked that?"

He furrowed his brow and gave the matter some consideration. "Here's my take on it. Priscilla was unpleasant and a snoop. Anybody could see that. She hinted around enough about the identity of Tori's killer that people believed her. I know that I did. It probably got her killed. After eliminating one person, maybe the killer figured why take chances."

Our discussion had extinguished any spark of romance that might have been in the air. Soon afterwards, Roddy thanked me for taking on the project and left. No more shakes, squeezes, or significant looks. Another romantic strikeout by yours truly.

Chapter Sixteen

I brooded about my exchange with Roddy and did penance by spending the next two hours reading Tori's compendium on Sherborne School. Good thing she was a gifted artist. Tori could have published her writing as a drug-free soporific and made a fortune. It was well past midnight when I rubbed my weary eyes and called it a night. Fantasia put her head in my lap and gave me a soulful look, letting me know that in her eyes at least I was still a hero. It was tempting to just peel off my clothes and climb into bed without following my usual routine but in my mind, Aunt Violet's words rang out.

"Always remove your makeup and apply moisturizer before going to bed, Marky. And for goodness' sake, don't forget eye cream. That undereye area deteriorates first without proper care."

I refused to become a hag. Not when I operated a cosmetics emporium and lectured customers about proper skin care. Besides, that routine was mechanical and provided a degree of comfort in an uncertain world. Just as I doused the lights, Fantasia emitted a fierce growl. Someone was turning the front doorknob. Fortunately, I had fastened both the deadbolt and the chain, so despite what sounded like a key turning in the lock, my visitor's efforts were frustrated. I called out, using my most menacing voice but I suspect it was Fantasia's warning bark that deterred the intruder. Who could it be? More importantly, who should I call for help? Roddy would still be awake but that was a non-starter. I couldn't expect either Claire or Gin to venture out and put themselves in danger. Instead, I chose the only rational course of action. I placed a chair under the doorknob, grabbed a wooden baseball bat from the broom closet, and dialed Gemma's number.

* * *

Sleep eluded me that night even though the conversation with Gemma bolstered my spirits. Leave it to my pragmatic pal to point out that with secure locks and Fantasia at my side, I was unlikely to be in danger. Wait until the morning, she said, and get one of those portable alarms for the door. Or Gemma being Gemma, she urged me to fling myself into Roddy Park's arms and beg for protection. Tempting but not an option.

I spent extra effort that morning deep conditioning my hair and applying a soothing face masque. Nothing buoyed my spirits quite like those small steps and besides, I intended to boldly confront danger and exude self-confidence. Easier said than done since I had no clue about the identity of my putative assailant. After inhaling two lattes, I ventured out to the park with Fantasia close by my side. Plenty of joggers, cyclists, and power walkers populated the area at that hour so I had little to fear. Still, it was heartening to see both Claire and Raleigh as we turned the corner. She noticed my grooming efforts immediately and applauded them.

"Wow! You look as sparkly as a star today. Anything I should know?" She turned her head to the side and gave me a long look. "Gin mentioned that you saw Roddy last night."

Nothing was secret in a closed community of academics with wild imaginations and limited social lives. I brushed off the romantic illusions and focused on my unwanted visitor. Claire immediately embraced me.

"You must have been terrified. I know I would have been. Why didn't you call me?"

"I was petrified but Fantasia kept me sane. Tell me this. Did Tori give anyone else a key to her flat?"

"Probably. I have one. You know how it is. We swapped keys in case of emergency. Besides, sometimes either Gin or I walked Raleigh for her." She sniffled. "Never thought of returning it but I will if you want me to."

I assured her that it wasn't necessary and that I was probably overreacting.

That didn't stop Claire from broadcasting my experience at breakfast that morning. My colleagues displayed a range of reactions from horror to disbelief. Gin clutched my arm, Roddy looked aghast, and Harrison openly sneered.

"Bit of an overreaction, wouldn't you say, Marky? We certainly don't need another drama queen around here. One was more than enough."

Coleman Ross grabbed a seat at the head of the table just as Harrison spoke. "What's all this about?" he asked. "Not another incident, I hope."

I slunk down in my chair, praying for the gift of invisibility. "Nothing, headmaster. Forget it." I chose not to remind him that two murders hardly qualified as "incidents" and were full-blown tragedies.

Roddy quickly changed the subject to the Sherborne School Anthology. "Marky's agreed to finish the project. That's a big relief for me. Can't wait to read about incidents from all your misspent youths."

"I for one refuse to participate in any more grilling," Harrison grumbled. "Leave well enough alone, for heaven's sake."

Harrison was an easy target, and Roddy couldn't resist. "Oh, I don't know, Harry. All your sainted ancestors would enjoy reading about themselves. Most of us don't have your kind of background."

Talk about touching a nerve! Harrison's cheeks grew crimson. He crumpled up his napkin, tossed it on his plate, and stormed off.

The rest of us exchanged puzzled looks. "Touchy, touchy," Gin said.

Roddy's eyes twinkled as he shrugged off the scene. "Guess I better find Harry and do a mea culpa." Coleman joined him, leaving Gin, Claire, and I to giggle about it.

"You know, most folks don't care about their antecedents. After all, it's what you accomplish that counts. But Harry is just rabid about that stuff." Gin scoffed. "Makes a mutt like me feel pretty good. I've had to scrap for everything I ever got. No helping hand from the relatives. I'm the first one in my family to even start college."

"But you have so much to be proud of." Claire gave her friend a hug. "Talent and persistence. It got you into Julliard and landed you a spot here. Clara and I got a helping hand from our school guidance counselor, but it was up to us to stay the course. No free rides, as they say."

I didn't contribute much to that conversation. My artistic talent had helped me get accepted into the Chicago Art Institute but there's no doubt at all in my mind that Aunt Violet smoothed the path for me. Harrison's reaction gave me pause. Suppose his blood was not quite so blue, and Tori found that out? She was too kind to publicize gossip, but Harrison might not believe it. Would he strike out to ensure that his secret was safe?

I pondered this as I headed for my classroom and the group of eager students it contained. Painting soothed the spirit and unleashed creative juices. Most of my proteges had completed their entries for the charity art auction and were applying the finishing touches to their canvases. In honor of Tori, one of her best works had been donated by Senator Jenkins, and it stood to fetch a tidy sum. Aunt Violet had also donated one of her own paintings, a particularly lovely oil of a young girl who looked very familiar. I recalled posing for her over a decade before. Violet captured all the optimism and hubris of a teenager who had never failed and whose future was limitless. Since that time, I'd learned a lot, taken some hard knocks, and was all the better for it. If anyone recognized me in that painting, I planned to steadfastly deny it.

I'd given a lot of thought to my own entry in the show. Most of my works were inspired by the Impressionists, particularly Cassatt and Morisot. Their depiction of female subjects was so vivid that it totally captivated me. One of my personal favorites, which had later been praised by several critics, featured a woman lounging with her dog in a garden. Aunt Violet said it was my best work. Fantasia and Gemma were my models, and I felt quite satisfied with the results, although Gemma swore that I had idealized her. Artists revealed so much of themselves through their work. Claire's compassion and sensitivity rang out in her novel while Gin's grit and determination to succeed were evident in her plays. I wasn't quite sure what secrets my work revealed, and I didn't care to think about it.

No one could deny that Tomas expressed intense emotions through painting. He favored abstract art, particularly that of his idol, Kandinsky. Vivid splashes of paint, bold colors, and freedom from form or traditional rules characterized his work. I admired the lad's talent and vowed that one way or another, I would help him realize his potential. That presumed, of course, that Sergeant Stevens didn't tag Tomas for two murders and relegate his talent to craft sessions in the big house.

I wandered over to his easel and lingered there, absorbing the power of his work. Tomas looked up but didn't acknowledge me. He was in a world of his own, absorbed by creative forces outside our classroom. No wonder Tori had doted upon him. How often does a teacher find such a gifted acolyte? Suddenly Roddy's warning rang in my ears. Had Tomas, this brilliant, passionate youth, poured his heart out to Tori and been spurned? My aunt had cited raging hormones, a factor for most teenagers who hadn't yet learned the lessons of maturity. But no. I refused to accept such a facile explanation.

"Your painting is exquisite, Tomas. Ms. Aaron would be so proud of you."

His reaction told me that Tori's loss still plagued him. Tomas bit his lip and gulped. "Sometimes I feel like she's still with me. Does that make me sound crazy? I hear her voice telling me to take my time and trust my talent. Stuff like that. She never gave up on me. Not like everyone else in my life. I loved Ms. Aaron. She meant everything to me."

I didn't know what to say but sometimes silence is the best response of all. I patted his back and moved over to Ru Taylor's easel. His study of a seaside harbor was all Ru, bright, cheerful, and totally unlike the work I'd just seen. It also had a pedestrian quality to it that separated good intentions from true art. I made a few suggestions which Ru readily agreed to.

"Good thing I'm content to be an amateur, right Ms. Davis?"

I laughed but chose not to comment.

"That's okay," he said. "My parents think I'm a genius. The next Winslow Homer. They have two of Winslow's paintings at home. Guess parental love is blind after all." Natalie crept up behind him and chimed in. "You are a genius, Ru. Just not an artist." The look they exchanged told me that these two were still very much a couple.

"Where's Abigail," I asked.

"Oh! She's over in the drama department with Ms. Hastings rehearsing.

All puckered up to play Juliet with our Romeo here." Ru pointed to Tomas and winked. "Method acting. They take it very seriously. Always perfecting their lines. Stravinsky would be proud of them."

"Aren't you practicing your part?" I asked.

"I prefer the less structured approach," Ru said airily.

"He means he's just lazy," Natalie teased. Ru grinned and acknowledged the truth of her statement. I left them and ventured over to the covered canvas that had belonged to Priscilla. She hadn't finished it, although the influence of Georgia O'Keefe was evident. Staring at the half-finished work saddened me. I hadn't liked the girl and certainly didn't miss her, but her murder and Tori's savage attack still stained the otherwise carefree campus.

Perhaps I would include a brief tribute to Priscilla in the anthology after all. No need to lie or pretend she was the beloved student mentioned by Coleman Ross. I scribbled a few notes into my folder, focusing on Priscilla's fierce desire to achieve in the arts and her talent. Perhaps Gin could suggest something appropriate. After class, I ventured over to the drama department, where Gin and a few students were busily exchanging views on Shakespeare and the parts they had been assigned to. Abigail and another student debated whether Romeo and Juliet were star-crossed lovers or romantic fools who sacrificed their lives for nothing. I was astonished at Abby's passion and vigor. She had always been rather shy, unwilling to court controversy, unlike many of her peers. Gin listened closely to both teens but didn't take sides. Aha, I thought. The mark of an inspired teacher—encouraging the students to think for themselves. Ultimately the debate ended, and class was dismissed. Gin turned my way and chuckled.

"Ah. The passion of youth. Personally, I've always thought Romeo and Juliet were saps. There's nothing romantic about being shoved into a coffin with dirt heaped on you. They probably would have loathed each other after a decade of marriage and five brats."

"My my. Awfully cynical today, Ms. Hastings." I asked her for any anecdotes about Priscilla that I could include in the anthology.

Gin grimaced. "You really intend to finish that piece of folderol, I suppose. Stick to Priscilla's love of Georgia O'Keeffe and Shakespeare. You know who her favorite character was, I suppose."

I shook my head. "Not a clue."

"Iago. That backstabbing liar ruled by jealousy. Go figure. Tells you everything you'd ever need to know about Ms. Priscilla, doesn't it?"

I decided it was wiser to skip that part. "Weren't you two close? She bragged that you were her sponsor to Julliard."

Gin closed her eyes. "Not likely. She was a pest and an irritant. Always stirring the pot. Tori had to watch her like a hawk. Priscilla was supposedly helping with the anthology, but she was really digging for dirt. Do you know that girl even hinted to Claire about her sister's death? Vile."

"Wow! Maybe I'll err on the side of less is more. A few kind words but nothing extravagant. By the way, is there any special nugget about your misspent youth that you'd like to share? I'll bet your pals at Julliard could tell a tale or two."

Gin folded her arms. "Suit yourself but leave me out of it. My life was too dull to interest anyone. Now Roddy or Coleman might have some skeletons in their closets. Dig away. You can't do too much damage in two weeks." She gathered her scripts and briskly dismissed the class. As they exited the theater, several students were still hotly debating the issues raised in Romeo and Juliet. No wonder Shakespeare's words were as relevant today as they were in the seventeenth century. Those universal themes spoke to the human condition, something that sparked the imagination of all ages. I scurried back to my cottage and rescued Fantasia. The sunny weather was perfect for an outing in the park, and by her reaction, I could tell that Fantasia agreed. I filled a backpack with a few snacks and my computer and strolled toward a likely picnic spot. Tori's notes were mostly straw, but I knew that with some hard work and a pinch of imagination, I could spin them into gold. Just call me Rumpelstiltskin! Unlike that fairytale imp, I didn't even need or want to claim anyone's firstborn as my prize. A completed project would satisfy me just fine.

At least one aspect of the project showed great promise. The file contained tons of photos, most of them thoroughly engaging and some equally revealing. Most experts advised that photos drew eyes to one's work much more effectively than prose. I scanned through images of teachers, students, and events from Sherborne School over the prior twelve months. Though I barely knew her, it hurt seeing glimpses of Tori surrounded by a gaggle of kids, bent over her easel, or gazing into Roddy's eyes. Candid shots of Gin and Harrison made me grin, as did impassioned photos of my students engaged in the *Jeopardy* competition. Seeing Claire's warm smile as she groomed Raleigh made me realize how much I had grown to care for her. She was no killer. No one could ever convince me of that. In fact, with a few exceptions, I doubted that any of the Sherborne crew was homicidal. And yet...two women had been viciously murdered. Two lives callously discarded. Someone was responsible, and the culprit was likely among the smiling faces I was looking at.

"Need any help?"

I was so absorbed that I hadn't heard Roddy approaching. Fantasia had, of course, but although she remained alert, she didn't appear to sense any danger.

Although I tried mightily to deny it, I was also growing attached to Roddy. His smile, intelligence, and general good cheer made me welcome any encounters I had with him. That wasn't smart. I would soon be returning to Harbor Bay and the life of an entrepreneur while he would be scaling the heights of academia. Our brief encounter was merely a summer flirtation meant to last but a few months. We hadn't even kissed, for heaven's sake! Good sense told me one thing, but my errant heart ignored it. Some day when I was too old and crotchety to move, I would tame my base impulses. Not for a while, though.

Roddy spoke again. "Making any progress? I know Tori got really frustrated. She said some things should remain secret, whatever that meant. She was so ethical that it tore her up if she found something amiss. Even something relatively minor." He grinned. "Personally, I'd rather enjoy it. A bit of muck can be fun, but sometimes it's deadly."

The look on his face puzzled me. "What are you talking about?"

"You know, too much poking and prodding into other people's lives can be harmful."

I considered the material I'd reviewed in this anthology. Most of it was mundane to the point of utter boredom. Was Roddy hinting that something in this mass of trivia had gotten Tori killed, or was he sending me a warning? I hadn't found any kryptonite among the anecdotes or biographical sketches, yet Priscilla apparently had.

"Did Tori give you any idea what was bothering her? It had to be something big. Otherwise, she would have ignored it." I considered Claire's novel, Abigail's prank, Tomas's juvenile record, and Harrison's suspect heritage. They were embarrassing true, but surely not important enough to kill for. On the other hand, the embezzlement of school funds was serious stuff. Tori would insist on publicizing that type of crime.

Roddy folded his arms and gave me a stern look.

"Don't you ever listen? I'll tell you what I told Tori. Mind your own business. There. It may be trite, but there's some wisdom in it too. Tori was troubled right before her murder. She'd uncovered something that could hurt Sherborne, and she was intensely loyal to the institution. What she found, I don't know, but she made an appointment to meet with the headmaster and discuss it."

I was dumbfounded. This was dynamite, and unfortunately, it pointed straight at Claire. Who else had a secret that could hurt the reputation of the school? Had Tori told Coleman Ross about it? Did Sergeant Stevens know? My mind was flooded with questions but before I said another word, Roddy stopped me.

"Remember what she was like. Tori was the epitome of fairness. Tediously so at times. Before meeting with Ross, she intended to verify the information. Give the person a chance to respond. She told me all about it the night of the Jeopardy contest."

I knew what came next. Fair, ethical Tori arranged to meet someone that evening. She obviously didn't fear whoever it was. That was her mistake. Tori wanted a calm, rational discussion, but her killer thought otherwise. Whatever secret she uncovered, it had to be explosive.

Roddy's face was anguished. "Don't you see? It's my fault that she died. I should have gone with her. Should have insisted. She brushed me off, and that got me mad. I put my ego over her safety."

Without thinking, I clutched his hand and squeezed it. "How could you possibly know? For heaven's sake, this is a school, not the mean streets of Detroit. If Tori wanted help, she would have asked for it."

As his eyes met mine, Roddy pulled me close. We stayed locked together long enough to attract the attention of several students. Ru Peterson, accompanied by Natalie, bounded up in front of us like two pups on the loose. His eyes popped open as he saw us, but Natalie looked away and averted her glance.

"Wow! This is awkward." Although he feigned embarrassment, the boy wasn't bothered at all. It was obvious that he delighted in finding two teachers caught in a romantic clinch.

We broke apart, and Roddy gave them a stern look reminiscent of what I had termed my father's dragon stare. It had always quelled rebellion in me as a child and seemed to have the same effect now.

"Yes, Peterson," Roddy said, foregoing any explanation. "What was it you wanted?"

Ru sputtered and stuttered. "Nothing, Mr. Park. We're just passing by."

"See that you do, and while you're at it, remember that paper of yours on the Cold War. As I recall, it's two weeks late."

Natalie giggled and pulled Ru down the path toward the exit. Roddy rolled his eyes and pulled me close again. "Now. Where were we? I've wanted to do that since we met, but I held back."

"Why?"

He shook his head. "Oh, I don't know. I didn't want you to think I was some kind of sleazy lothario. See, people misunderstood about Tori and me. They cast me in the role of grieving lover, but that wasn't accurate. We'd sort of abandoned the romance thing a while back and were just friends. Good friends, though. I really cared about her. She was a fine person." He grinned. "Besides, you're probably used to guys hitting on you, looking the way you do."

"If you only knew. My record with men is dismal."

My head was spinning with these latest developments. I wasn't consumed by romantic notions, although they were certainly pleasurable enough. It was Roddy's comment about the night of Tori's murder that confirmed my suspicions. The killer had to be someone-either student or faculty—from Sherborne. Someone she trusted and didn't fear. Any of those kids or teachers would have appeared harmless enough. I would probably have made the same mistake. Tori was a strong, independent woman who believed she could fight her own battles without a male protector standing in the wings. Somehow, Priscilla had intuited the identity of the killer as well and probably tried her hand at blackmail. Hubris. Both women had been slain by excessive confidence and pride. My task was to find the identity of Nemesis without suffering the same fate.

"Hey. Are you listening? You seem a million miles away." Roddy eyes were deep brown, a very captivating sight under normal circumstances. I hated to break the spell, but the romance was secondary to finding the killer. Gemma would have had plenty to say about my poor choices when it came to men. Small wonder that I was cruising toward thirty without any serious prospects in sight. Aunt Violet would have understood, but she would also have counseled me to seek balance in my personal life and other pursuits. Moderation. That French approach felt very far afield at this moment.

"Did you tell Sergeant Stevens about Tori's discovery?" I watched Roddy closely, searching for any signs of guilt.

The look on his face told me all I needed to know. "Not really. I mean, I started to, but everyone seemed so positive that it was a mugging. So, I just backed off. It was easier to tell myself that."

I tried mightily to remain neutral, but it was a hard sell. Roddy felt my disgust immediately.

He hung his head for a moment before answering. "Let's face it. I was ashamed of myself, and I took the easy way out. Isn't that what you're thinking? I'm not proud of it, but it's true."

Honesty may be the best policy, but it's hell on romance. I squeezed his hand and tried a less direct approach. "We could see Stevens together. He brushes me off whenever I suggest anything, but with you there, he might listen. I think he's probably sexist. You know, women as alarmists. Plus, he basically accused me of being a fantasist because I read mystery stories."

Roddy chuckled and hugged me. Once again, I found the sensation tolerable, even pleasant. "What about me?" he said. "I read spy stories. Between the two of us, he'll really think we're conspiracy buffs."

Fantasia stirred, put her head on my knee, and gave me a soulful look that said she was hungry.

"I have a suggestion," I said. "Let's analyze each potential suspect for motive and opportunity for both Tori's and Priscilla's murders. We'll do it independently and compare notes before we broach the issue with Stevens."

Roddy nodded. "Objectively and dispassionately too. Exclude no one, even someone we may like."

He meant Claire. I knew he did. Still, I couldn't argue with his logic. It was far too easy to be blinded by friendship. Tori had discounted someone and paid the ultimate price. Priscilla had underestimated her foe and suffered the same fate. I didn't plan to repeat their errors.

"Remember," Roddy cautioned. "Tell no one what we're up to. Promise me that. A double murderer is roaming around here, and we have no idea who we can trust."

He was right, even though the idea was loathsome. I'm basically a blabbermouth, so that meant monitoring every word I said. It would be onerous, and people who knew me would probably wonder what was wrong. On the other hand, discretion might save my life. After a moment, I finally agreed.

"Okay," I said. "I promise."

"One more thing." Roddy put his arm around me. "Make sure you include me in your list of suspects. I could easily have killed them both."

* * *

That evening as I settled down to my task, Roddy's words haunted me. What did I really know about him? True, he was brilliant, gorgeous, and career-oriented but that didn't mean he wasn't hiding something. He could easily have slipped out of the room during the Jeopardy competition without anyone taking note of it. Most men used the restroom at least once during an evening. Women were less likely to do so, except to make repairs to hair and makeup. Once again, I chided myself for making essentially sexist assumptions although in this instance, I believed they were accurate. Thinking about that made me shiver, double-check windows and the front door. I also placed a chair under the doorknob. That wasn't paranoia. It was plain common sense. Who knew how many keys to Tori's flat were floating around Sherborne? As an additional safety measure, I phoned Aunt Violet and shared my plan. She listened patiently, as she always did before voicing her concerns.

"Seems like you're on the right track but don't underestimate your adversary. Remember. Priscilla was murdered right under our very eyes. This killer is smart and audacious, Marky. Cool enough to fool a smart cookie like Tori Aaron and arrogant enough to kill Priscilla in the open."

I assured Violet that nothing was off the table, and no one was above suspicion, even my dearest friends and students at Sherborne. She knew Claire's secret and had already heard Abigail's confession. Neither one seemed likely to damage the school, although Claire might lose her job if it became known. The headmaster bragged incessantly about the famous author on his faculty. A scandal like that was no small thing in the gossipy academic and literary world. It might provoke even a gentle soul like Claire to violence.

"I meant to call you anyway," Violet said. "I spoke with a few of my contacts about Harrison Putnam."

"Oh yeah?" If Harry was the murderer, I wouldn't feel guilty at all. Not one bit. In fact, I might feel jubilant and relish it.

Violet continued her narrative. "Anyhow, seems like the Putnam family is indeed well-connected, wealthy, and socially prominent, just like Harrison says."

There went my hopes for seeing Harrison ensconced in the Big House. What a bummer.

"There's only one catch." Violet gave a dramatic pause. "His side of the family isn't part of that bunch. Harrison comes from the other side of the tracks, relatively speaking."

Unreal. Despite his endless bragging and ancestor worship, our Harrison Putnam was merely a cipher, a hanger-on, who probably yearned for the occasional invitation at Christmas time or the stray crumb of affection from his betters.

"Would that bring actual harm to Sherborne?" I asked. "Embarrassment perhaps, but enough harm to incite violence?" I reminded myself that normal people wouldn't care about their progenitors, but Harrison was scarcely normal. The man's obsession with Tomas proved that.

Violet didn't speculate. However, she did say that Coleman Ross's wife was the ultimate snob who might freeze Harrison out if it became public knowledge. "That woman lives by the social register. Perhaps Harrison considered the humiliation unendurable. You said he and Tori were enemies."

I doubted that Tori would publicize Harrison's secret shame. She was far too compassionate. Priscilla, on the other hand, would have reveled in the knowledge and wouldn't have hesitated to use it to her advantage.

I longed to call Roddy and share the news about our esteemed colleague, but something restrained me. Better to plod on and construct a full list of suspects. Harrison had not joined the *Jeopardy* crowd, but that left him free to arrange a meeting with Tori that evening. He remained on the likely list and even moved up a few notches.

Considering Claire as a suspect aroused every guilty bone in my body. True, she had motive, opportunity, and means, but her genuinely sweet nature ruled her out or at least put her at the very end of my list. Besides, Raleigh loved Claire, and he would have been traumatized if he had witnessed her brutally slaying Tori. My reasoning was weak, but I stuck with it. Didn't everyone always say that animals were excellent judges of character? One day I would puzzle out who spread this "everyone says" nonsense. Until then, I was content to go with the flow.

Tori's scribblings and Priscilla's vague hints were hard to decipher. Gin's name had but one notation beside it. "Find class photo and yearbook from her Julliard graduating class." Like many of us, Gin likely had some less-than-flattering photos or fatuous sayings in the yearbooks. Six years ago, her view of the world was probably very different than her current somewhat jaded perspective. Idealism flourished in academia, but it soon dissipated in the trenches of the real world. I put that task off to the side and focused on Tomas Devereaux. Tori's notes remarked on the talent and potential of her favorite student, and she included several snapshots of his work. I stared at a charcoal sketch of a nude, enraptured by the depth and power it displayed. Then it occurred to me that there was something very familiar about the model. Although her face was turned away, I saw in her profile the familiar features of one Tori Aaron! Every nerve ending in my body exploded. Oh no! I'm no prude, and I understood that artists and models don't always have physical relationships. However, I now understood why so many at Sherborne had remarked that Tori got too close to her students. A school like Sherborne would punish both Tori and Tomas if this became public. Heads would roll. Coleman Ross would levitate, and the parent advisory board would condemn everyone involved, especially the headmaster, for fostering a den of iniquity. That possibility made me scrutinize Ross more closely. He might strike out to deter Tori, but he was not present when Priscilla was murdered. Could he have enlisted the aid of his disciple Harrison Putnam to subdue Priscilla? It all seemed too fantastic to be real. More like the complex plot of a potboiler than life at an upscale prep school.

There were other explanations. Perhaps Tori had not posed for the artist. It was possible to paint or draw a nude from a sketch of a fully clothed model or to superimpose facial features on another body. I decided to confront Tomas directly the very next day before discussing it with Roddy, Claire, or anyone else. The implications were simply too volcanic to ignore. That concluded my detective work for the evening. Instead of pouring myself a good stiff drink, I chose another route. I telephoned Gemma.

Chapter Seventeen

Gemma reacted in typical fashion. The mere idea of a sex angle to the murders thrilled her.

"I'm flabbergasted," she said. "Of course, that Tomas Devereaux has a certain animal magnetism that might tempt any woman even a straight arrow like Tori. He doesn't look like a kid even though I guess he is, technically."

I'd read the Michigan statute and generally, the age of consent was sixteen unless—and this was the big kicker—unless an authority figure like a teacher was involved. Then the age of consent rose to eighteen. Tomas was seventeen. Either way, that left him well within the range of trouble with a capital T.

"We probably shouldn't presume that anything happened between them." My voice sounded prim and oh-so-proper even to my ears. "Most artists don't really see their models as sexual objects. More like something inanimate. Furniture."

"Huh!" Gemma's voice radiated disapproval and disbelief. "I'm no scholar, but I've read enough to know how that works. Tell me this. Did you ever pose nude while you were in art school? Were you somebody's muse, Marky?"

"Certainly not! They hired professional models at the Art Institute. Get your mind out of the gutter and help me think. I need to speak with Tomas first thing tomorrow. Why speculate until he explains things." I shared the scoop about Harrison Putnam and merely a hint about my contact with Roddy.

Gemma chortled at that tidbit. "Good grief, you have been busy. Not that anyone would blame you. That Roddy is one hot number. I'd jump on him right away. Didn't I tell you I sensed something between the two of you?"

I hung up before Gemma started planning my trousseau. She meant well but was fixated on finding Mr. Right for me. That presumed, of course, that she had already found her own prospective mate. I closed my eyes, visualizing the dreadful Deputy Soto, Gemma's current partner. Not a pretty picture.

Fantasia cuddled next to me that night, giving me a sense of comfort and security. No nocturnal visitors disturbed my sleep, and my dreams were rated strictly PG.

The next morning, I scrambled over to the cafeteria, hungry for sustenance and information. Roddy patted an empty seat next to him and motioned to me. "Make any progress last night? he asked, sotto voce. "I got a few ideas."

Gin narrowed her eyes. "You two are up to something. Come on. Give."

"No big deal," Roddy said. "Just finishing up that stupid anthology. Tori left it in a big mess."

I recalled one uncompleted task that might be easily resolved. "Tori wanted your yearbook from Julliard but couldn't find one. May I borrow yours?"

Gin's voice rose. "Absolutely not. If you think I want some truly hideous shots of me bandied about you're crazy! I told Tori that was strictly off-limits. Besides, I never bought one of the stupid things anyway."

Once more, Claire played peacemaker. "I told Tori the same thing. Why resurrect the past when we're focused on the future? She unearthed a copy from Wellesley anyway though. Nothing could stop that girl when she was on a mission. Natalie's aunt had one. Called it 'keeping memories.' You should see the weird hairstyles Clara, and I had." She shook her head at the thought. "Don't be surprised if she has the Julliard one too, Gin."

I listened to their conversation with only half an ear. Today's breakfast servers were Tomas and Abigail, a stroke of luck that I intended to pursue. After crumbling a piece of toast on my plate, I excused myself and set out to confront my gifted student.

Stay calm, I cautioned myself. No accusations or recriminations.

I tapped Tomas on his shoulder and plastered a phony smile on my face. Abigail immediately looked up and flashed that sweet smile of hers. "Hey,

Ms. Davis. Can I get you something?"

"I just need a moment of your time, Tomas. Meet me in the classroom when you're finished here."

He didn't look like a killer, and his reaction was untroubled. "Uh, sure. Will thirty minutes be okay? I'm not in trouble, am I?"

I reassured him that all was well, although it occurred to me that the art studio would be deserted this time of day, leaving me alone and very vulnerable if Tomas became violent. But no, I refused to even consider that possibility. There must be a simple explanation for the nude in the charcoal sketch. Tori Aaron would never take advantage of a student, even a besotted one like Tomas.

I waved goodbye to my colleagues and trudged over to the art studio. True to form, the corridors were deserted, and the lights were dimmed. Coleman Ross had his own ideas about energy saving, and they corresponded to cost reduction for the school. Old buildings creak and moan at the most inopportune times. I forced myself to subdue my imagination, unlock the door, flick on the lights, and stand by my easel as I awaited Tomas. Both my palate and painting knives were at the ready, and while their edges were blunt rather than sharp, they still afforded me a measure of protection. The time passed slowly, each moment seeming like an eternity. I had no strategy for dealing with Tomas. Honesty, that best of all policies, was my only hope. When the door finally swung open, my heart leapt to new heights. Fortunately, I come from strong stock. Tomas edged into the room with a look of trepidation on his face. He was a burly fellow, but I reminded myself that, after all, he was still only a teenager with all the insecurities that entailed.

"I reviewed some of Ms. Aaron's notes and found several of your sketches, Tomas. She was quite a fan of your work."

He hung his head, looking warily at me out of the corner of his eyes. "She inspired me," he said. His voice was reverent, almost a whisper. "Before Ms. Aaron, I had no confidence. It means a lot when someone believes in you. In your talent."

I pulled the charcoal sketch from my folder. "This work is very powerful,

202

Tomas. I'd never seen it before." His muscles tensed, highlighting the anguish that he felt. Time for truth-telling.

"This model looks very familiar. Is it Ms. Aaron? Did she pose for you?"

Tomas's eyes opened wide. "What? Oh no. You've got this all wrong, Ms. Davis." The boy was genuinely surprised and somewhat relieved. "I admit using Ms. Aaron's face, but only that. Please believe me. The torso was someone else entirely." Tomas blushed. "A friend who was kind enough to model for me."

I said nothing. Felt nothing. Merely looked at his face and took a deep breath. Tomas was telling the truth. Every fiber in my being told me that.

"Explain," I said.

He did so in a few short sentences. It was quite simple, really. Tomas needed a model, and Abigail volunteered. She had but one requirement. To avoid embarrassing her dad, she asked that someone else's face be used. Tori had agreed to the proposition.

"People said all kinds of bad things about Ms. Aaron, but they weren't true. She would never have done anything, you know, physical, with one of us. Abby and I...we care for each other."

Shakespeare couldn't have written it better. Our young Romeo and Juliet had something special that Tomas had expressed in that sketch. Love, lust, or something very much like it.

"I had to ask," I said. "Forgive me for prying."

His smile was radiant. "Forget it. Did you really like my work? I'd never worked much in charcoal before." We embarked on a long discussion about the elements of clarity, theme, and creativity that characterized fine art. By the end of our session, both of us, student and teacher were satiated.

Roddy couldn't wait to discuss our project. His enthusiasm was contagious, and I proudly shared my finds about Harrison and Tomas's charcoal sketch.

"No kidding!" You are some detective, lady. My efforts weren't half that good." He had drawn some interesting diagrams, however, showing the positions of each person on the evening of the Jeopardy competition and the bus ride from the DIA. We agreed that the bus ride was a muddled event since almost everyone passed by Priscilla's seat to access the restroom.

Coleman Ross was the only person we ruled out. He was miles away when Priscilla was killed. I floated the possibility that Harrison served as Ross's henchman, but Roddy was unconvinced. Too complicated, he said. Priscilla's killer struck quickly, using that Hermes scarf as a weapon of opportunity. Nothing appeared to be preplanned. More than likely, some incident had occurred during the trip that made her elimination worth the risk. Knowing Priscilla, she probably taunted the killer or made exorbitant demands. The girl saw no limits when her interests were at stake. I closed my eyes, trying to visualize her interactions with students and teachers on the bus. Priscilla's face always sported a perpetual sneer. I'd never seen a genuine smile or friendly expression on the girl, so it was hard to isolate any one incident. She'd annoyed Harrison and been suitably chastised. Roddy had once again openly snubbed her attempts to vamp him, and Priscilla had been insolent to both Claire and me. Par for the course for that little madam, hardly a prelude to murder. I finally recalled something significant. Priscilla said that she had slipped out during the Jeopardy contest. Harrison and I both heard her hint that she had seen Tori's killer. I thought it was mere bombast, but suppose the killer heard It too? Would Priscilla be foolish enough to tease that person knowing the possible consequences? Absolutely. I suspected that she blackmailed the culprit or intended to do so. So many teenagers, even sophisticated ones like the Sherborne students, lived in a surreal world populated by super-heroes, podcasts, and internet rumors. Death rarely intruded on their worldview, and they certainly didn't expect tragedy to grasp them in its cold clutches. No doubt Priscilla saw herself as an invulnerable combination of Lady Macbeth, Wonder Woman, and Iago. Instead, an unlovely fate had cast her as a modern-day Ophelia, doomed to die alone and un-mourned in the back of a school bus.

I'm no quitter, and I'm certainly no coward. But I longed with all my heart to forget Sherborne, murder, that blasted anthology, and detective work. I wanted to return home. I missed my friends and like the Sirens of old, the soothing song of cosmetics beckoned to me. The killer had defaced Tori, using cheap mascara to send a message. Surely Sergeant Stevens would nab the guilty party. Ultimately. He was a plodder, but with the clues Roddy and

I had assembled, the end was near. I glanced at the charcoal sketch that bore Tori Aaron's face. She was a fearless fighter for justice, but I was merely an artist who beautified the world whenever possible. It was unnerving to face my colleagues and students each day, knowing that one of them was a ruthless murderer. Trust was a luxury I simply couldn't afford, but cynicism didn't suit me either. Face facts, I told myself. Beneath someone's placid exterior, witty asides, and intellectual depth, evil lurked. It was both profoundly disheartening and exhausting to even consider that. My pledge to Aunt Violet had been naïve and presumptuous. I had failed her and Tori Aaron.

"Marky, are you okay? We need to finish that anthology this weekend."

Roddy's look of alarm brought me back to earth. I'd been woolgathering when I had some very pressing responsibilities to fulfill. "Don't worry. I just need to assemble a few more things. Funny, though, we don't have anything about the headmaster. Maybe I'll drop by and see about that."

Roddy's frown told me he disagreed. "You know how stuffy Coleman is. Just stick with the formal stuff from the school website. He won't welcome any candid photos or anecdotes unless they laud him for his devotion to Sherborne. He certainly won't like any prying into his private life."

"You're probably right. I was able to snag some old yearbooks from Julliard and Wellesley, though. Natalie's Aunt Carolyn came through like a champ. Claire coughed up some old shots of her and her sister Clara too. Boy, it was like pulling teeth to get that stuff. Gin refused any part in it and Harrison echoed that. According to Tori's notes, she had to plead for cooperation and didn't always get it. I thought we'd call it the Sherborne Chronicles. Make it a retrospective of the school year with a shot of levity added."

Roddy suggested that they include a slideshow to liven up the art auction. Aunt Violet had agreed to conduct the proceedings, and she loved the concept. I heard that Senator Jenkins also planned to attend, but my aunt was circumspect on that topic. Either way, the entire weekend was a festival, complete with the Shakespeare Unbound presentation and the fundraiser. It was a fitting end to the summer term and served a good cause.

That evening at dinner, Claire asked for a favor. She had completed the first draft of her novel and wanted feedback. Honest feedback, she insisted. "Gin and Roddy will join us later. I value their opinions, but they might feel obliged to be kind rather than honest." Claire laughed. "After all, they must face me every day. It pains me to say it, but you, my dear, will soon return to the real world. You can afford to take a risk."

We agreed to meet at eight o'clock. Fantasia was waiting for her supper, so I scurried back to my lodging to feed that good girl. Afterwards, the two of us trotted over to Claire's.

She was anxious. I could tell by the feverish light in her eyes and the spots of color that dotted her cheeks. I took the first five chapters and settled into the wing chair with Fantasia curled up at my feet. Once again, I was captivated by the first sentence by Claire's moving account of dealing with a sister's passing and the survivor's guilt it entailed. The title was *Reverie*, and its power was so compelling that I sped through those five chapters yearning for more.

My absorption was such that I barely noticed when Roddy and Gin arrived. Claire hastily collected the manuscript and ignored Roddy's quizzical look. Closed communities like Sherborne offered very little excitement and therefore bred an almost unnatural interest in the lives of others. Gin was either too well-mannered or otherwise occupied to notice. I knew that the forthcoming Shakespeare event consumed most of her waking hours. Gin was a perfectionist who agonized over every negative possibility and demanded the same standards from her students.

Both demanded an update on the Sherborne Chronicles saga, especially Claire, who offered to pen a dedication and tribute to Tori. Her eyes teared up as she said her friend's name, and Gin gave her a generous hug.

"Don't cry, Claire. Tori wouldn't want you to be sad."

Roddy agreed. "We should be celebrating her life, not mourning her death. You know, I almost abandoned my dissertation until Tori read me the riot act. She was all about achieving excellence no matter what the cost."

Claire and Gin agreed, although Gin reminded us that living up to those high standards wasn't always easy.

"Tori dealt with absolutes and that could cause angst, especially from the kids. They lived to please her."

That brought me back to motive. If Tori spurred others on to greater heights, she would have been outraged by pretenders, those who were false prophets. Apparently, she had uncovered such a poseur lurking among the students or faculty at Sherborne and proposed to out the offender.

It was a wonderful evening full of friendship and good cheer. We discussed our students, sipped hot apple cider, and toasted the draft of Claire's novel. Roddy and Gin demanded to see those same five chapters I had read, and in the end, Claire relented. Just before midnight, we scattered for home. Fantasia joined Raleigh for a romp and a final comfort break before turning in. As we approached my apartment, her fur bristled, and she uttered a low, menacing growl. I looked around but saw no one. The front door was firmly fastened, and all seemed in order. "What's the matter, girl? Did some strange animal walk by here?" I patted her silky fur and unlocked the door. That's when my blissful night ended.

Chapter Eighteen

T he entire living room was the scene of chaos. Papers were strewn about, pillows askew, and worst of all, the lovingly assembled work on the anthology was either missing or destroyed. Fortunately, my laptop was still intact, but Tori's outline and Priscilla's notes were gone along with assorted photos and the yearbooks from Wellesley, Julliard, and Amherst. The destruction stunned me. A normal, sensible reaction would have been to immediately flee the apartment and notify the authorities. I proved once again that my synapses weren't always firing. I plopped into the damaged wing chair, clutched Fantasia, and fumbled in my purse for my cell phone. This time I had absolutely no pride. I dialed Roddy's number immediately.

His approach to a crisis was far superior to mine. Roddy responded immediately after calmly urging me to call the police, step outside the apartment and await his arrival. A rumpled and slightly irascible Sergeant Stevens followed closely behind him, looking as if he had just awakened from a sound sleep.

Stevens made no attempt to coddle me. His manner was gruff and openly suspicious.

"No forced entry," he observed. "You sure you didn't leave things this way?"

My first reaction was outrage. Weren't the police supposed to protect and serve? That's what it said on their cruisers. I didn't cry although I felt perilously close to doing so. Roddy pointed out that in this complex several people shared keys with their neighbors. No one had much worth stealing in our academic paradise and many had plants or pets that needed attention.

Stevens narrowed his eyes and sneered.

"Two murders don't count, I suppose. Especially when Ms. Davis here has been snooping around and playing detective. You people are something else. No sense of survival. No wonder a killer has it made."

I bristled at that, but Roddy put his arm around me and squeezed. No sense in alienating Stevens even more. Besides, it was late, and I lacked the energy to fight back. If I expected him to summon a full forensic team ala *CSI*, I was doomed to disappointment. Stevens advised me to check the windows and door again, get some sleep and change the locks in the morning.

"I'll be gone in two weeks," I protested. "Why bother."

Stevens lowered his glasses, but before he launched into the stern lecture that I truly deserved, Roddy intervened. "I plan to stay with her tonight, Sergeant. Don't worry. She'll be safe."

My hopes were dampened when he added, "The couch looks comfortable enough."

Once we were alone, I unfolded the futon and handed him a pillow and blanket. "You didn't have to stay you know." I couldn't help adding. "But I'm glad you did. This whole mess has me shaken. I'm usually more courageous."

"Who can blame you?" Roddy said. "Besides, after a few hours' sleep, we'll try to sort everything out." He checked his watch. "Wow. It's almost one o'clock already. Close your bedroom door and take Fantasia with you."

If there was any lust in his eyes, I missed it. Like me, Roddy was probably tuckered out. I followed his suggestion, turned off the light, and burrowed under the covers with my faithful canine companion. Despite my misgivings, I immediately fell into a deep, dreamless sleep.

* * *

Roddy slipped out of my apartment early enough to avoid the prying eyes of my colleagues. At the communal breakfast, I shared the sad, scary saga of my brush with the killer. Claire was speechless. She put her hand over her mouth and stared, bug-eyed. Gin had plenty of questions but very few insights.

"What will you do about your project?" she asked. "Forget it, I say. Somebody wants you to and isn't shy about showing it. Your safety is more important than that stupid anthology."

Harrison merely raised one eyebrow and smirked. "Funny what some people will do for attention, isn't it? Who would risk being caught for something that inconsequential?"

His implication was clear. Once again, Harry was suggesting that I had fabricated the incident. I lacked the energy to respond, but Roddy stepped in.

"For once in your life, Harry, try to act like a decent human being. Marky was terrified. I saw that myself."

All heads swiveled his way and exchanged knowing looks. Roddy flushed but didn't flinch. "Cut it out, you guys. I slept on the couch. No hanky-panky, just concern for a friend."

Too bad his words were true. Fantasia kept me nice and warm, but Roddy's arms would have been even more welcome. His scowl told me that he hadn't finished with Harrison yet. He faced his colleague without flinching. "By the way, where were you last night? You could easily have broken in while the rest of us were at Claire's."

Harry's outrage was almost comical. "How dare you accuse me. I'll have you know I was with my family last evening."

Before hostilities escalated, the solemn figure of Coleman Ross appeared. He touched my shoulder in a rare display of emotion. "Are you all right, Ms. Davis? Sergeant Stevens just called me." He finger-combed his silver mane. "This outrage must stop. What will the trustees say?"

No one had the answer to that, but we could all speculate. Murders and mayhem were scarcely the portrait of Sherborne that inspired confidence in parents or donors.

"Perhaps we should consider canceling next weekend's events," Coleman said. "No need to arouse outside interests."

Claire and Gin immediately intervened. "Headmaster, I beg you not to do that," Claire said. "Questions would arise, and the impact on our scholarship drive would be devastating."

Gin echoed her concern. "We've publicized the event throughout the area, and the students have worked so hard. They would be heartbroken."

Roddy nodded in agreement, and even Harrison concurred.

Coleman closed his eyes for a moment. "I suppose you're right. But for heaven's sake, forget about that anthology. No document is worth this fuss." He glared my way as if I were the culprit. "Simple biographies will suffice, Ms. Davis." With that, the voice of authority spoke, leaving the rest of us with our marching orders. Coleman did an about-face and marched for the door with Harrison trailing in his wake.

My students were assembled in the studio, applying the finishing touches to their paintings. From the side glances they threw my way, I realized that word had spread about my nocturnal visitor. Not surprising in a closed society where gossip was an accepted currency. Ru Peterson finally summoned the courage to ask. "Are you okay, Ms. Davis? We heard you got clobbered by the killer, and Professor Park saved you." Natalie cringed at the thought, but Tomas kept his head down.

"Not true," I said. Natalie heaved a sigh of relief after I filled them in. No doubt they remembered the grisly fate suffered by Tori and, more recently, Priscilla. Personally, I preferred to forget those images and move on. "Here's some good news. The headmaster agreed not to cancel our art auction and drama presentation. That means you guys must hoof it. Violet Davis and Natalie's Aunt Carolyn will start evaluating your projects bright and early next weekend. No exceptions."

That piece of news sobered them up immediately and inspired my students to stop chattering and get to work. At noon I hustled back to my apartment to rescue Fantasia for our lunchtime walk. My approach was tentative, even though I realized that with a vigilant collie in residence, an intruder was unlikely to strike. I gathered up our gear and set out for the park at a brisk trot, stopping only to quell the persistent ringing of my cell phone. Not surprisingly, my aunt was already on the case. She assessed my state of mind and made a few deft suggestions to assuage my anxiety. "Sounds like you hit a nerve with that anthology business," Violet said. "It seemed innocuous. Can you think of anything that might spark a violent response?"

I confessed that my efforts were pedestrian, hardly more exciting than the average Facebook or website bio. "The yearbook photos were amusing enough. Kids would enjoy seeing their teachers in unguarded moments, I suppose. Luckily, I uploaded most of the snapshots to the cloud, so no harm was done there. I'll finish it and take it over to the Office Depot. Let them print the programs."

Violet paused. "Sergeant Stevens was right, you know. You should change those locks or do something to protect yourself."

Visions of Roddy Park floated unbidden through my mind. They were only slightly salacious but very satisfying.

When Violet suggested that I bunk in with Claire, I confessed the awful truth. "Suppose Claire is the killer? She has a lot to lose, and let's face it, she was on the scene of both murders." The list of suspects I had compiled included Claire, Gin, Harrison, and even Roddy, in addition to several of my favorite students. It pained me to admit that Tomas, that superbly talented artist topped my hit parade. I hoped I was wrong. Prayed that I was.

"I gave some thought to your situation," Violet said. "Expect a surprise to arrive this afternoon. It will help you feel safe."

That brightened my day. Leave it to my dear aunt to think ahead and protect my interests. She wouldn't send a weapon of course but perhaps it was some sort of burglar alarm. After class, I sped back to the apartment, feeling a sense of anticipation. An hour later, the doorbell chimed, and Aunt Violet's surprise arrived.

Gemma Reed stood on my doorstep!

* * *

She held out her arms and gave me a big hug. I normally avoid such displays, but this time was different. Near-death experiences will do that to you.

"You're my surprise?" I asked. "Who's minding the store?"

She gave me her trademark eye roll. "So practical. My mom and Violet have things under control. I'm your official guard dog and protector." Gemma bared her teeth. "Sorry, Fantasia."

I ushered her into the living room and stowed her valise in the closet. "I missed you. Things have gotten so crazy here and I'm not sure who to trust. How long can you stay?"

Her response was enigmatic. "As long as you need me. Between the two of us we might just make something of this hash."

I brewed a pot of tea, unearthed a package of semi-stale biscuits, and settled in to discuss the case with my friend. Watching Gemma lean forward and brush aside her russet curls unleashed a wave of nostalgia. How many times over the years had we repeated this ritual? We rarely resolved anything, but airing our views added clarity to seemingly insoluble problems. Gemma's approach was intuitive rather than intellectual. She brought insight and a keen sense of human nature to any issue. Unlike me, she was seldom blinded by affection or misguided loyalty, except in the case of Benny Soto. That was a very different matter, however. Love can indeed be blind.

I shared my analysis of suspects, motives, and opportunity, watching as she studied each name. Gemma scratched her head when she finished reading.

"Gee, I don't know, Marky. None of this jumps out at me. Except for Claire. That stuff with her novel is a big deal, isn't it?"

I closed my eyes and mouthed a quick prayer. *Not Claire. Please, Lord.*

"I suppose it could be. What about the others? Anything strike you?"

Gemma curled her lip when discussing Harrison. We both agreed that discovery of his inflated heritage could have tipped the scales toward violence. "He's such a creep," Gemma said. "Ugh! Does he have the guts to strangle Priscilla right in plain sight? I wonder." That got me thinking. Our killer was intelligent, cool, and cunning. Those adjectives could fit Harrison under the right circumstances, but they were equally applicable to several others, including Roddy, Gin, and Ru. Tomas was passionate, likely to erupt unexpectedly, while Natalie and Abigail would agonize over any violent act. Coleman Ross, that aloof aristocrat, would be more inclined to delegate an undesirable task to one of his menials.

Gemma scrutinized the dry-as-dust biographies of students and staff and yawned. "No big deal. I suppose these colleges mean something to your crowd."

"Yeah! Wellesley, Dartmouth, Amherst, Julliard, and of course, the Art Institute of Chicago. They're part of the gold standard in academic circles. I'll bet you won't find even one teacher at Sherborne without that type of pedigree."

"Humph," Gemma snorted. "Doesn't mean they're any smarter than other people, does it?"

She was sensitive about that issue, so I immediately tried to reassure her.

"Guess they'd think someone like me was just dirt." Gemma took a mighty sip of her tea. "Snobs. I hate snobs. Everyone here probably came from a rich family."

"Not really," I said. "Claire and her sister had a middle-class upbringing, and Gin was the first in her family to attend college. Tomas and Natalie are scholarship students."

That mollified Gemma somewhat, although I could still hear her grumbling as she unpacked her things. Fortunately, dinnertime was upon us. I dangled the prospect of chicken pot pie before Gemma and immediately activated her taste buds. Although she was tall and svelte, my pal had the appetite of a lumberjack. "Lead me to it," she said.

Dinner ended up being a festive affair. Everyone greeted Gemma like an old friend, and the conversation was light and lively, devoid of any mention of murder or mayhem. As expected, the entrée was lip-smacking good. Gemma and Roddy both dove into second helpings while the rest of us cleaned our plates. Lemon tarts, one of my favorite sweets, completed the meal.

"Any chance of booking a massage while you're here," Gin asked. "My muscles ache from hauling all that stage furniture around."

When Gemma agreed, the floodgates opened. Claire and Roddy also scheduled a session, as did the unflappable Ru Peterson. "Kind of young for that type of pampering, aren't you?" Roddy teased.

"No, sir. Hunching over my computer takes a toll. That paper on the Cold War that you assigned almost finished me off."

I gazed fondly at my colleagues and students, knowing full well that we were unlikely to meet once I returned to Harbor Bay. Fingers crossed, I hoped that Roddy would be the exception to that rule. Gemma reached into her bag and retrieved a small box. "Violet sent this for you, Gin. Lancôme's best. It doesn't smear, and she recommends it."

Roddy leaned over and snatched the parcel. "Mascara? What's that about?"

Gin and Claire bowed their heads. Roddy realized his mistake and apologized. "Gee, I'm sorry. That stirs up some bad memories. I'm such a clod!"

Claire, ever the peacemaker, patted his shoulder. "Don't fret. Men don't use this much."

Gin followed up by asking about the anthology. "I suppose the final version is a mere shadow of its former self."

I agreed. "More like a wisp than a shadow, but it should do the trick. I managed to save a few choice snapshots, though, including one of Tori with her students. Even a clip of Priscilla with a smile on her face." Our group scattered after that, although Roddy paused to chat with Gemma and me.

"Will you two be okay tonight?"

Gemma scoffed. "I defy anyone to try messing with us." She made a muscle. "Massage training makes for strong arms."

He insisted on walking us back to the apartment and waiting while we checked for any problems. Gemma, the perpetual matchmaker, herded him into the living room for a spot of brandy.

"Might as well toast Sherborne, the students and faculty, and those kids." A lump formed in my throat as I said that. What would become of those eager teens with their bright eyes and big dreams in the years to come? Tomas would head for the Chicago Art Institute if I had any influence whatsoever. Most of the others were slated for the Ivys or similar institutions. For them, it was the beginning, while for us, an important phase was ending. Sad but a vital part of life.

Roddy settled into the loveseat while Gemma claimed my couch. She struggled to get comfortable, rearranging cushions and reaching under the bottom. "This thing is ready for the junk heap," she said. "What'd you stuff it with anyway? Feels like cement?" Gemma pulled a lump of paper from underneath and laughed. "Hey. Aren't these those yearbooks you were squawking about?" Sure enough, copies from Amherst, Wellesley, and Julliard tumbled out of her hands and littered the floor. I'd already salvaged mine from the Art Institute.

"Let me see those," Roddy said. "You probably won't recognize me." He was wrong, of course. How many hunky guys with thick black locks and trim bodies exist, even in college? The only difference I could detect was a Fu Manchu mustache and the length of his hair. Roddy sported a ponytail during his senior year. He had since trimmed it to meet the rigorous standards of Sherborne School.

"Oh man," he said. "The Pride of Amherst." I grabbed the Wellesley yearbook and quickly located Claire and her sister Clara in the literary section. Gin must have studiously avoided the photographers because I could find nothing from her time at Julliard. My images from college were presentable. I proudly stood next to my easel, grinning broadly, and displaying my senior project.

"We'll use some of these shots during the opening ceremony," I said. "Give the kids some hope that they can do better."

After toasting our misspent youths, Roddy departed leaving Gemma and me to clean up. "That guy's a keeper," she said. "Don't let him slip away."

She meant well, but I'd found it was wiser to ignore her matchmaking efforts. We locked the door, placed a chair under the knob, and checked the windows. "Only a pygmy could fit through those," Gemma groused. "Man. I am really tired." She yawned and headed for the bedroom to ready herself for the night. Fantasia usually slept with me, but even a queen-sized bed wouldn't accommodate three of us. I placed her pillow on the floor with a blanket and ignored the pitiful glance she gave me. Tomorrow was the final weekend before the auction. The finale. Somehow that word sounded ominous rather than descriptive. I resolved to avoid even thinking about it.

Chapter Nineteen

Weekends mean nothing to aspiring artists and actors. We dove into our projects head-on, determined to finish them up in style. Although she knew virtually nothing about art, Gemma surveyed each of my students' efforts and pronounced them perfect. She was too tactful to mention the unfinished work left by Priscilla. I'd considered removing the canvas, but it felt like a callous act, as if I were erasing the artist as well. Perhaps I was motivated more by guilt than altruism. Even in death, a malevolent air surrounded the girl, and everything attached to her. Mourning someone like Priscilla was no easy task.

Gemma was more intrigued by the Shakespeare Unbound rehearsals that Gin with the help of Claire, was shepherding. Since the role of Ophelia had been vacated by Priscilla's death, Gemma agreed to step in. I believed that she was secretly thrilled to participate in the event. No doubt Soto and the regulars in Harbor Bay would be regaled with snippets from the program.

As the term ended, I experienced several emotions: guilt at my inability to avenge Tori, and sadness at the thought of leaving Sherborne and the people I cared about. On the plus side, I felt justifiable pride in my work with students. By guiding their efforts and bolstering their confidence, I had contributed to their future. Violet had already agreed to sponsor Tomas for a scholarship to the Art Institute, but there were other options as well.

"Doesn't Julliard have a visual arts program?" I asked Gin. "Tomas might fit in there, and you must have contacts."

She shrugged. "Not really. As drama students, we stayed pretty much to ourselves. Someone like Natalie's aunt might be a good source." I was surprised by her indifference but said no more. When the Fall term started, other mentors for my students would emerge.

Meanwhile, Roddy's exuberant mood enlivened the entire lunch table. He'd received great news about his dissertation, and the prospect of an assistant professorship at Michigan was dangled before him. In between bites of pizza, he teased Claire about her college yearbook photos. "You looked so serious," he said. "Your solemn pronouncements about literature were inspiring." He stole a glance at Harrison. "And you, Harry. Dartmouth never had a more dapper mathematician."

That drew a grimace from Harrison, who nevertheless chose to ignore the jibe. "Good to see you in such high spirits, Park."

Gemma explained that we had unearthed the yearbooks after all. "Stuffed under the couch, can you believe it? Your local cops didn't do much of a search."

That comment drew a universal groan. "Stevens only cares about real crimes," Gin said.

"Really? Is that why he's solved our two murders so quickly?" Harrison asked. "Face it. The guy's a hack. For the record, I never had a key to Tori Aaron's apartment or anyone else's either."

Claire tried to play peacemaker by changing the subject. "I haven't even looked at those old yearbooks in ages. Carolyn was in the first two, but then, of course, she transferred to Julliard."

Tomas, our designated server, appeared with a fresh tray of cheese pizza. I'm ashamed to admit that we quickly demolished another pie. I made some desultory comments about his art project, which he acknowledged with a brusque nod. The lad's social skills were indeed lacking. Fortunately, his artistic ability compensated for them. After he left, Harrison made a trademark comment. "Looks like Senator Jenkins has his hands full with that fellow as a prospective son-in-law. Not exactly cocktail party material."

"Ah, come on," Roddy said. "Abigail and Tomas are just kids. Too young to get serious."

That inspired a spirited discussion about romance, with several of us providing vivid examples of love gone awry. Romeo and Juliet figured prominently in our arguments, as did Othello and Desdemona, and Hamlet and Ophelia.

Gemma zoned out of the conversation when it took a literary turn. She focused instead on her massage schedule. Gin claimed the early slot, pleading for help with her aching back. "You lucked out, you know," Gemma told her. "No trace of you in that yearbook. Not like Roddy here. His mustache took up the entire page."

Our meal ended as Roddy mounted a vigorous defense of hirsute males at Amherst, which we immediately shouted down. Gemma and I scurried back to the apartment to free Fantasia and gather our materials. Time was tight, and when my pal offered to walk my furry friend, I jumped at the chance. "Make sure you lock the place up," I said. "Don't take any chances."

She waved me off and hitched up Fantasia's harness while I sped off to class, eager to evaluate my students' efforts. Ru's completed work was perfectly adequate, although in no way spectacular. Despite that, I knew that his parents would proudly display the canvas and brag about their offspring. Natalie was still working feverishly on her collage, an amalgamation of photos, fabric, and news clippings that celebrated her time at Sherborne. She termed it a pastiche, a remembrance of good times, but I noted that a sizable portion of the work featured glimpses of Tori. I applauded her creativity and moved back to Abby's easel. Her painting, a delicate watercolor of the lake area surrounding the campus, was no work of genius, but it displayed a sensitivity and delicate touch that rendered the canvas appealing. I never compared any of my students to Tomas. Quite frankly, he was a true artist while they were mere dabblers. No problem. There was room in my class for all sorts of creative outlets.

We worked later than usual and when I saw the time, I was astonished. Our absorption was such that nobody had complained or even noticed. I shooed them out, carefully locked the room, and sped toward the apartment to find Gemma. A surprise awaited me there: Gemma was entertaining a visitor.

Chapter Twenty

"Not here already for your massage, are you? I thought we agreed on later tonight."

She was perfectly composed; hands folded and smile affixed. The Julliard catalog, an eight-inch boning knife, and a tube of cheap mascara lay by her side.

"Where's Gemma? And Fantasia?" I forced myself to remain calm although a note of panic crept into my voice.

"Don't worry," she said. "Gemma's taking a nap, and Fantasia is fine. I would never hurt an animal."

"What did you do to Gemma?"

She shrugged. "Nothing fatal. Not yet. You see, I brought a bottle of wine. A nice neighborly gesture. I'm afraid it didn't agree with her. She gulped down a big glass of

the stuff and then had to rest. I don't suppose she has an alcohol problem, does she?"

"What's going on? I don't understand."

Gin Hastings bared her teeth. "That's your problem, Marky. You don't understand. I tried everything but you wouldn't let it go. Now look where we are." She moved over to the front door and fastened the latch.

The woman was obviously mad, in the bat-shit-crazy sense, not angry. This petite redhead with the engaging manner had murdered two people and planned some grisly fate for two more. I hadn't a clue what motivated her.

"If this is a joke, Gin. Stop it. I'm not laughing." I took a deep breath, fighting to maintain my composure. Her complacency was the most frightening thing of all. Hard to recall that I was facing a double murderer with the face of a friend.

She picked up the knife and fingered the blade. "Ooh. That's sharp. Should more than do the job. They say hunters use it to cut through bone. I oppose killing innocent creatures, of course, but most humans aren't so innocent. Naturally, I'll be hysterical when I find your bodies. I'm a terrific actress, as you know."

If she expected kudos, she was mistaken. Oddly enough, the only emotion I felt was anger. "Stop this nonsense right away and tell me what's going on. Is it some kind of drama thing you're practicing?"

My cell phone rang, but I knew better than to answer it. Gin's repressive frown was enough to end any ideas I might have had.

Remain calm. Act nonchalant. Pretend to have a rational conversation.

"Why kill Tori? I thought you liked her. Priscilla, I can certainly understand. I wanted to choke that hussy myself on several occasions. But why Tori?"

Gin blinked away a tear that formed in her eye. "I adored Tori, just like everyone else. She was my best friend."

"Then why...?" I was truly puzzled.

"Tori found out my secret. I begged her not to tell, but she said she was honor bound to alert Coleman. Honor bound! Her very words. Never mind what it would do to my life."

I still had no earthly idea what her secret was, but the longer we spoke, my odds of survival increased.

"What could you possibly have done that was so bad?"

Gin grabbed the Julliard yearbook and thumbed through it. "Look at this." She pointed to the last page, where the names of the graduates for that year were listed.

Gin hissed. "I knew you were thick, but this is ridiculous. Tori got it right away."

My stupor only fueled her rage. Gin flung the book across the room, hitting me in the shin. "I said look at it, Marky."

"Ouch! That hurt." No need to pretend.

Her reaction frightened me, and I feared that things would not end well.

"Look at that list again, genius. You're supposed to be the great detective, aren't you? To tell you the truth, I don't even think you're much of an artist." Gin snarled. "Family connections. That says it all, doesn't it?"

The list of Julliard graduates was lengthy, but one name was missing. Virginia Hastings.

"Where's your name, Gin?"

"You finally figured it out," she said. "That's my big secret. I never graduated from Julliard or any other University. I failed. Got kicked out. They sugarcoated it, but the result was the same. I wasn't good enough for their precious community. Without a scholarship, I was up the creek. No Aunt Violet to bail me out, no ma'am."

No wonder Tori Aaron reacted. Gin's duplicity was a firing offense and might affect state accreditation if an audit were conducted. Somehow, she had gamed the system, relying on the laxity so common in many institutions.

"Weren't you afraid the school would find out?" I pictured Coleman Ross clutching his chest in a death spiral.

She laughed. "At first, I was terrified. Never thought I'd get away with it, but I did. Then I became part of the Sherborne scenery. Good old reliable Virginia Hastings. Until Tori stuck her nose in."

Gin was animated as she relayed the events leading up to the murders. It almost felt like a scene from Shakespeare Unbound. Tori had contacted her for a private meeting, certain there had been a mistake that could be rectified.

"I begged...pleaded with her to ignore it. After all, it was my life hanging in the balance. But she didn't care. Integrity was more important than my future."

Gin's face contorted in a mask of hatred as she waved that tube of mascara in the air. "I had a Darwinian choice. Survival of the fittest. I chose to survive. Little Miss Perfect didn't like cosmetics, so I gave her a deluxe makeup job with this cheap junk."

As I listened, it became apparent that Julliard had made a huge blunder.

Gin was a consummate actress, academy award caliber. She'd played the part of the cheery sprite perfectly. No one, including me, would cast her as the killer.

My cell phone buzzed yet again, as if it were an impatient insect ready to sting. Gin didn't seem to notice it. She was far too involved in recounting her tale.

"I suppose Priscilla found out somehow?"

Gin nodded as if it were a pleasant memory.

"Nasty piece of work. Deserved what she got. All those hints about Tori's murder. I couldn't take the chance. When I distributed those chocolates on the bus, I nipped over and garroted her with that scarf. No one even noticed. It was surprisingly easy."

Our conversation was surreal, but it was coming to an end. I had to think fast if I wanted to survive. "So. Where does that leave us now? You can't possibly handle both Gemma and me."

Her grin was malevolent. "Oops! Forgot to tell you. I took some precautions. Gemma is tied up good and tight, and Fantasia is in her crate." She waved the knife. "That leaves only you, and I'm up to that task."

Gin rose slowly and walked my way. I edged toward the back of the couch, searching frantically for a weapon, anything that might deter her. Too bad ashtrays were no longer in vogue, and firearms were in short supply. Then it struck me. If only I could reach my backpack, there was hope. Earlier that morning, I'd packed Fantasia's leather lead and a small container of pepper spray in there. Gin wasn't the only one who could take precautions but outrunning that boning knife was a dicey proposition.

Some subtle gesture must have given away my plan. Gin eyed the backpack and quickly moved beside it. "Sorry, Marky. That's not going to work." She flung my only hope far away and continued her forward march. I positioned myself next to the end table. As I grasped it, I felt something solid and heavy. That leatherbound unabridged version of Shakespeare's tragedies with steel engravings fit neatly into my hand and gave me a final chance to save my life. Just one but that was enough.

I heaved that volume at Gin's head and scored a direct hit. The heft of it stunned her, causing her to cry out and drop the knife. I wasted no time. Before she recovered, I scooped up the boning knife, grabbed my cell phone, and stampeded out the front door, screaming for help at the top of my lungs. The rest of the story was rather a blur. Doors flew open and familiar faces appeared. Roddy came running, and Claire, with Raleigh at her side, hastened to my aid. While she phoned the police, I rushed back to free Gemma and Fantasia. Gin was still groggy and presented no problem when Sergeant Stevens arrived to take charge.

"Quite a weapon," Roddy said, pointing at the book. "Ironic that the tragedies stopped her. Gin always loved those plays."

I couldn't help making a jest. "Truly an example of Shakespeare Unbound."

* * *

Gemma had a monster headache but was otherwise unharmed. Fantasia apparently slept through the entire episode. The next few days were a blur of police statements, official interviews, and attempts to console our students and explain the incomprehensible. Against all odds, the charity art show and drama presentation went on as scheduled the next weekend. Aunt Violet assisted with the auction, and Natalie's Aunt Carolyn guided the drama presentation to a rousing success. Despite or perhaps because of the notoriety, we attracted twice the crowd we had planned for and raised an astounding amount for the scholarship fund.

On my final day at Sherborne, colleagues and students feted me with good wishes and more than a few tears. Even Harrison had warm words for my contribution to the school, although he never said he would miss me. Coleman Ross presented me with a handsome plaque commemorating unspecified services to Sherborne.

I knew I would stay close to Claire, who had become especially dear to me, and hoped the same held true for Roddy. He reminded me that his new post in Ann Arbor was a mere two hours from Harbor Bay, a distance that could easily be bridged. As fervently as I longed for home and the comforts of that familiar landscape, a part of me remained at the school alongside Tori

Aaron. A small sketch by Tori now held pride of place at Poppet. Somehow, I knew that this woman, who I had never met, would be pleased.

About the Author

Former Treasury executive Arlene Kay is noted for sophisticated mysteries with a touch of snark and plots that bedevil and delight readers. Her published works include traditional mysteries, romantic suspense, and two cozy mystery series that combine wit and whimsy with a cast of unforgettable characters, sleuths, and suspects.

SOCIAL MEDIA HANDLES:
  Arlene Kay author (Facebook)
  ArleneKay1 (Twitter)
  AK mysteries (Twitter)

AUTHOR WEBSITE:
  www.arlenekay.com

Also by Arlene Kay

Intrusion

Die Laughing

The Abacus Prize

The Boston Uncommon series:
   Swann Dive
   Mantrap
   Gilt Trip
   Swann Songs

The Creature Comfort Series:
   Death by Dog Show
   Homicide by Horse Show
   Murder at the Falls

The Cosmetic Crimes Series:
   Murder at First Blush
   The Mascara Murders

www.ingramcontent.com/pod-product-compliance
Lightning Source LLC
Chambersburg PA
CBHW030423120726
47903CB00003B/776